Forgetting Tabitha

By Julie Dewey

Forgetting Tabitha

ISBN: 978-0-578-17231-6

Library of Congress Control Number: 2015920667

Publisher's Cataloging-In-Publication Data
(Prepared by The Donohue Group, Inc.)

Dewey, Julie.
  Forgetting Tabitha : the story of an orphan train rider / by Julie Dewey.

    pages ; cm

  Previously published: [North Charleston, South Carolina] : [CreateSpace], Ā2013.
  ISBN: 9780578172316

  1. Orphan trains--Fiction. 2. Homeless girls--New York (State)--New York--Fiction. 3. Mothers and daughters--New York (State)--Fiction. 4. Street life--New York (State)--Fiction. 5. Survival--Fiction. 6. Historical fiction. I. Title.

PS3604.E949 F67 2016
813/.6

Book design by Sabach Design, sabachdesign.com

Published & Distributed by
HOLLAND PRESS
7640 Edgecomb Drive
Liverpool, New York 13088

www.juliedewey.com
info@juliedewey.com

Printed in the United States of America

DEDICATION

Dedicated to my beautiful mother
Who never wavers in her support
Who has taught me to be a better person
Who has encouraged me to go after my dreams
Who has loved me unconditionally.
Thank you, Mom!

CONTENTS
❧

PROLOGUE

❧

1920

In my reverie, an old lady settled in a creaking wicker rocker, beside a bounty of lush gardens, I recall mama's stories about my birth and our early years, both on the farm and in the city. I hear the whispers from yesterday creeping backwards through time, reminding me of who I am, where I came from, and how I came to survive my plight. Certain moments flutter by like the seeds from a dandelion blowing wishes in the wind, but others stand out and bear the weight of my shaping.

I close my eyes and recollect our spread out farming days in the summertime. I recall the gentle nuzzle of Oliver's velvety nose as I fed him a juicy apple picked fresh from our very own tree. He had a soft mane and calm nature as he guided me through our pastures, always steady of foot. I relive the harsh winters spent huddling together with mama and da by the fire to stay warm. We shared steaming cups of nettle tea to fill our trembling bellies in the lean months. My most prevalent memory is of the spring, when the daffodils and crocuses came to life, when the earth thawed, and mama always began with my birth story.

My story begins among the wild meadows. I can see the landscape of budding flowers and hear the comfort of my parents' voices by my side. The voices fill me with the memories I hold dear once more and pass down to my children now.

I was birthed just as the violet crocuses nudged their dainty goblet-shaped heads through the thawing soil announcing, with their arrival, spring. It was a chilly but clear morning when my mother woke early, feeling the strain of an overripe bladder. Retracing her steps toward the outhouse, she counted her paces and filled her lungs with the crisp morning air. She wasn't due for several weeks but the pressure on her pelvis had increased, inconveniencing her by doubling her trips to the outhouse. Upon her return to the farmhouse, she lit a fire and began to prepare the morning meal of oat groats. She stoked the embers and rearranged logs when she felt a syrupy substance stream down her thigh. Standing in a puddle of her own making, she contemplated whether or not she emptied her bladder in its entirety. Looking down, she saw blood mixed with her waters and simultaneously felt pain pulse through her abdomen. The pain stole her breath. She lowered herself into a crouched position and alternated between cradling her immense belly and holding her ankles for balance. The contractions were hard and fast, keeping her low to the ground. Da finished the milking chores and quickened his pace back to the house to ease his wife's burden with breakfast. He entered the kitchen with a fresh pail of the sudsy drink he craved and found his wife laboring on the cold wooden floors. Da jumped immediately into his rehearsed role of midwife. He placed fresh towels across the bed they shared and filled a basin with warm water. He hefted my mother from her crouch to a more comfortable position on the bed. He climbed in behind her massive body, pulled her dress off, and massaged her cramping back and belly.

Maura had not given birth before and without the advice of a midwife, she followed her instinct. My da, having witnessed many animal births, helped prepare my mother by massaging oils around her delicate tissue so that she wouldn't tear. When she felt the urge to push, da rearranged himself in front of her belly, and together with four loving hands entwined, I was brought gently into the world.

"A girl!" da exclaimed, out of breath, worry etching itself across his brow in deep furrows.

The seconds ticked by and I hadn't mustered a cry. My airways were clogged with birthing matter and mucus and my skin was turning blue. Da resuscitated me by putting his large mouth across my small nose and lips and sucking deeply. Suck-spit-repeat, he did this several times to no avail, finally he held me upside down and whacked my back. On cue I wailed, no longer safe in the warm confines of my mother's womb.

The year was 1850 and I was blessed and named Tabitha Colleen Salt. Tabitha was my name alone but Colleen was a tribute to my paternal grandmother whose blessing and purse made it possible for us to be on American land, farming our small plot of acreage in Westchester, New York. Salt, our surname, was assumed and passed down by our great, great grandfather who worked in the salt mines in Northern Ireland near Carrickfergus. The story goes that grandfather Salt lived to a ripe age of one hundred and seven; his longevity, he claimed, due to the healing properties of the mineral.

CHAPTER 1

❧

CITY LIFE, 1860

My head was itchy, particularly on the base of my skull and behind both ears. My fingernails had dried blood under them from the scabs I scratched open sometime during the night. Mama was clawing at her skin too, not just on her head but also on her woman parts. One time I saw her woman parts when she climbed out from our washbasin and reached for a towel. I didn't mean to look but was curious and surprised to see a little puff of hair "down there" too. Now she was itching that place a lot. The schoolteacher called it "lice."

"Tabitha Salt," Miss Marianne pulled me aside one morning, "you may not be present in school until your head lice are gone. They are highly contagious and with all of your itching, you are disrupting the other students. You can hardly sit still." When I told my mama why I was sent home, she cried softly into her hands before pulling me in for a hug. "Alright then, we'll get rid of the lice at once and get you back into school," she said with a conquering nod of her head and far-away gleam in her eyes. If there was one thing my mama was determined about, it was that I receive a proper education. She and my da didn't risk their lives on board the *Emma Prescott* in 1847 only to die from starvation or stupidity once on solid ground. Together they sailed from their beloved Galway toward religious freedom and a brighter future in America where they believed education was the key to a better life.

The lice came in on one of the shirts we laundered, which was not unusual given that our clientele included manky sailors and dockhands. The critters attached themselves to our hair and got into our bed sheets. They bit us repeatedly and feasted on our scaly dry skin before laying eggs. The nits were barely visible so you couldn't pick them off or swat them away like a pesky fly. We had no choice but to cut our hair and bathe with harsh lye soap. We also had to wash our sheets and clothes in scalding water. Our mattresses were stuffed with straw, horsehair, and old rags to even the lumps, but now they would have to be burned. We would sleep on the floor until we had enough money to buy or make new ones. The thought of freshly plumped straw mattresses was pleasing because my back was stiff from the old ones. Plus, they smelled rank, but mama said we had to make do for now and that's what we did.

We walked hand in hand to the barbershop on Bowery Street that offered shoeshines and dental work, as well as haircuts and shaves. The barber was settling a customer into a reclining red leather chair and draping him in a cloth when we asked how much it would cost to cut our hair. Without looking up, he said rather rudely that he didn't cut girls' hair and sent us to a salon house down the street.

"Well, we certainly don't need up-dos, do we? If the barber can't help us we'll tend to it ourselves." We left the barbershop and went home; when we arrived, mama got her sewing scissors and cut my curls herself. The shears weren't sharp so the tugging hurt badly and I cried when I saw my red, curly hair on the floor all around me. All my pretty tendrils surrounded my feet and soon after, all my mama's pretty curls did too. We sobbed and then laughed when we swooshed our heads back and forth; they felt so light and airy now. Still, we had to cut them closer to the scalp where the eggs were laid. We went back to the barber and asked if he would shave us now and after he dipped his razor into a bluish liquid, he did, for a nickel each.

Mama and I wore red handkerchiefs over our heads to cover our baldness, but I never thought my mama, Maura Salt, looked so pretty. Her blue eyes sparkled with flecks of gold and her freckled cheeks looked fuller, her right cheek looked rosier too.

She said she had a toothache, but when I looked at it from underneath I didn't see a hole or black spot among the grooves indicating a cavity. Mama could only eat soft, tepid foods because anything that was pointy, cold, or hot caused her discomfort. She chewed on her left side and in a few days became sluggish and bedridden. Several days passed and mama remained in pain; finally she gave in and sent me to fetch a dentist. She could have asked the barber to look at it, but preferred someone with only one specialty. The dentist came at once and, after an initial exam, told her the tooth that was causing her pain needed to be pulled immediately. The cost for the extraction was going to be two dollars.

"Tabitha, go into the bedroom and open the top dresser drawer. Behind the stockings that need mending, there is a leather pouch. Count out two dollars in change and bring the coins to me, please." After I counted the money, I replaced the pouch. I felt uneasy because it was nearly empty now and I knew this was our life savings.

Two burly men accompanied the dentist when he came back for his appointment in the evening. The men filled up all the space in our undersized two-room dwelling that we rented from our landlady, Mrs. Canter. The men offered my mama a three-finger-full shot of Jim Beam whiskey, which she threw down her throat quickly, anxious to get the procedure over with.

The men offered me a shot too so that I could sleep through all the bellowing but I said, "No thank you, I am much too young for whiskey and I need to help my mother." I held my mama's clammy hands tight while the big man with the black suspenders and graying white shirt that desperately needed laundering held her shoulders back and down. The smaller mustached man sat across her lap. The dentist put a large metal tooth puller that resembled a key into her delicate mouth. He counted to three and twisted the instrument clockwise before pulling with all his might at the tooth. The tooth cracked in several places, blood poured down my mama's chin, and the dentist wiped away the sweat that ran into his eyes. He said he would have to charge more to get all the splinters out. By the look of his grimace, he didn't like causing my mama pain any more than she liked receiving it. Tears flowed from her eyes and I kissed her hands and squeezed them tight to give her courage.

"It will be all right soon," I said. Mama, frozen with fear, nodded and mustered the strength to withstand the increasing pain in her mouth.

"Sir, maybe you ought to have a shot of that whiskey," I said, facing the dentist.

He chuckled as if I had told a good joke and wiped his sweaty brow once more. Then he opened my mama's mouth and poked around inside.

Mama nearly passed out from the combination of agony and whiskey. Helpless, I ran into the kitchen where Mrs. Canter was baking bread and staying close in case she was needed. I asked what I should do and she lent me a dollar bill for the extra fee. She wiped her hands on her apron and walked into our quarters with me, nearly fainting from the sight and smell of all the blood. The dentist gave my mama another three-finger-full shot of whiskey and wedged a piece of sanded wood wrapped in cotton in her mouth so that it would stay open while he worked. One of the men held a lantern closer so the dentist could decipher the problem. Mrs. Canter filled our basin with warm water and held a fraying rag to her chest in preparation for cleaning up; I noticed that she looked pale and was swaying. The gore didn't bother me but I thought my mama was dead because she wasn't talking and her eyeballs were rolled backwards into her head. I started to cry hysterically.

"She's just passed out from the drink; now she won't feel a thing," the dentist assured me.

"What's your name, little girl?" the man with the filthy shirt asked me.

"Tabitha, what's yours?" I asked, wondering what kind of name belonged to this huge man.

"I'm Big Joe. Come over here and look at my teeth." The man opened his mouth and showed me three empty spaces where his teeth used to be. "It's the same man that took these teeth and I'm fine, just like your mama is going to be."

I didn't feel any better after looking at his mouth; his gums were swollen and he had foul breath. But I knew my mama would brush and at least she'd wake up after she slept off the booze.

The dentist used long metal tweezers with razor sharp tips, his newest tool, to pull out all the splinters of teeth. He was perplexed because the tooth he pulled had three roots holding it in place, which was rather unusual. He said she would be swollen in the morning and in a good amount of discomfort for the next several days. However, she could drink and eat soft foods when she felt up to it. He gave me a dozen whole cloves wrapped in a ramie cloth that mama could put inside her cheek when she woke up. The cloves would help dull the pain. I thanked him for not charging me for the remedy and put them right beside mama's bed.

After the surgery, the dentist took a long swig of the whiskey.

"She made me work for my money, Tabitha, you take care of her now," he patted my back and left at once.

"Tabitha, quickly, go get an armful of rags from under the kitchen sink. We're going to need more if we are going to get your mama cleaned up," Mrs. Canter said.

I did as I was told. I rummaged through stacks of folded towels and shreds of cloth, thankful for the help of this kind woman. Together, we wiped the dried, caked blood from the corners of my mama's mouth and the drips that ran all the way down her neck collecting in the folds of her skin before drenching her shirt collar.

"Help me turn her over, she'll sleep better that way," Mrs. Canter ordered after the bathing was complete. We laid her on her left side and propped her up with numerous pillows. I covered her with our patchwork quilt and tucked her in so that she was nice and snug. Mrs. Canter went back across the hall with all the dirty rags and returned with clean strips of material for the morning. She also brought me two warm oatmeal cookies with raisins.

"Now, get some sleep, dear, your mama will be needing you in the morning," she said, running her hands across my fuzzy head before leaving me to take care of her own family.

Sure enough, my mama woke up in agony. She hollered out in pain and swished her tongue into the hole where her tooth used to be. She looked crooked because one side of her face was swollen like a chipmunk and her left eye was black and blue, which confused me since it was her mouth that had work done. I put a nice warm cloth on her cheek and she said it helped. However, when she tried to stand up to use the john, she held tight to her stomach and swooned.

"Lie back down, mama. I will do the laundry today." I was more than confident in my ability to get all of our work done.

I had been my mama's laundry helper for a year now and even though I was only ten years old, mama said I did as good a job as she did when it came to getting out stains and wrinkles. I worked on the white-collared shirts first and paid extra attention to the underarm stains. I used lemon and vinegar when I scrubbed and was careful not to scrub too hard or the acid would wear a hole right through the fabric. After I cleaned the shirts, I let them air dry. In between all the washing, I ironed. I was careful not to let the iron get too hot or it would burn the cotton and we'd be forced to buy the patron a new shirt; we had learned this the hard way.

"I took care of everything, mama, look," I said that afternoon. I held up several stacks of fresh smelling, neatly folded shirts and trousers. I took my time with the folding so I didn't leave any creases in the wrong spot.

"Be a good girl and ask Mrs. Canter to be sure the bundles are delivered," mama said. She had several cloves tucked inside her cheek and drifted in and out of sleep all day.

Mrs. Canter rewarded me with a shiny penny for my hard work and sent me to the penny candy store on Orange Street. I bought a sack worth of butterscotch balls that I could share with my mama and went home at once.

"Mama, here, I bought you your favorite candies." I unwrapped a piece of butterscotch and put it in mama's mouth. She savored the salty flavor on her good side and gave my hand a squeeze.

"I am so proud of you, Tabitha. If we stick together like this we will be just fine, won't we?" We may have managed to fail the farm, but so far, we were managing in New York City.

CHAPTER 2

❧

THE FIVE POINTS

After my da died a year ago, we moved from the country to the city and settled into the first affordable place we found with a vacancy. We lived in one of a dozen identical, five-story, red-brick buildings on Cross Street in the notorious Five Points District. City life was crowded, costly, and challenging for us and unfortunately, the vacant room we found was in a building with mostly German immigrants, not Irish, as we had hoped to find in order to reacquaint ourselves with kin.

I could see Paradise Place outside my window and often sat for hours watching the spectacle below. Women wearing colorful bonnets waltzed through town carrying baskets in the crooks of their arms that were full to the brim with ripe fruit, meats, cheeses, bread, and wine. They hustled their children toward the used clothing shop to sell their old clothes or purchase new ones. After shopping, they ate lunch at the Chinks Oyster Shack or The Yard House Tavern. Once their bellies were full, they picked up articles of clothing that the tailor had taken in or let out, and finally ducked into the barber shop with its twirling red-and-blue striped pole out front. Here, they got shoeshines as well as quick snips.

Other individuals, mostly men, drowned their sorrows at the corner tavern next to the brewery building. Here drinks could be purchased with ears and noses as long as they were from an opposing gang. Mama told me the remains were placed in glass canisters filled with a cloudy liquid that lined the bar for all the patrons to admire and try to recognize.

Immigrants and other folks in dire circumstances made stops at the money lender shop, always leaving with their heads down. Mama and Mrs. Canter agreed that taking a loan in this city was a last resort because the high interest rates made it impossible to pay back the lender. The lack of reimbursement caused a great need for henchmen who sought those who didn't pay, taking ears, noses, fingers, and toes as retribution. We didn't want to lose any of those so we paid for everything with cash on the barrel or we went without.

Brothels, missions, and theaters lined Anthony Street, providing various forms of entertainment at one establishment, food and redemption for those who lost themselves in the other. Occasionally my mama and Mrs. Canter would take in a show when time and money permitted.

"But, why can't I go too, mama?" I pleaded one day.

"Because there are unsightly businesses along the way and you are far too young to have your eyes ruined." I wondered what she meant by that. Years later, I learned.

Priests, pastors, ministers, reverends, and rabbis led their congregations to worship in Paradise Park while their various cathedrals, churches, and temples were constructed. Anyone seeking solace at the end of the day could find a place to bow his head. Children donned their Sunday best to attend worship. For the boys that included button-down shirts, trousers held up with suspenders, topcoats, and occasionally, caps. Gentleman dressed similarly, but on Sunday they appeared more dapper in their low cut plaid vests that displayed fine starched dress shirts, colorful cravats, and long, knee-length topcoats. On Sundays, the men wore their best toppers too, often reaching an impressive twelve inches in height. Little girls and young ladies wore a wide array of bonnets and dresses, some with hoops and lace shawls, others in coats and muffs when the weather warranted.

New York was a city of clans; thousands of immigrants in different colors, shapes, and sizes came fresh off famine ships and streamed onto the streets daily. Adding to the chaos, the immigrants spoke different languages, looking as confused by us as we were by them. If luck was on their side, distant family members who had previously survived the crossing of the shifty waters and had now settled into life in New York, greeted them at the harbor. Others who weren't so lucky were left to their own devices and struggled to find work and shelter in the midst of this cauldron.

Looking back now, I recall that sometimes sisters from the Mission met boats with warm bowls of soup and cups of steaming tea; when money allowed, they gave out clothing and held free checkups too. The Sisters of Charity tried desperately to steer the depleted newcomers to a Godly life that held promise rather than a broken one on the streets.

Wealthy do-gooders, flanked by constables, fanned their jowls and mingled among the poor in the Five Points, taking in the populace as you would a P.T. Barnum grand traveling circus with wide eyes, disbelief, and curiosity. They covered their noses with handkerchiefs, aghast by our squalor and confined living spaces, as well as the swampy smell we became accustomed to. Concern regarding our poorly draining Bestevaer Swamp was evident in their eyes as they noted the demise of our ramshackle buildings and sliding tenement homes resulting from the poorly engineered landfill and waterway problem. The water problems not only caused the structures to sink and fall in on themselves, but also, sewage leaked into the streets, fostering disease and death. Our conditions were unsanitary at best and uninhabitable at worst. But for the poor who could not afford to live elsewhere, it was home. However, having the Manhattanites in town served a purpose for pickpockets and thieves dressed as sweet children. Any angler worth his salt used the opportunity to his advantage when up-towners were here. They were often rewarded with their best get of watches, wristlets, medallions, coins, or rings that were immediately melted down at the pawn shop before any claims could be made.

Trolleys and carriages stopped at each corner in the Five Points between the Fourth and Sixth Wards all day long delivering passengers to their destinations. The city bustled with life as people walked their schnauzers, wiener dogs, and retrievers, or stood singing and playing instruments such as fiddles for money on the corner. My favorite was the organ grinder with the poodle that danced while he played. Bums with missing limbs held up signs begging for food and charity. Some were too forlorn to beg and just lay sleeping on the brick pavement, hoping a Good Samaritan would drop a few coins while they slept.

"He-She's," as my mama called them, stood at the street corners waiting for a certain clientele to approach them. It didn't matter if it was daylight, they shared flasks of gin and danced eagerly in anticipation of the evening's events. If we passed them, mama shielded my eyes so I wouldn't see the drunken, ludicrous behavior that included much fondling.

Ours was a crumbling civilization, to say the least. Streets were in desperate need of repair, rubbish stood putrid on every corner and storefront. In the Five Points, jobs were scarce, medicine hard to come by, and the level of noise increased with all the construction continually going on. Construction was a fortunate evil though, because it was one place immigrants could find work. Unsafe conditions had many natives opt out after seeing accidents and death, one after the other.

The only time the streets were quiet was during the draft for the Civil War in 1861. Men of a certain age abandoned the tavern and gambling halls in favor of their reclusive homes or hideouts, hoping not to be found and summoned. In the years to come, coffins carrying dead soldiers would line the harbor's docks, causing a panic for young men who then went to extremes by mutilating themselves; cutting off their fingers or bashing their eardrums purposely in order to fail the necessary physical. If they could afford to pay a large fee of three hundred dollars, they avoided the draft and disfigurement all together; otherwise it was the law. The draft riled the Native American Butchers as well as the Bowery Brothers, Roach Guards, and Dead Rabbits, who joined in with the Daybreak Boys, Forty Thieves, and Swamp Angels all in opposition to the wealthy buying their own sons' safety. The city's gangs grew and the violence got worse.

Mama tried to shield me from the horror but I could hear gunshots at night and heard stories from the Canter boys about the murders occurring here nearly every day. All I had to do was look out my window at an opportune moment and I could see gangs fighting each other in the daylight using makeshift weapons such as axes, bats, bricks, knives, and cleavers. In the morning, men lay dead at our doorway. It often took several days before the municipal workers came with shovels and scraped the stiff, reeking bodies into an open top carriage and carried them to a mass grave where they were covered in dirt, omitting the opportunity to say a proper goodbye or blessing. Orphans and chiselers patrolled the streets for fresh dead bodies, which they collected and sold to hospitals for research. If there was a way to make money, the resourceful people of the Five Points found it.

Usually it was a drunkard or gambler who lay dead outside our door, but lately kids from our own block showed up. They had made the mistake of getting involved in the senseless gang fighting that took place over territory, politics, and religion. The Dead Rabbits scared us the most. Gang members wore a red stripe on their pantaloons and carried a dead rabbit impaled on a spike with them into street fights. They fought the Roach Guards most of the time over territorial rights and, unfortunately for us, our home was at the intersection smack in the middle of the scuffle. We couldn't afford to move just yet, but my mama decided if we rented two rooms in Mrs. Canter's flat instead of our own apartment we could reside with her family and save a few dollars each month. We pared down our belongings in hopes of saving our pennies to get ahead with nothing but the promise of living further north spurring us on.

Mrs. Canter had six rotten smelling boys that always slagged around, and she had no husband either. All her lads shared a bed with each other and were directly across the hall from my mama and me; we could hear their snoring and farting all night long. Worse, we had to share a toilet basin with them and they always left crude pee stripes or sticky crap smears on the seat. One time I woke in the middle of the night to use the john and sat right in something sticky and thick. Sure enough, it was crap from one of the vile boys. I told my mama about it the next day and she nodded in acknowledgment and scrubbed the stains she was laundering even harder than normal. We had to wash our laundry in the kitchen sink and hang the clothing to dry where it would soak in the stench from the filthy streets below.

Several of Mrs. Canter's lads were being recruited by the gangs already. It was Liam, her five year old, who was caught for stealing and thrown into jail with a gang of ruffians. The thugs from the Dead Rabbits saved him from rape in the slammer and now he was indebted to them, bringing the threat and promise of gang life to our front door.

Lots of men from opposing gangs approached my mama, dazed by her vitality and beauty, even with her short hair. She was fiercely protective of me and had a quick temper the men admired. She was young and had more teeth than most women her age because she brushed regularly and ate her greens. She managed to push off most of the advances because the gang members were deeply involved in politicking and gambling.

Brian Kelley showed up at our door on numerous occasions after he had been drinking; he tried desperately to lure my mama toward a better life with him. He pulled at her slender hips with his grimy hands and kissed her right in front of me. He had dimples and a wide grin, but his eyes had lost their sparkle. He had seen death too many times and since he was a founding member of the Dead Rabbits, mama thought he had done his share of killing. When we found out he was murdered, mama clutched her chest and sank to the ground. I didn't understand why she was mourning over a man who wasn't my da.

After da died, we naively moved from our spread out farming days in the country to the constraints of the city. We thought it would be easier to manage our life where work, food, and medical care were closer. We also had foolish hopes to find more of our kind, Irish immigrants. Mama had to go door to door in town asking for work as a laundress. We worked all day and night scrubbing and ironing to get our work done. One day shortly after we were settled, mama had looked up at me and said, "Da and I made a promise to each other that any child of ours would get a proper education. We are set up well enough now that I can handle the laundry." Just like everything else, when she made her mind up about something, it was done. The next day, she had marched me to the schoolhouse and registered me for classes.

One room in the schoolhouse was for elementary students like me and the other was for the older children who already knew how to read, write, and figure arithmetic. Most of the students were Irish immigrants like myself, so we all had the same way of pronouncing our As. My teacher was a woman named Miss Marianne, and I adored her. She had the patience of a saint when she taught me to read from my first primer and this filled me with hope.

Mama walked me to school in the mornings and collected me in the afternoons. The city teemed with people now and she wouldn't allow me to walk alone in case I got caught in a scuffle, or worse, was kidnapped and sold into prostitution. In the afternoon, we delivered the day's laundry and stopped by the grocers for dinner. Usually we bought day-old bread, because it was cheaper and only a tad stale, cheese, and whatever greens they had. I helped prepare our meager meal when we got home and after we ate, I read from my primer while mama knit. She often told me far-away stories of Galway and my da. I grew to associate the sound of her needles click clacking together, knit and purl, knit and purl, with peaceful evenings. We would fall asleep to the harmonies of the city outside and to the Canter boys tooting along.

One dismal morning on our walk to school, our routine was interrupted by the Sisters of Charity shuffling kids from discarded boxes and out from doorways onto the sidewalks with offers of bread, sweet milk, and lollipops. The children were orphans or had parents who were alive but had fallen on hard times, and were known therefore, as half orphans. I stared at their ratty clothes and bare feet, unable to peel my eyes from the toddler among the group.

"Mama, how can we help them?" I asked.

"Uppy," the wee toddler with the opaque eyes and green snotty nose held his arms up in the air for someone to pick him up.

"I'm afraid we can't, we are making just enough for ourselves at the moment, but you can put your penny in the collection for the Sisters of Charity at church this week. That would be more than generous and the sisters will see to it that the children are taken care of."

Orphans were all over the city. When we walked the short block to buy penny candy, I saw one child looking into a garbage container and another chewing on moldy orange peels. Another time I saw a child sleeping on the sidewalk mid-day. I wondered about these children day and night and felt guilty that I was more fortunate than they were. I was curious about how they survived the harshness of the city. What did they eat besides garbage and who told them what to do? It was already getting chilly in New York and it was only October, but surely the sisters had rooms for them to rest at night. Was there anyone else to take pity on them?

❧

My hair was starting to grow back in and I was teased relentlessly at school for looking like a boy. I wanted to wear my handkerchief to class but it was forbidden so I suffered the abuse and focused my energy on my penmanship. One day however, Owen Kenville teased me so badly that I stomped on his foot and made him cry. "That's what you get," I yelled at him, feeling zero remorse. He never teased me again.

Mama's hair was growing in too, but now she had some gray strands around her ears and temples and it made her depressed. I thought she was beautiful but she said the gray hair made her feel old. Her shoulders drooped a bit after a long day's work and she lost some of her steam.

"I'm feeling a little sluggish today," she said one morning. "I'm sure it's nothing to worry about, but since you did such a good job with the laundry a few weeks ago, would you mind helping again?" she asked.

"Of course, mama, I can help." I was determined to do a good job too, because mama looked shagged and needed the rest.

By nighttime, she was howling in pain. The tooth next to the one pulled several weeks ago was hot to the touch. Her gums looked funny and there was a pimply spot on them with yellow-colored pus that oozed out. I gave her a few leftover cloves and told her to keep them between her gums to numb the pain. I ran for Mrs. Canter, who fetched the dentist. He came at once carrying his black satchel of tools, including a new instrument that looked like a wrench. Mama's fever spiked and we had no money left in the drawer for a second pull. Besides, my mama didn't want to lose any more teeth and suffer with ill-fitting dentures. We brushed every day with baking soda on our cotton ramie cloths, and were careful to swish afterward, counting to ten before spitting. We even scrubbed our tongues.

But the dentist insisted the tooth was infected and the white pustule was an abscess. He offered to pull the tooth immediately and we could owe him the credit. Everyone agreed to the plan and the doctor filled my mama up with Jim Beam once more for the pain. He pulled this tooth with far more ease than the last and didn't need two men to help hold her down. She was lethargic and tired the entire next day; not only was her cheek swollen, but now she had subtle streaks of red that ran down her neck. The streaks reminded me of the branches on our old willow tree the way they spread out like vines. Throughout the night, my mama's fever climbed, making her eyes appear glassy. Her breathing became shallow and she looked pale. I offered her tepid ginger ale and wiped her brow to keep her cool, pleading with her to eat or drink to regain her strength. She had no appetite. She passed away sometime during the night. The dentist said the infection poisoned her bloodstream, possibly from the tooth that was pulled weeks earlier.

I sat alone in the room with my mama dead beside me, getting stiffer by the minute. Her beautiful face was swollen and bruised. It struck me as odd, just then, that we never took the time to pretty up our place. We had nothing on our walls, no framed pictures, samplers, or artifacts. Time had double crossed us, there would never be a moment that belonged to my mama and me again.

Mrs. Canter poked her head into our room, "Tabitha, allow me to prepare your mother for her burial."

"Okay," I said, rather meekly.

"What would you like to dress her in?" she asked as she looked into my mama's wardrobe, pulling out her Sunday outfit.

"She'd like that," I said, and so Mrs. Canter and I dressed her in the emerald green ensemble she wore to worship, complete with thick cream stockings and matching shoes. Mrs. Canter applied pink rouge to the cheeks of the corpse disguised as my mama, and covered her head with the red handkerchief.

A few customers stopped by to collect their laundry and apologize for my loss. Some even tipped me shiny pennies, but none offered to take me in, not even Mrs. Canter.

"You'll need your nourishment, Tabitha, eat this," Mrs. Canter gave me a thick roll of ham with extra mustard and a glass of frothy milk sweetened with sugar. She left me alone after all of the laundry was collected and the last of the visitors had come by. I picked at my food and wondered what was going to happen to me now. We had been living in the city for less than a year and we didn't know many people outside our building. We didn't make friends or find anyone close enough to resemble family.

I took the handkerchief off my mama's noggin and rubbed at the stubble that still felt velvety soft beneath my fingertips.

"Mama, mama, why did you leave me?" I cried, noting how the gray hair that spread from her temples to her crown had grown in straight when it used to be curly. I wiped off the rouge and lipstick and climbed on to the table where she was laid out. I draped her arm across my shoulders and curled up with her for one last time until the men from the morgue arrived to take her away. I screamed and clawed at the men, kicking their shins and begging them not to take her, but they did anyway. The only memento I had now was her red handkerchief and it was the color of blood so I didn't want it. The Canter boys had to help the men from the morgue get my mama down the small stair well. They checked on me once or twice that night too, but I told them to go away.

The following morning I woke up alone for the first time in my life. I was numb. Waves of confusion and shock tugged at me from all sides, threatening to pull me under a thick hovering cloud. I jingled the pennies in my pocket; the ones I had saved for the Sisters of Charity. I had to find them now because they were the only people who might be able to help me. I knew the way to the stoop where they often gathered orphans. Now that I was an orphan, I could give them the pennies in exchange for their help in finding me a new home. Even though I looked like a boy because of my short hair I wasn't ugly, and maybe, God willing, someone would want me.

My legs didn't want to work; I sat motionless on the floor staring into space. I wasn't able to focus on anything, I wasn't hungry or thirsty, I was alone and frightened. I was an orphan.

The word "orphan" sat thick on my tongue like cotton. I couldn't swallow it no matter how I tried. I was afraid I would become hysterical so I concentrated on breathing deeply in and out through my nose to calm myself. I needed a plan but my head was spinning and I wasn't able to think straight. First, I had to get my legs to work. I rubbed my shins and flexed my feet to get the blood circulating. I stood up and tried walking; it was like being on air. I felt no pressure beneath the souls of my feet. I didn't stumble or fall, I just put one foot in front of the other and counted my steps out the door. I felt nothing and everything all at once.

CHAPTER 3

❧

ALONE

Sister Agnes was patrolling the streets for children when I stumbled upon her.

"Excuse me, miss, can you help me?" I asked, feeling frightened. The woman, who I knew was a Sister of Charity based on her habit, looked at me with smiling eyes that put me at ease.

"Why sure, my child, what can I do for you?" the sister asked.

"I have nowhere to go..." I stammered. My courage no longer sustained me and tears rolled down my cheeks.

"There, there, it will be alright. What is your name and how old are you?" she asked.

"My name is Tabitha Salt and I'm ten, almost eleven."

"Do you go to school, Tabitha?" she inquired.

"I do. Miss Marianne is my teacher, but now I don't have anyone to walk me and my mama doesn't like me to walk that far alone."

"Where do you live, Tabitha? Where are your mother and father?" Sister Agnes asked gently, probing for answers.

"Well, I lived over there." I pointed with a shaking hand to the tenement building. "But my mama just died so I have to leave because there is a new renter coming in."

The sister put her arms across my shoulders and led me to a bench. She sat me down and held my hands tight while

I told her about my da's death on the farm and my mama's bloody tooth.

"So now I am all alone," I repeated.

When I was done talking and sat spent, Sister Agnes soothed me by rubbing her thumb back and forth rhythmically across my tiny wrists. Sitting quietly for a moment, deciding the best way to approach my situation she finally launched into a solution that didn't involve an orphanage but rather an orphan train.

"I know this is a lot to take in right now, but I would like to help you if you'll let me. Will you let me help you, Tabitha?"

"Uh uh," I said quietly.

"Have you ever heard of Reverend Brace?" Sister Agnes asked me.

"No, who is he?"

"Well, he is a very important man who is trying to help children like yourself. He started a movement on behalf of New York City, a city that is failing its children. The needs of the city's indigent are simply not being met," the sister said sternly and it sounded like she had rehearsed this many times over.

I didn't know what indigent meant but assumed I was one. She went on to explain that the orphanages and workhouses were not well funded and the inhabitants suffered abuse, mistreatment, and often further neglect. "Many children run away from such facilities and it's certainly not a good fit for you," she said, speaking more to herself than to me. She further detailed how the reverend worked with several other humanitarians and Children's Aid servants to find a solution to the growing epidemic. He did not believe in charity for its own sake and felt certain that soup kitchens and handouts fostered dependence. Instead, he had an idea to help society by establishing newsboy lodging houses, industrial schools, and night schools. Sadly, these too fell short, furthering the reverend's belief that without familial life, true reform was lacking. His thoughts fixated on the growing dangerous criminal activity that lured thousands of children. The only option available, it seemed, was sending the homeless waifs and half orphans west. The westward expansion of the railways would help make this possible. The idea was radical and ingenious and enormous effort went into it. Want ads were circulated ahead to cities on each train's route with details regarding the children available for adoption or work. Children were given Bibles, new clothing, and had their hair cut. They used cardboard suitcases for their belongings. All the children were given a lesson in manners and new identities before being sent on their way.

Sister Agnes was animated as she described the massive locomotives and it was clear she held Reverend Brace in very high esteem.

"The sisters and I personally draft and circulate want ads so that someone could be waiting for you when you arrive at a stop. If you're willing to board the train, you could have a new home, just like that."

The orphan trains were filled with children from the poverty-stricken city and transported west on the Erie line where they were fostered by new families or selected to become laborers. Sister Agnes detailed the countryside out west, describing the fresh air and wide, open fields with roaming animals. While I could create a picture in my mind of flower gardens and flapping hens, I couldn't bear the thought of new parents. Most children in the sisters' care were given a ten-day waiting period for any of their family members to claim them, but I knew that wasn't going to happen for me since my parents were both dead.

"How do you feel about what I've just explained?" Sister Agnes asked me, breaking my concentration. I was confused by all the big words she used, had never heard of Reverend Brace or his school for boys. What about girls? Why weren't there schools for us? Terror filled my veins, the thought of boarding a train heading some place unknown, while alone, did not sit well with me.

After meeting Sister Agnes and hearing about the trains, I ran up the familiar stairwell into Mrs. Canter's apartment and asked her what she thought. My landlady already knew about the trains and had asked the Sisters of Charity to kindly consider taking me along on their next departure. It would be charitable, she said, considering my age. Most families only wanted to adopt babies and the kids that were older were hired for work. Perhaps because of my laundry skills I could be useful to someone even though I'm ten and any potential I had for cuteness was lost with my curls.

I didn't have time to let the shock of losing my mother settle in. I couldn't allow myself one tear or it would turn into an unstoppable fountain of self-pity and body numbing grief. Furthermore, the city was my home now.

I pleaded with Mrs. Canter to let me stay with her, "Please, Mrs. Canter, I won't be a bother and I can help you with the laundry and other chores. I won't go to school anymore," I cried. I didn't want to go on the orphan train with the juveniles, but Mrs. Canter already had too many mouths to feed.

"No, no, that won't do. I have enough on my plate already. I am sorry, Tabitha." Reluctantly, she sent me away with warm cookies and told me to gather my belongings and clean out my room for the new renter, who would be arriving tomorrow. I grabbed my laundry bag and filled it with my primer and the only other dress I owned. I only had two pairs of underwear and stockings and even though they were riddled with holes we had yet to mend, I put them in along with a needle and thread. I reached under our clothing hamper and found the one thing I would treasure. Mama kept the photograph of us under the hamper where it was dark, she never wanted it to fade or crumple. "Someday we will have it framed and maybe we can even have another taken to go along side it," she had said, but my mama's voice was nothing but a memory now. I looked at the picture of us; it was taken when we first got to the big city. We were giddy and apprehensive at the same time. Neither of us was smiling so that our teeth showed but we had a sparkle in our eyes and were clearly full of ambition. That's how I will remember my mama always, with sparkles in her eyes and ambition in her heart.

Miss Marianne, my teacher, heard that my mother passed away and did her best to soothe my worries and concerns about the orphan train. She said I could keep coming to class as long as I was kempt and clean. She didn't ask where I was planning to stay, so I didn't tell.

ॐ

I was the first orphan under the stoop that night but by midnight there were three more. Tommy was the oldest scoundrel and his nose was crooked from being bashed so many times.

"You just gotta learn how to steal food, or sneak into houses at night to get warm," Tommy said, as if breaking the law were no big deal.

"There are other ways a girl could get warm in the big city," Karen said with a dirty laugh, inching her skirt up her leg and giving me a wink. That one would lie down in a bed of nettles for certain. She had dirt under her fingernails and violet hollows beneath her sad eyes. Tommy leaned in closer to Karen and they cuddled up together away from me and Scotty. Scotty was slightly older than me but had been on the streets a long time. He smelled like something from the sewers and slept with one eye open in case anyway dared to bother us at night.

"I've been in a home for boys once already and I ain't going back."

"Why not?" I asked.

"Cuz they got too many rules and they whip you good if you don't follow 'em."

"Well, at least they fed you, didn't they?" I asked, already wondering about my next meal.

"If you can call the slop they put on our plates food. I just gotta be careful not to get caught. I've been seen with the Roach Guards and if I get picked up, it's more trouble for me."

I didn't think Scotty was a delinquent but he did steal us bread for dinner and gloves for my freezing hands. Tommy and Scotty both swept the streets and sold Sunday papers for coin but sooner or later they would have to join one of the gangs for protection. Neither one of them knew what it really meant to be initiated but both worried about the prospect.

"I can help you get a job you know," Scotty whispered in my ear, his stinky breath hanging thick between us like fog.

"Thanks, but I'm going to try to get a job tomorrow doing laundry. I'm good at that, I did it with my mama. Plus, Miss Marianne said as long as I am clean I could still go to school." I picked at my fingers, pulling off the hangnails until they bled.

"Awe, isn't that swell, she did laundry with her mama, guys." Tommy threw the crusty heel of his bread at my legs. "You better grow up fast, your mama ain't here no more," he said and cracked his knuckles one at a time before pulling on brown gloves that covered his scabs.

"You're just jealous she had a mama, you prick, Tommy, leave her alone." Scotty moved in front of me and threatened to beat Tommy up if he kept bullying me.

"You really think you can go to school and work?" Scotty asked. Of the three scoundrels under the stoop with me, he was the only one with any hope and still had a gleam in his eyes.

"Well, it's my plan and I have to try. Do you know a place where I can get cleaned up in the morning?" I asked, remembering my promise to my teacher.

Before the sun lit up the morning sky, the Sisters of Charity were at the stoop ushering kids out with offers of dark bread and hot tea. Sister Agnes was not among the flock. Their offerings were tempting but Scotty grabbed my hands and pulled me to my feet and together we ran for it, adrenaline pulsing through my body, until we mixed in with the city dwellers.

"What do you need to get cleaned up?" Obviously Scotty hadn't washed in a while, so he didn't know where to go to find a fresh water basin and baking soda for my teeth. It had already been a full day since I brushed and my teeth felt slimy. I decided to talk to Miss Marianne about this. I would ask for a clean basin of water to wash with before school and in return, I would gladly clean the chalkboard and erasers.

Miss Marianne agreed that this was a good idea. Then she asked me where I had been sleeping, and right then I told my first lie. I told her I was bunking on Mrs. Canter's floor for now and explained there were too many people in the small apartment for me to expect fresh water for a bath.

After school, I began my search for a job doing laundry. Heaven knows I knocked on dozens of doors with my mama a year ago hoping to find work. I would knock on them again today and pray that someone would remember me. On account of my short, boyish haircut, no one did; I was shooed away and treated like a pest. I walked toward the docks and asked the sailors and workers if anyone needed laundering done. Everyone sent me away, thinking I was just a beggar boy.

It became clear that this line of work wasn't going to happen. So the second day after my mama died I went around town with Scotty and asked store clerks if I could sweep their storefronts for a penny. Five stores turned me down but the sixth was owned by a matronly woman who took pity on my poor soul and gave me the job, even though she called me, "boy."

I encountered a problem immediately; I had no place to store my nice school clothing and primer while I was at work sweeping and no place to keep my work clothes while I was at school. If I talked to my teacher about this, it would just make her suspicious so instead I talked to Scotty. We devised a watch out system for our stoop that involved taking turns guarding our territory while the others were working. Scotty and I became fast friends and helped one another in other ways too. Often he would bring me supper, or share what little he had, and in return, I would wash his spare socks in the leftover water basin at school. Whenever Tommy bullied me, Scotty stepped in as my protector, threatening to break Tommy's nose again, and he could too. Tommy was slightly built and not very strong. Scotty was only eleven but stronger and sturdier than Tommy was at thirteen. He knew more than his share about fighting too, the way he held his arms and fists made me wonder more about his past.

One night Karen came to the stoop crying, her dress was torn at the hem and there was blood mixed with mud on her legs. She had noticeable scrapes and cuts and a pink-tinged streak of blood slowly made its way from her thighs down the backs of her knobby knees, staining her ankles. Tommy was livid and unable to comfort Karen because he was focused on killing the animal that did this to her.

"What happened?" I asked, clueless as to how she was injured.

"You really are just a kid, aren't you?" Scotty replied, looking at me with pity.

It was the first time I felt insulted by him and I cried softly into my hands, feeling like an eejit for not understanding what took place. Tommy cradled Karen in his arms and whispered sweetly to her until she was asleep. Then he and Scotty left us alone and went out to seek revenge.

I was unable to sleep, unable to imagine what tomorrow would bring. I missed the click clack of my mama's knitting needles as well as the smell of her loving arms wrapped protectively around me. I imagined that she was with me, sheltering me from harm as she always had. She hummed softly into my ears and I allowed myself to feel her presence and, for a fleeting moment, the heaviness I felt weighing me down lifted.

❧

The next day at school, I was overwhelmed and distraught. I gave in and told my teacher all about the incident with Karen. Miss Marianne asked me again where I was staying and, because it was against my conscience to fib a second time, I told her I had been living under a stoop with several other orphans. I explained that we were friends and helped each other find food and stay warm. She refused to allow me to go back there after school and took me instead to the Elizabeth Home for Girls. At this particular home, I would learn sewing skills and typing skills so that I could find a job and become a productive member of society. I would have a cot to sleep on at night and two square meals a day. I would also have a place to wash.

I hated this place; the girls, fifty-eight in all, were crammed together in rooms often two to a cot. The showers were communal and older girls made fun of my "buds" and short boy hair. I was teased and bullied to no end and it made me miss Scotty something awful. I even missed Tommy and Karen and was upset I never had the chance to tell them I was going away. Nor did I get to tell the shopkeeper that I wouldn't be there to sweep away the grime from her sidewalk. I remembered how the blood-tinged loogies and spit got stuck in the broom making it wet and harder to use. The job was lost to me now, like so many other things in my life.

I wasn't allowed to go to school in Lower Manhattan anymore and I missed Miss Marianne's kindness terribly. Most of the girls at the home were older and had no reason for schooling; instead they had plans to become secretaries or dressmakers. Many of them were delinquents who got caught smoking fags in their rooms or sneaking out to meet boys. One girl even got pregnant while living at the home. I quickly learned the ways between a man and woman and finally understood what happened to Karen. I prayed Karen wasn't doing "it" to make coin, because she was only thirteen. The thought made me shiver and I promised myself that no matter how desperate my circumstances became I would never, ever, sell myself.

I had been living at the home for three weeks and shared a bed with a fourteen-year-old girl named Mira. One morning, when I woke up later than usual, I noted my belongings scattered all over the floor. Lying on the ground, ripped into pieces, was the photograph of my mother and me. I couldn't control my anger, I was a good Christian girl but this stirred something inside me and I went crazy. I found Mira in the shower and clocked her one right in the nose. I punched, kicked, and slapped her with everything I had inside until her friend, Dottie, was able to pull me off. Mira told me time and again that I was nothing but a spoiled, bratty kid. She said I had it easy and that I needed to toughen up and forget my mama. She heard me crying at night in my sleep and knew I had something special tucked under my side of the mattress.

Mira was bleeding profusely from her nose and I was glad to see her pain. All the anger I had bottled up since my mama died seeped from my veins and I couldn't control it, nor did I want to.

Tears streamed down my face in torrents and mixed with snot, which I wiped on my thin woolen blanket spread out across my portion of the bed. My breathing was rapid and I clenched my teeth, not sure what I was going to do next.

I wasn't allowed to eat supper that evening and was scheduled to meet with the ward of the Elizabeth Home at six o'clock. While everyone else was in the dining hall eating their gray slop, I grabbed the few belongings I had left, along with the tattered pieces of my photograph and ran for the door. I ran without stopping until I was back at the stoop on Mulberry Street. I sat down breathless, finally allowing my anger and sadness to pour out of me. I cried and punched the stairs until my fists bled. I waited for Scotty, Tommy, and Karen to show up all night but none of them came. It was cold and blustery and I was all alone. I tried to stay awake and make myself unnoticeable by pulling my knees up to my stomach and sinking deeper in the corner. I worried about the drunk men who would be leaving the pubs soon. I woke to street sounds, bootblacks setting up their stations, trains and horns screeching and honking at one another, and people shouting. I had fallen asleep sometime near dawn, and now my fingers were swollen and blue, and my toes were numb. I walked to the shop and asked for my job back but the matronly woman shooed me away saying that I was unreliable. I had nowhere to go and nowhere to turn. I was alone and scared.

I missed my da and the old Irish tunes he sang to mama and me after supper, and the way he was always coddin' around. I missed my mama for more reasons than I could count. I even missed Mrs. Canter and her boys. It seemed that now I had only one choice...I wiped my bloody hands across my dirty skirt, pulled up my knee socks, sucked in my breath, and walked toward my destiny.

CHAPTER 4

❧

ORPHAN TRAIN

"Children, line up for your breakfast," the sisters ordered. They clapped their hands to get our attention and organized us in a single file line before leading us into the mess hall where we would receive a hot morning meal of porridge with chunks of fruit and a glass of sweet milk. After we ate, the sisters ordered us to bathe; they put our old clothes in a grate to be burned, claiming that "cleanliness was Godliness." I thought it was wasteful and remembered how my mama wove scraps of old material into her knitting giving it new life, but here we were to dispose of our old clothing in case it was infested with lice or fleas. We were stripped of our personal belongings too, but I managed to smuggle the remains of my photo into my underwear before anyone got a hold of it. The girls had their hair washed, brushed, and braided or put back in headbands if it was short like mine. We were given new dresses, complete with bows tied around the middle. The boys were outfitted in suit coats, long socks, knickers, and dress shoes. All of us were instructed to use proper manners at all times. For example, the sisters told us over and over again, "Don't speak unless you are spoken to," as well as, "Clasp your hands together and stand still, no fidgeting." We were told to smile and be expressive when meeting prospective families. We needed to hide our pain and bury it deep.

Once we were properly fed and dressed, we were lined up and given new names.

"You will be named Mary." Sister Agnes handed me a Bible and told me to hold it close to my chest at all times.

"Mary?" I stuttered.

"Yes, it's a very comely name and it suits you well. It's time for you to erase anything about your past, including your religious beliefs. Can you read, Mary?" she asked.

"Yes, I can," I said.

"Well then, I suggest you study the Bible, fill your mind and heart with pure thoughts, and think about becoming the best Christian you possibly can. Can you do that?"

"Uh huh," I muttered quietly.

❧

The next morning we were lined up to board a massive train that followed the Erie route west, heading for Illinois; it would travel northwest through New York before making stops in all the major cities in Pennsylvania, Ohio, and Indiana along the way. Our stops were coordinated ahead of our arrival by the sisters who corresponded with churches at each of our destinations. They did their best to describe the ages and demeanors of the children on board the orphan train in order to interest local families who wanted to add to their family or were in need of farm hands. The laboring children were given over freely in exchange for their care, which consisted of clothing, a bed to sleep in at night, and a few hot meals throughout the day. Most of the children were hoping they would be loved as well.

WANTED:

HOMES FOR ORPHAN CHILDREN

A group of orphans under the auspices of the Sisters of Charity will arrive in Philadelphia, Pennsylvania on November 1st. Children on board looking for homes and or work include:

Baby girl of 6 months, good disposition

Sisters ages 11 months and two years, both in good health

Boy of 4, small for his age, good demeanor

Twin girls, age unknown, criss-crossed eyes, shy, otherwise good health

Boy of 6, blue eyes, blond hair, quiet and shy, adequate health

Siblings 7 and 8, a boy and girl respectively, friendly and hard-working

Girl of 10, short hair, malnourished, previous work experience as laundress

Twin boys age 12, hard workers, experience with horses

Boy of 13 with reading and writing skills, good singing voice

2 boys of 14, well fed, disciplined, respectful workers

4 lads, 15 years old with various work experience, all capable and healthy

Please note:

SIBLINGS KEPT TOGETHER WHENEVER POSSIBLE

Sister Agnes had frizzy brown hair that always strayed from her bun. She wore wire spectacles with thick glass making her eyes appear like large saucers. Her body was wiry like her hair but she was otherwise unremarkable in her appearance, it was her genuine kindness that became evident to all the children she chaperoned on the trip. She pushed her glasses higher up the bridge of her nose and took a deep breath, already overwhelmed by the task of managing so many orphans. There were a dozen and a half of us for the trip and at the last minute, a blubbering five-year-old boy was added to the mix so there were nineteen of us now. The boy was very small and undernourished and looked pathetic. He was given the Christian name Edmund.

"Mary, will you be kind enough to look after Edmund today?" Sister Agnes asked, placing the child in a seat beside me and settling him in with a snack.

Several hours later, she approached the two of us again, "Well then, he seems to be doing quite well in your company, maybe he can be your charge for the trip. Would that be alright with you?" she asked.

"Certainly, sister," I responded, unwilling to do or say anything that wasn't Christian. I had never cared for a child before but remembered my mama's words, "We do what we must to help others and get by."

Edmund was a clingy child who was not on the want ad because of his late addition. It was obvious he had not been properly cared for as he wasn't fully potty trained and had very few words to his vocabulary. He sucked his thumbs and had difficulty making eye contact. He was ornery and sickly, always crying with snotty boogies, eye mucus, and a whistling sound emanating from his chest. It gagged me but if I were to become a Christian, I would have to do my best to care for Edmund. This meant wiping his snot and patting his back so he could cough up the thick phlegm plaguing his chest and causing him respiratory distress. He held onto me for dear life, making me wonder what his five years had been like up until now. I asked Sister Agnes about Edmund's past but she said, "Never mind about that, all that matters is what happens now." It would be a difficult placement, not only because Edmund was in poor health, but because he also had pressing dark features. His skin was olive toned and his hair was dark like his eyes. If he was mistaken for a Spaniard, he had no chance whatsoever for adoption. His nose was big for his face and his lashes were long and dark; he was a pretty boy, although he remained painfully shy.

I was also going to be lucky if I got adopted. I was a freckle-faced ten-year-old girl, had untamed spiky reddish hair that made me look like a boy in spite of my headband and calico dress. I ate like a boy and fought like one too if anyone tried to cheat me. I had developed a chip on my shoulder according to Sister Agnes. Adoptive parents wanted babies and darling children or conversely, they wanted strapping lads who could work a farm. Edmund and I were neither and as we found at our first stop, we were not wanted.

The first stop on our journey west was in Pennsylvania. It only took us half a day by train to get there so when we arrived we weren't too weary from the travel, although our bums were sore from the wooden bench seats. Typically, the youngest children rode in the carriages with Sister Agnes while the older charges traveled in the boxcars, becoming known as "boxcar" children. We wore our traveling outfits aboard the train and upon our arrival were instructed to change into our Christian attire. I put on my dress with the comely bow, put the remaining shreds of my cherished photograph snuggly against my underwear seam, and smoothed my skirt as I had often seen my mother do. Next, I changed Edmund's nappy. Changing him gagged me given the gigantic turds he delivered. He held in his bowel movements for days, causing himself tremendous stomach cramps, and when he finally did go it was gross. He only had one alternative outfit so I changed him frequently. We didn't have washbasins so if he had an accident he would be in a pickle. I dressed Edmund in the suit he was given for such an occasion and thought he looked rather cute.

We were told to forget where we came from, forget everything about our old lives, including our names. However, I could never and would never forget my mother.

I squeezed my eyes shut to prevent the tears that were welling from spilling out. My heart ached as I tried to put the city and all its memories, both good and bad, behind me. My mother and father were dead and I was alone in the world. As I held Edmund close to my chest, feeling the vibration from his wheeze, a lonely tear escaped. I quickly wiped it away and sucked in my breath. I was determined to look forward now and try my best to find myself a new home.

As the train neared its destination, we were given further instructions on how to behave on the platform.

"Remember, only speak if you are spoken to. Your new families want respectful children, show off your good manners, and be sure to smile!" Sister Agnes handed out lemon-flavored lollipops and allowed us a few moments to suck on them. Several of the orphans were crying and others clutched their stomachs in fear. Sister Agnes assured us that we were God's children and there was a place for each of us. She told us to hold our chins up and think of our bright futures. When all the lollipops were finished and everyone's face was wiped clean, sister inspected our clothing and ushered us from the train to the platform, touching each child in some way, a gentle hand on the shoulder or a pat on the back, her way of providing comfort to us.

"Stay together now, children, line up in order of height like we practiced. Taller children stand in the back, smaller ones up in the front please." Sister Agnes spoke gently as we took our places on the stage in Philadelphia's town center. The sugar surge from the candy helped to lighten our spirits and energize us before greeting the families that gathered in anticipation of our arrival. I held Edmund's tiny hand for a moment before lifting him to my hip. I wet my fingers and wiped his sticky chin, then smiled my brightest smile. Someone had to think I was worthy. I was a hard worker and was able to read and write. I tried putting Edmund down on the ground next to me to stand on his own but he wouldn't have it. Nor would he go to Sister Agnes. He fussed and cried, which brought on a coughing fit that caused a spectacle and ensured that no one from this destination would want him. However, when he got back into the fold of my arms he calmed down immediately and laid his sweet cheeks on my neck. His tears and snot wet the rim of my dress collar but I didn't mind, when it dried I would just flake it off. My arms grew tired from holding him but my heart wept; poor Edmund, what had happened to him in his short life? He was endearing himself to me and I would do whatever I could to help him find a loving home.

After an hour on the splintered wooden platform, paraded like cattle, four children were officially adopted. Two big strapping fellows who rode in the boxcar were taken together by a dairy farmer; the boys seemed happy and thanked Sister Agnes for her kindness. It was very Christian of them and I would be sure to do the same when my time came. Then two of our youngest went to a couple who must not have been able to have children of their own. The proud new parents held the babies, delighted with the addition to their family.

Sadly, fifteen of us remained orphans and boarded the train once more. We had an uncanny mix of apprehension and excitement as we headed toward our second destination in Ohio. The younger children were terrified of the dark and had difficulty sleeping. Edmund's lungs rattled and wheezed at night and his coughing fits kept the majority of us awake. I laid him across my lap and pat his back with cupped hands; this seemed to help bring up the phlegm that clogged his airways. He had no place to spit the mucus so he swallowed it down once more, gagging as he did so. Sister Agnes did her best to quell the fears of the kids by singing lullabies at night and sacrificing her own sleep to ensure that everyone was comfortable, warm, and felt safe.

Aside from a quiet thirteen-year-old boy, I was now the oldest charge in the carriage portion of the train so I did my best to help calm and entertain the children. I told them stories from my days on the farm, describing the funny things the animals did. I shared how Harriet the hen chased me around her pen whenever I tried to collect her eggs, she would cluck and flap her wings, and try to peck my legs while I gathered breakfast. I told them about my pony, Oliver, too, and how I used to brush and braid his long tail, sometimes adding wooden beads into the braid for decoration. However, when Sister Agnes heard me recounting my days on the farm she reminded me I was supposed to forget everything from my past. I had difficulty making up stories, so I relied on the few my mama told me; *Hansel and Gretel* and *Little Red Riding Hood* were favorites.

I learned later that many of the children on board the train were from my Ward and that some of them even had parents that were alive. Nonetheless, they were handed over to strangers for numerous reasons. Some folks were doing hard time in jail, others were drunkards or drug addicts who had fallen prey to the opium dens. The majority, however, were financially incapable of caring for their children. The poverty-stricken city produced so much crime resulting from immigration that even those with good intentions handed their flesh and blood over to the sisters, hoping they would have a better life in the country. The thirteen-year-old boy with the lovely singing voice and sunken eyes told me that his mother was a prostitute and could no longer care for him. I held his hand tightly, knowing full well that he felt abandoned and unwanted like I did. I thanked my lucky stars above that I had a good mother who would never have sold me out or sent me away as long as she was alive. I felt a little remorse toward the girl who I beat up at the girls' home because she must not have had any love before and didn't know just how nice a comfort the memory was.

As the train rolled along westward, we made several stops at churches, opera houses, and town halls. Sister Agnes handed out sweets and repeated her instructions, and then we cleaned our faces and marched onto the platform where we put on our best show, smiling, being delightful, and praying for a family to want us. Many boys didn't necessarily want families but rather work and often that is what they were offered. As long as they were fed and had a bed to sleep in at night the family could legally adopt them for free in exchange for labor. The next two boys adopted out went to a mill owner who planned to expand his operation. The boys were given room and board in exchange for work and seemed comfortable enough about the arrangement. They said their goodbyes to those of us left on the train and began their new lives at once.

Several more babies and toddlers were adopted by families who were sure to love them as their own. You could see it in the eyes of the new parents, the tenderness they showed when examining their prospective new child, counting their fingers and toes and kissing their pudgy cheeks. There was love in their embrace and when the paperwork requirements were met, they were able to take their son or daughter home. It was something to marvel at, the way parents just knew which child was meant for them. I couldn't deny the children this love although I was growing more anxious and insecure as the train traveled further west, changing lines from the Erie to the Lackawanna in Chicago.

Edmund was painfully shy and guarded. He gripped my hand tighter than ever and particularly so on the platform. An eager man came toward Eddie, as I had begun to call him. He tried to be friendly and get Eddie to talk before he stuck his grimy, dirt-ridden fingers in the little guy's mouth to examine his teeth. Eddie chomped right down on them, spitting out the yucky residue left by the stranger's fingers and proceeded to wail so loudly that any attention he called to him or to me for that matter, was negative. I took Edmund back in the train that afternoon and cuddled him as if he were mine. He was a lovely child once you got past his quirky behaviors, fears, and snotty nose. As long as I had Eddie to care for I would surely never be given a home. But secretly, I liked that Eddie needed me and I grew to adore him even more.

I decided to make the orphan train my home with Eddie. We were fed and had a bed to sleep on at night and nowhere else to be. I began to sing Eddie the ABCs and taught him to count to ten. We counted our fingers and toes and he laughed when I pretended I captured his nose. His smile was devilish, and boy, was he squirmy, turning to spaghetti whenever it was time to change him into his traveling clothes. Sister Agnes had a few children's books on the train and as I read them out loud and pointed to the pictures, Eddie and the others were able to forget their pain momentarily.

At night, we often slept at hotels or in church halls that were prepared for us ahead of time by the Sisters of Charity. The boys and girls were divided and separated into rooms by age and gender. But Eddie and I always remained together. No one else could get him to fall asleep; he needed me to pat his back and rub his hair just so, and to sing his favorite lullabies such as "Rock a Bye Baby." He held onto my thumbs with his tiny hands and when I woke in the morning, he would be staring adoringly into my eyes.

Sister Agnes was fearful that Edmund was growing too attached to me and tried to take him upon herself, but he proved to be too much trouble when she had so many other children to chaperone. The older orphans were growing restless and it was reported that they were smoking and using profanity in the boxcars. One of the teenage boys had plans to jump from the train and run away but he was forced to sit in coach with us until his Christian notions settled in. Sister Agnes quizzed him on Bible verses, filled his mind with Christian ways and other nonsense until she was certain he would behave. When he finally made his way back to the boxcar, he leapt off and we never saw him again.

A family at our fifth stop inquired about me because they heard I was a skilled laundress. The family was rather wealthy and had three young girls. They had a nanny under their employ but she struggled with the care and keeping of the girls and requested they hire a girl strictly for laundry. I was much too small for their liking and they hated my cropped haircut. Still, they poked at my ears and hair, opened my mouth and inspected my teeth and gums as if I were a cattle specimen. They turned my hands over multiple times, looking curiously at my nail beds.

"She will do," the predatory woman said. She never once looked into my eyes and I started to shake.

"Fine, I will sign the papers. Meet me outside, dear," the man with the receding hairline said to his wife. She was already walking outdoors ahead of him without so much as a backwards glance. There was nothing cheerful about her and it was clear I would be no more than a piece of property to them.

I was about to become an indentured worker for a family that was incapable of loving me. What would happen to Edmund now? I had grown to love this little boy. He was pointing to all sorts of objects now and reciting them as well as reciting different animals and what sounds they made, "cat, dog, meow, ruff, ruff..."

"Now, Mary, I assure you that I will remain in touch. It's part of my job to follow up and see that you are thriving in your new environment." Sister Agnes spoke lovingly as she tried to comfort me.

"But it's not a family as I'd prayed for..." I let my voice trail off.

"I know, Mary. I know it isn't what we hoped, but you will be provided for and have everything you need. You can write to me yourself, we can be pen pals, would you like that?"

"I suppose that would be nice. Thank you, Sister Agnes."

I prepared to say my goodbyes to Edmund, kissing him gently on the forehead and whispering into his tiny ears that I loved him and hoped a nice family would come for him at the next stop. He put his little hands on my cheeks and I heaved a sigh of grief so great that I began to heave and throw up. I threw up all over my good Christian dress and all over Eddie's nice clothes. I had chunks of vomit in my hair and on my shoes. I looked into the face of the man who was supposed to take me home but he just snarled at me. He threw the pen back at Sister Agnes and said, "We've changed our minds." He walked out and never looked back. I was free to be with Eddie and Sister Agnes for another few days at least.

I don't know what overcame me that day, perhaps it was the fact we had been traveling for several weeks, having gone through New York, Pennsylvania, Ohio, Indiana, and Illinois and had paraded ourselves desperately in front of strangers, hoping to be wanted. Or perhaps it was my growing love for Edmund, who was softening me. Either way, I was grateful, for we only had one more stop before returning to the city. We only had to go through the flat lands of Iowa and would be turning back around heading east to pick up more orphans. I would be able to stay with the sisters until our next trip was scheduled.

Our very last stop on the way home was going to be in Mason City, Iowa. I had considered that I could be a ward like Agnes someday and she agreed I would do a fine job. She also agreed it was necessary to find Edmund a nice family home first, however, or I would be unable to help her on subsequent trips.

Most of the children had been adopted or exchanged for work at this point in our journey. There were five of us left including me and Eddie, a set of twin girls with criss-crossed eyes, and a lad about the age of seven who was sullen and not so bright. The lad repeatedly hit himself in the forehead and screamed out curse words in feverish torrents, frightening the younger children onboard.

We donned our finest clothes, Sister Agnes reminded us to display our good manners and to smile big for the crowd, and then we met up with the coordinating sister who led us to the town center for our appraisals. Only a few families had come in to see us but one family that was present was most certainly of the do-gooder variety. They had children of their own but felt it was Christian to adopt a child in need, bringing them into the folds of their family and showing them the ways of the Lord. The matriarch of the family held the Holy Bible tightly across her chest while glancing at the five of us before her. She whispered to her husband, a stout man with a neatly manicured mustache that curled up on each end. He pulled out his glasses and put them on so he was able to get a closer look at the twins. They clasped their hands together and smiled their best smiles that to me seemed to make their eyes cross even more toward their noses. The family walked toward the girls for introductions and soon laughter ensued because the girls learned they were going to be adopted by none other than an optometrist who could fit them with glasses to strengthen their eyes and redirect their gaze. They were giddy with excitement and thrilled that they weren't going to be separated as other siblings before them had been. The six-year-old twins ran to say their goodbyes to Sister Agnes and they hugged Edmund and me as well before skipping off hand in hand with their new parents.

I smiled inside my heart because if two little girls with mousy hair and funny eyes were able to get a family to love them, then surely Edmund and I could. We just haven't found them yet, or rather, they haven't found us.

⚬

The last three of us unclaimed children boarded the train with Sister Agnes a final time and headed back to New York City. I was looking forward to the hustle and bustle of the city after seeing so much boring countryside. The possibility that I might see Scotty again loomed large within me. I liked him and missed his mischievous ways. He was my one and only true friend in the city. I thought maybe I could convince him to ride the next train bound west with me and find a place of his own or at least find good honest work that he could get paid for doing. Scotty had a tough exterior but I suspected he was soft on the inside like the rest of us.

Our train pulled into the New York City Grand Central Station and, rather than being met by large crowds milling about, kids selling the papers or matches, we were met with emptiness.

"What's this?" Sister Agnes asked out loud, her eyes roving the quiet station.

Spring had brought a substantial rise and resurgence of cholera while we were traveling. The newspaper described it as an epidemic similar to the outbreak of 1831, one that took thousands of lives. Panic ensued. The widespread disease began taking lives shortly after we left on the orphan train. The sisters remained healthy but many of the children from the slums were sickly or had passed away. People in stagecoaches, livery coaches, or on horseback were leaving the city in droves, clogging the streets. Inhabitants were forewarned not to eat or drink too heartily and not to sleep anywhere there could be a draft. Posters lined the train station, warning people to tend immediately to problems of the bowels and not to take any medicine without a doctor's advice, not to get wet, and or drink cold water. Yet no one knew what really caused the cholera; only that it was deadly and spread quickly.

The symptoms of cholera appeared instantly. Someone who was healthy in the morning could become violently ill by mid-morning and have their skin turn a ghastly gray-blue tint; they would become severely dehydrated and die shortly after. The city's inhabitants walked on eggshells in fear for their lives.

"Children, it has been decided that we will not stay in the city a moment longer than we have to with cholera on the rise. Prepare to leave on the train tomorrow morning as we are heading out at first light. We will have a larger group this time, so please, do your best to be courteous and kind to anyone in need."

Typically, the sisters would pre-arrange trips with very specific stops along the route. However, in this emergent instance, children frantically boarded the trains that set out for destinations unknown. The conductor agreed to stop in all major cities bound west in hopes of finding the children new homes.

Edmund and I were once again under the guardianship of Sister Agnes as we headed northwest. Our route was slightly different this time, as we would head further north and go further west. We had nearly one hundred orphans on our train; all the children less than six years of age were with us in coach, while the older children were cramped into the quarters of the boxcars. It was my job to help Sister Agnes with all the small children, not just Edmund. Edmund was growing more plump and cheerful and had several more words in his vocabulary. He could even recognize letters now when I read to him. Although his dark features could not be disguised, he was a precious boy who would have no trouble at all being adopted this trip.

We had two additional chaperones on our trip this run. Thankfully, Mr. and Mrs. Porter volunteered their services to help with the dozen or more infants. The babies needed constant changing, dressing, holding, bundling, and feeding, which made me wonder why anyone who had a choice would prefer an infant that took so much time and energy as compared to a child like Eddie. I decided, somewhat selfishly, that I would train Eddie to use the potty like a proper big lad and alleviate the necessity to change his nappy any longer. He should have learned this skill years ago but given his upbringing he never did. He did very well on his first few tries. The trick was getting him to realize when he had to make a dooty and tell me in time to get him to the potty. The bathroom was several cars behind us and therefore took several minutes to get to.

Wanting very much to please me, Eddie eventually succeeded in becoming trained and this increased his odds of going to a good home. I imagined him with a loving mother who would dote on him endlessly and a father who would take him fishing and teach him to feed the barn animals along with other chores. Eddie already knew the sounds the barn animals made, although he has never heard them first hand. He could even sing a few lines from songs highlighting the animals, like "Mary Had a Little Lamb." His singing voice was squeaky and high pitched but precious nonetheless.

When I told Sister Agnes about our successful potty training she pushed her frizzy brown hair behind her ears and pulled me in for a tight hug. It was the first time I received a hug from an adult since my mother passed away and I stiffened at the sensation from the embrace.

"You did well, Mary. Now surely Edmund will be adopted and you can help me with the other toddlers who are in need of attention." She smiled at me briefly and then was off preparing for our first stop.

As usual, our first stop was in Pennsylvania. Despite the fact that our trip wasn't advertised in the paper, it was still a huge success. Eight of the infants were adopted and a dozen of the older children were taken in exchange for work by farmers, mill owners, and even hotels. Eddie and I were clinging to each other when a dapper couple came toward us. The young woman had copper-colored hair and a face full of freckles. Her curly locks attracted Edmund and as she approached, he reached out to feel her tresses. She put her hands out in hopes Edmund would go to her but instead he clung tighter to me. I leaned into the lady with Edmund and tried to unhinge his little fingers from my dress. I asked him, "Eddie, what does the bunny do?" and he replied by crinkling up his nose and making a snuffling sound. The woman laughed at this and tried again to pry Eddie from my arms. After much coaxing with a grape sucker, Edmund got down from my hip and stood at my side. He held tight to my calico dress while he sucked his pop loudly and drooled out the side of his mouth. The woman and her husband asked if he was a bright boy, they wanted to know if he slept through the night. They also asked if he was potty trained, and wanted to know if he had any trouble seeing or hearing things. I answered all of the questions thoughtfully. I told them about Edmund's nature to want to cuddle. I explained that he liked to be sung to sleep and have his head rubbed. They were enchanted with him and decided that they would love nothing more than to welcome him into their home as their son. Tears filled my eyes. Eddie would have a loving home, a real family, and he could grow up to be a businessman like his adoptive father, or perhaps he could learn a trade. He would learn to read and write, figure arithmetic, and one day might even have a wife and children of his own. More than anything, the family would see to his health and his ailing lungs. He hardly noticed me as his new parents bribed him off the platform with stuffed animals and toys.

Feeling a kinship toward me now, Sister Agnes placed her hands upon my sunken shoulders to offer comfort. "Mary, I will talk to the sisters about having you assist me with the other small children, would you like that?" I hugged her and stifled my tears. "Yes, I would like that very much," I said in reply. I felt my heart break at the loss of Edmund and suddenly I was overwhelmed with sadness and worry. I wondered what my own future had in store for me, it was clear that Edmund had become a crutch for me and now I was alone all over again.

Later I found out that Sister Agnes had approached the family about adopting me as Eddie's nanny, she showered me with praise for my ability to calm him when he was upset. They declined because they only had the financial capability to care for one child at this time.

I had numerous other children to look after now, but at every stop more of them were finding homes. Terrified siblings clung to one another in fear of being ripped apart; happily, most of them were taken together on this journey. All the infants were gone and most of the older lads and gals were gone too.

Sister Agnes always talked about the clean country air and when I closed my eyes, I could taste it. I remembered when both my mama and da were alive and we lived in a farmhouse with two rooms and a loft that my da built by himself. I had my own bed and starburst quilt and even had a window to see the constellations at night. The smell of fresh cut hay and the taste of the crisp apples that came from the trees by our stream filled my senses. I wished fervently that we could have figured out a way to stay on the farm, but the good Lord must have had a different plan in mind for me.

؞ﻩ؞

One day on the train when the youngsters were napping, I sat next to Sister Agnes and asked about her family. She cleared her throat before recounting her story. She fondled the cross she wore around her neck and got a far-away look in her eye. Her mother was a German immigrant in New York City struggling to feed her three small children. Her father left her mother for days on end, heading to the brothels or opium dens in the Five Points. Her mother, Anna, starved herself in order to feed her children the scraps she could beg or find in garbage cans around the city. Hearing the news that her husband had died in a bar brawl, she was overcome with shock and walked away from her children, leaving them alone for an entire day. When she returned, she had food and drink, blankets and a few spare coins for emergencies. She began going out at night, coming home in the early morning hours; often she was drunk and she was always sore down there. She reeked of cheap perfume and male body odor and more than once she came home with large bruises across her face. Sister Agnes remembered the time her mother's wrist was broken and she cradled it in her other arm; she never complained and was able to put food on the table despite the injury. When she was thirteen, her mother was gone so much of the time that she had to quit school and watch over her siblings. She herself would venture out in the daytime to sweep storefronts or beg for coin for food. One night, her mother didn't come home at all and she was found dead in the alleyway near their small home in Lower Manhattan. She had been brutally raped and beaten to death. When she was found, her shoes were missing and her skirt was removed, all that remained was her torn shift and the simple wooden cross she wore around her neck tied with shoestring.

Sister Agnes was separated from her siblings and brought to a corporately funded House of Refuge that already housed hundreds of neglected or abandoned children. The home for the refugees was poorly run and Sister Agnes spent many pointless days scrubbing floorboards and washing walls and windows. The children were given jobs to help keep them out of trouble but in many instances, they were whipped and beaten or deprived of food if the overseer didn't approve of their work. The children were often sickly and went without proper medical attention, some even died. Thankfully, the Sisters of Charity were in need of a few young ladies to help them in the new journey they were about to begin trekking across the countryside with orphans. In return for the help, the sisters promised to bring children from the refuge home along on their next trip.

Agnes fondled the smooth wooden cross around her neck, "This was my mother Anna's. She did her best to care for us. I will never know what happened to my siblings, but my destiny now is to help all of these children, and you too." A tear trickled down her cheek and she let it roll onto her habit. She had chosen a life of faith instead of the painful life she associated with family. She opened her Bible and began reciting the words to her favorite psalm, "The Lord is my Shepherd..."

"How old are you, Sister Agnes?" I asked, interrupting her.

"I suspect I am nearing eighteen," she answered without looking up from her Bible.

I crept back to my wooden plank seat in the last row of the carriage and thought of my life on the farm and in the city. I was never so grateful that neither of my parents agonized with death. The thought of my mama giving herself to men for coin was sickening. To think of that act at all was mind boggling, but I supposed that if it was with someone you loved it was okay.

I grew sullen as the days passed and more children were adopted into loving homes. It wasn't fair that my da died nor was it fair I had no mama; I had no one left in this life to love me. Scotty and Eddie were the closest things I had to family and now they were gone, too.

I was setting up my new plan when the train pulled into our next stop, this time in Ohio. I was thinking of turning to the Lord and becoming a sister, like Sister Agnes, when a familiar cry reached my ears. We were walking off the train when the sound captured my attention; it was Edmund's wail! He was being returned on account of his difficult nature. The gentleman who had signed the papers for him handed him to me and sought Sister Agnes. They were in deep, concentrated discussion about the situation.

"It isn't natural, ma'am, if you'll pardon my saying so." The gentleman had taken off his top hat while he spoke to Sister Agnes and gestured to Eddie, who was happy now that he was safely back in my arms.

Eddie clung to me as if his life depended on it. I wiped his snotty nose and kissed his cheeks. I missed him dearly and now that he was back, I would never let him go again. His eyes were puffy and red rimmed from all his crying so I kissed them too. I overheard the man comment on Eddie's unnatural affection for me and shook the thought aside. I was the closest thing he had to a mother and being separated from me caused him too much anxiety.

"Oh, Eddie, I love you!" I exclaimed, selfishly happy that he was back with me.

"Eddie wuvs you too!" the child said softly before nestling into my welcoming arms once again.

Sister Agnes had her hands full with the other orphans so she instructed me to take care of Edmund. I gave him a pail with sweet milk and a buttered roll, which he gobbled down immediately. He savored the tart green apple, letting the juices run down his chin, and holding it out to share with me.

A dozen orphans were adopted on that stop but more than half of us remained homeless so we pushed onward to the Dakotas. The conductor yelled, "All aboard," setting the train on a click clack motion that we were all used to by now.

Sister Agnes approached me cautiously, "We have a slight problem."

"Oh, dear, I hope it doesn't have to do with me, sister." I was afraid because she appeared very serious.

"Well, in fact it does. It seems Edmund simply can't be placed without you. He was inconsolable, crying for you nonstop." The sister fluffed Edmund's dark curls as he sucked his thumb and tried to make sense of our conversation.

"Oh, sister, do you mean it?" I asked. "Can we be placed as siblings? Is that possible?" I might not become a sister like Sister Agnes; there still remained a glimmer of hope for me after all.

"It may be impossible, it's difficult enough to find a home for a dark-skinned toddler and a red-headed girl, but we will try our best." Sister Agnes adjusted her cross and left us alone so that we could reunite. She had a wistful expression on her face as she turned away from us to tend to the needs of the other orphans.

The train rambled on a northwest route taking us through Wisconsin and Minnesota before stopping in North Dakota, then heading to South Dakota and continuing on through Nebraska and Kansas. We would eventually cross into Missouri and Kentucky, and wind our way back through Ohio, West Virginia, Pennsylvania, and New York. The journey took several weeks and everyone, including Sister Agnes, was growing restless. The Porters left us in the Dakotas because there were no babies to attend. I would spend the long hours braiding the little girls' hair and singing Christian songs to provide entertainment. The older boys played checkers and cards and arm wrestled in the filthy boxcars, and some even jumped from the train in an attempt to find their own way.

As we approached Pennsylvania and New York, Sister Agnes spent her time finishing paperwork. She continued to make notations in her folders for those of us still available as well. One day while she was bathing and dressing the elementary age kids, I found her notebook and snooped.

It didn't take long to find my name. It read:

"Mary is an insecure yet proud and capable ten-year-old orphan girl. Both of her parents are deceased and as a result, she is often quiet and reflective. On account of prior malnutrition she weighs approximately sixty-five pounds and is shorter than most girls her age. She has red hair that was shaved when she contracted lice, it is now growing in nicely. Mary is skilled at laundering and pressing clothing, she is also quite capable of taking care of younger children. If given the opportunity she would be best placed in a home with Edmund, if not as his caregiver, then as a sibling."

I sifted through the paperwork until I found Edmund's name. Under his description, it read: "Edmund is an underdeveloped five-year-old boy with a peculiar demeanor and unusual attachment issues."

That night I said a heartfelt prayer. I prayed to God and to my mama and da, I prayed to Edmund's family and anyone else that would listen. I promised to be good, I promised to always take care of Edmund, if only a family would come for us. I recited this prayer over and over hundreds of times before drifting off into a restless sleep.

❧

The next morning we were greeted and paraded in front of the good people of Binghamton, New York. It was a small city several hour's train ride from New York City, which meant we were nearly done with our trip. It was sad that so many of us remained unadopted and unwanted.

Edmund and I were paying attention to ourselves when an older woman wearing a plaid dress and matching bonnet approached us. She smelled of verbena and talcum powder and appeared to be in her late forties. This woman had no children of her own and spent her time as a volunteer at the hospital.

Her husband was the local pharmacist and they were well off but not at all snooty like some other folks we encountered on our journey. She spoke directly to me, asking if I liked to read. I told her about my first primer and Eddie and I sang her the ABCs. Eddie clapped his little hands together and the nice lady was smitten. A gentleman wearing a crimson vest and high top hat approached our group and began speaking to me.

"Why, hello there, young lady, what is your name?" he inquired.

"I am called Mary," I replied sheepishly.

"Mary, I am Jonathan Pearsall. It's a pleasure to meet you. Tell me, Mary, what is it you enjoy doing?"

"I don't know what you mean, sir. I always work hard and help look after the children, especially Eddie. I don't suppose I have time to enjoy too much when my chores and duties are done." I scratched my head and thought about his question. I repositioned my pink headband so it wouldn't slide down my forehead.

"Well, that is a shame," he said while shaking his head and smoothing his beard with his right hand.

"My wife and I are more than happy to open our home to a young girl like yourself, someone with whom Edna could share her love of reading and sewing." When he finished speaking to me, he and his wife smiled at one another and clasped their hands together.

I was overjoyed. After months and months on the train, a family finally wanted me! They actually wanted me as their own daughter, not as an indentured servant. Still, I had Edmund to consider and remembered he was hopeless without me.

"I would love to learn to read harder words, sir. I could also try to find the patience for sewing, but I am afraid I have this little boy here to think of. He can't seem to get by without me; he was adopted once already and returned," I explained. With that admission, I took Eddie's plump fingers in my own and turned away from the couple. I felt defeated. We walked across the platform and after I sat down with my legs crossed, I positioned Eddie in my lap.

Eddie and I played a game of patty cake while we waited to re-board the train; however, the couple approached us again.

"Dear, my name is Edna. You remind me very much of someone I once knew. I would like to have you in our home." Edna gentled me with her soft warm hands and said she might have a solution for Eddie.

Her sister and husband lived nearby and might be interested in the small boy. If we could delay the train, she would travel in her own buggy to collect them and bring them to meet Eddie at once. Edna explained that while she and her sister both dreamed of having children, neither was able to conceive. If we lived close to one another, perhaps Eddie and I could thrive even if we were in different homes because we would be secure in the knowledge that we were only a few miles apart.

The opportunity for a real family overwhelmed me. I nearly wet my underpants and could hardly speak. I was excited and afraid at the same time. I didn't know how to express my feelings so I crossed my fingers and tapped my leg, waiting impatiently for Edna to come back with her sister in tow.

Several hours and introductions later, Eddie and I were officially adopted. The paperwork was signed and we clung to Sister Agnes while saying our tearful goodbyes. She promised to write to me directly over the course of the year to make sure everything was going well. I promised to keep up with my schoolwork so that I could write back to her myself.

CHAPTER 5

❦

MARY: BINGHAMTON, NEW YORK 1860

"Welcome to your new home, Mary." Edna held my hand and Edmund lurked close behind while she gave us the tour through her grand Victorian style house on the outskirts of Binghamton. It boasted six bedrooms, four brick-laid chimneys, and two baths, each with a claw foot tub to soak in. The home had gingerbread latticework along the roof line and white siding that was kept clean. The floors and banisters were made from chestnut wood and large, lead diamond-shaped patterns adorned the windows. The porch wrapped itself around the home, culminating in the large central foyer complete with chestnut columns. The center foyer led to a full kitchen in the back of the house that smelled of freshly baked bread. I noted the orderliness of the room; clean aprons were hung on several decorative hooks across from the stove, pots and pans were stacked by task and size, as was the white porcelain dinnerware that lay across open shelving. Across the hall, there was an ornate dining room and adjacent to that was my favorite room of all, the library. The entire room had floor-to-ceiling whitewashed bookshelves full to the brim with books of all shapes and sizes. Several over-sized leather chairs sat stoically upon a deep burgundy-colored Oriental carpet with center medallion. They faced the backyard and overlooked a bountiful garden that boasted roses, daisies, and more. The inviting chairs were adorned with soft blankets and fluffy pillows that Eddie and I sank into. Soon a tea service appeared with finger sandwiches and cookies. We ate our fill and chatted cautiously with our new families, enjoying the fact we were now cousins.

I was hard pressed to believe someone, even sweet generous Edna, would see fit to let children in her parlor with so many knick-knacks and breakables around, it just wasn't practical. Edmund didn't have the same concerns; he picked up the miniatures one by one and played with them as if they were his very own. I was afraid of breaking anything and being sent away so I kept my hands to my sides at all times and only looked with my eyes as my mother had taught me on our sojourns into city shops.

Edna was perceptive and welcoming. She asked me which miniature I liked the best and when I told her I liked the porcelain pony, she allowed me to have it even though I protested. I carried it painstakingly up to my room on the second level and secured it on my dresser next to a crystal lamp. I would admire the trinket each morning when I woke and stroke the salty colored mane on the horse each night before bed. Edmund sulked when I was given the miniature pony and because he made such a fuss, Edna allowed him to also choose from her collection of treasures. He chose the rabbit with the pink floppy ears and cotton tail, which I was certain was Edna's favorite. Edmund objected to having just one because this rabbit came as a set that she herself made. Selfishly, he wanted the rabbit that wore a blue bonnet as well as the one with the pink ears. He needed to learn some manners. But for now everyone seemed to appease him when he cried and sulked, myself included. I was fearful Edmund would become spoiled and forget his manners.

Because Eddie and I weren't separated right away, he went more willingly to his new family as time went on. Sarah and Samuel Whitmore were his parents now. Samuel was a banker and Sarah, like her sister, spent her free time volunteering. Both had acquired money and enjoyed a menagerie of fine things. They had Oriental rugs and furnishings in every room, paintings, curtains, as well as both formal and every day dinnerware. I had never heard of such a thing and found it very extravagant. I reminisced about the cracked plates that mama and I used to sup on and the threadbare sheet we hung for privacy across our single window in the slums.

Settling in was easy for me, I had never been so doted on before. My hair was tended by a hairdresser who softened my unruly spikes into curls, giving me a more feminine look. My clothes were made by Edna's personal dressmaker. The seamstress came over to my new home carrying a basket full of youthful materials in a variety of colors and patterns. She got out her measuring tape and asked me what colors I liked while she measured my outstretched arms and took notes. I was given dolls and clothes to dress them in. Edna gave me my very own afghan too. It was a lovely purple cotton yarn with red, pink, and white stripes throughout it that she knit herself. She promised to teach me to knit and thought that making a scarf for the upcoming winter season would be the perfect beginner project.

I treasured the blanket and hugged Edna tightly. "Thank you, Edna!" I cried out.

"Mary, would you like to call me mom?" she asked pensively.

I was confused, I had a mom and Edna wasn't her. My tattered picture was safely tucked away in my top dresser drawer and I was tempted to pull it out and share it with Edna.

Sensing my distress, she said, "Why don't you call me Edna for now okay, dear? Perhaps later we will settle on a special name for me."

I nodded in agreement. "We are supposed to forget, but I can't say that I want to. I'm sorry, ma'am." My knuckles tightened around the blanket and a small hole appeared where I was digging my fingers as a result of my anxiety.

Instead of getting scolded, Edna pulled me in for a grandmotherly hug. "I would never expect you to forget your family, Mary. Every step you have traveled has led you to us and we couldn't be happier." Edna smiled as she held me to her bosom.

I stood up from Edna's embrace and opened my dresser, sifting through the underwear and stockings until my hands found the photograph. I held the shreds out for Edna to see. She pieced it together and stared at it for a moment.

"Oh, my." Edna clutched her chest before continuing. "Your mother is beautiful, and you look just like her."

"Really, Edna, do you think so?" I asked.

"I certainly do, it's not just the hair, but your eyes and smile are just like hers. What was her name?"

"Her name was Maura Anne Salt," I stuttered.

"I would like to say a special thank you to her every night in my prayers. Will that be okay with you?" she asked.

I assured Edna that it was okay and proceeded to think about her name, Maura. Maura and Mary weren't so different, yet "Mary" still felt uneasy to me. It wasn't my real name after all, but for Edna I would do my best to accept it and her.

"Do you like it here, Mary, with us?"

"Oh, Edna, I do, I really do," I said. "I can't think of a better place for me, or Eddie."

Sarah and Samuel were smitten with Eddie. He still clung to me and cried for me to kiss his boo boos but more often now he could be distracted with brightly painted tops that spun and other wooden toys like carvings and blocks. The first few days, he and I shared a bed at Edna's but by day three, Eddie hugged me goodbye and went home with his new family who lived only one block away. I saw him for our breakfast meals; the sisters donned their aprons and cooked up a storm for us. They fed us johnnycakes with real maple syrup and chocolate shavings on top. Eddie was cheerful and energetic and Sarah proved to be very patient with him. His cough was better for the time being and I hoped it didn't cause too much trouble in the future.

After several weeks of living with my new family, I became accustomed to our routines and rules, of which there were only a few. I accompanied Edna on her daily errands and spent time in the local library where she volunteered once a week. She allowed me to read from the children's section and I wished I could bring one or two books home to share with Edmund. But the library did not yet have a system in place to circulate books. Once Edna realized how well I could read, she decided I was settled enough into my new life that I could begin attending the elementary school in the city. In preparation, we bought a new notebook and canvas bag to carry it in, two pencils, a lunch pail, and several new pairs of shoes to match my dresses and ribbons that went in my hair. For my first day, I was going to wear a cream-colored dress with smocking across the bodice and a red ribbon at my waist. My stockings were cream and my shoes were patent leather. A matching red headband was made to hold my hair out of my eyes. I was nervous because I had missed an entire year of learning, but I was also excited to make friends and to wear my new outfit, although I didn't think the light color of my dress was practical for a child my age to wear. Mama and I always wore dark colors that didn't show stains.

Edna assured me I would like the teacher, Miss Kate. After making the proper introductions on my first day, she left me in her care. There were six rows of six wooden desks and chairs, making for thirty-six students in the classroom. I was assigned a seat in the second row on my first day and sat fidgeting with my fingers while the remainder of the children filed in so that we could begin the day's lessons.

The blackboard at school had rhyming words on it like cat, hat, mat, and rat. But when a young man was called upon to read them, he quietly refused. The young man was called to the teacher's desk where she took out a ruler and smacked his knuckles. Miss Kate cringed with each smack she doled out. But when the young man with curly brown hair turned back around and walked toward his seat, I screamed.

"Scotty!" The words were out of my mouth before I could scoop them back up; it was the most wonderful surprise I could have asked for. I beamed, jumped out of my seat, and clapped my hands to my chest.

"Miss Mary, please do get a hold of yourself. I will give you some leeway as this is your first day, but such outbursts are not allowed in this classroom. Furthermore, this is Matthew, not Scotty." But I knew it was my dear friend Scotty and he, grinning from ear to ear, knew it was me.

We could hardly wait until lunchtime recess to get reacquainted. We grabbed our lunch pails when the school bell rang and ran toward each other.

"I thought cholera got you," I said, hugging Scotty.

"Not a chance, but the sisters did," he chuckled, reminding me of our time back in the city, spent telling jokes under the stoop.

"You sure have grown up, your hair, it's so curly now." I studied him and realized he was now twelve. He had broad shoulders and appeared far taller than other boys his age.

"Look at you, Tabit..." He let my name trail off before catching himself. "I mean, Mary, is it? You're still a shrimp. What happened anyway? I couldn't find you. I looked everywhere, I even went to the Canter's but they said you'd gone on the train. So I went to see the sisters and ask, but they said you weren't on it. The police were already after me for stealing and a few other things so the sisters gave me a choice, I either get on the train or I would be taken to a juvenile house of reform. I chose the train."

I explained to my friend, whom I would always refer to as Scotty, that I spent time at the Home for Girls, but then ran away and went back to the stoop expecting to find him there. I told him how I slept alone that night and how scary it was. I told him how I went door to door in search of work but couldn't find any. I worried about him and the others dying from typhoid, or life on the streets, and he said he would have been more worried about me if he had known I was alone. He said things had gotten pretty rough around the city and what had happened to Karen was just the beginning. He said I was lucky I was left alone and not killed. The gangs were more pronounced and territorial, there was more theft, and it was becoming scary, even for him. When Scotty spoke about New York City, his right eyebrow spasmed and he clenched his fists.

"A tough guy like you, scared?" I teased.

"Yeah, it was scary, even for a tough guy like me." He grabbed my head into a cradle and dislodged my headband as he ran his knuckles back and forth playfully.

"So where do you live now?" I asked, hoping we were close enough to each other that we could walk to and from school together.

"I live out past the mill at the Wright Farm." He kicked the ground and stirred the dust when he said, "farm." I knew what it meant for him; he was adopted in exchange for work. He didn't have a family to love him like I did.

"Well, at least you get to come to school. That's pretty lucky." I offered the encouragement while shading my eyes from the bright mid-day's sunshine.

"Mr. and Mrs. Wright are good people; they want me to be educated so I can help keep the books someday. But you know me; I don't have the patience for arithmetic. I am, however, good with my hands." He wiggled his eyebrows up and down and then pushed up his shirtsleeves and flexed his well-toned muscles.

"Right now I fix the fences, do the whitewashing, and help feed the animals, that kind of thing," he said.

He pulled a butterscotch candy from his pocket and handed it to me. I opened it and popped it right into my mouth. It had been a long time since I had butterscotch and it reminded me of our old penny candy store. I started to cry at the image the memory evoked.

"What's wrong? Don't you like it?" he asked, concerned.

"It's not that. Remember how my mama had her teeth pulled? Well, I bought her butterscotch to suck on after, that's all. It just made me think of her." I pushed the thought far from my mind and stared into the eyes of my friend.

Scotty hugged me tight against his chest. "Everything will be all right now," he said in my ear.

I believed him.

When school got out that day, I grabbed Scotty's hand and ran with him over toward Edna, who was waiting for me with Eddie at the corner.

"Oh, Edna, you'll never guess!" I ran to her and hugged her.

Edna could see my joy and clapped her hands together. "Have you made a friend already?" she asked lightheartedly.

"It's even better, Edna. This is my old friend, Scotty. He's from New York, we were best friends there!" Scotty blushed at the endearment, but I didn't think anything of it, it was true. Scotty was the truest friend I had ever had.

"Well, that is splendid news. Scotty, can you join us at the house for some milk and cookies? Then you two could tell me how you are acquainted."

"I would like to, ma'am, but I have to get back to the Wright Farm and do my chores. Thank you for the offer though." He was very polite, making me feel curiously proud.

With that, he gave me a soft nudge in the upper arm and said, "See you tomorrow, Red!" I guess that was his new nickname for me and I liked it, it was fitting.

Scotty headed off in the opposite direction from town and Edna and I swung Eddie between us on the way home. It was a splendid day indeed and not just because of my shiny new shoes.

"So, Mary, how was school?" Edna was full of anticipation and pulled a chair right up beside me so we could have a good chat. Eddie played with the frosting on his cookie and listened intently as well.

"It was the best day ever, Edna! Miss Kate is smart and kind, and keeps the kids in line if I don't say so myself. She even posted the classroom rules on the blackboard."

Edna laughed under her breath when I said this but I knew after spending time with Sister Agnes on the train just how difficult a task it was to keep a large number of kids in line.

"She advanced me to the fourth grade primer and said I would catch up to the others in my group in no time at all. Why, she even said I could help the smaller children from time to time if I wanted. It seems they like me, I guess." I straightened my shoulders and looked at Eddie who gave me a big frosting grin that I kissed right off his little gooey lips.

"I have homework to do, so I suppose I should get to it. I have to read a chapter in my primer and then write all the words that rhyme with ball and bat. I have to do it in my best handwriting too. Soon I will even get to learn to write in cursive." I finished my cookies and milk and swept my crumbs onto my plate before bringing it to the sink and setting it in the basin.

"Why don't you study in the library and close the door so you can work in peace." Edna cleaned the dishes and walked Eddie home to be with Sarah.

School progressed well and before the year's end, I had advanced to the fifth grade level. Scotty had a difficult time juggling his studies with farm work; he became frustrated and stomped out the weeds during recess, explaining to me that he didn't have time to do his homework once school let out because his farm work kept him busy until nighttime. Not doing his homework got him put into a corner at school and it was purely humiliating. He wanted to learn his letters but it was harder for him than others. He got his letters all jumbled up and confused and found reading difficult as a result. At the farm he worked so hard that he was dog-tired in class and it was hard to keep his eyes open and pay attention. The true realization was that he had to work in order to have a place to live, so his chores were the priority.

"Let me help you, Scotty. You have always helped me and now it's my turn. I used to live on a farm; I could do the milking while you fix the fence posts. With what time we save I can teach you grammar rules. It could work, we have to try."

Scotty shook his head and his curls swayed freely, as they had grown out way past his ears. "What do you mean, you lived on a farm? All I ever knew was that you lived in tenement housing, Red."

"Well, you don't know everything then, do you?" I grinned at him and we made a deal that I would help him two days a week as long as Edna and Pap agreed it was okay.

That night I sat down with Edna and Pap and described Scotty's situation. I asked if they would allow me to help him. I added that I thought it would be very Christian of me to do this. They expressed their concerns to me as well. They worried that I spent too much time concerned with Scotty's welfare and that my own grades could suffer as a result. When they saw the tears welling in the corners of my eyes they promised they would give the idea some thought. They wanted to come to terms with how much Scotty meant to me but they also wanted me to put my old life behind me. They were very delicate as they expressed concern about my troubled past. Some nights I woke up crying and screaming and it was always Edna who rushed to my bedside, reassuring me when my dreams were fraught with images of a dying mother, bloody teeth, or anything else from the streets.

I wondered if I should tell them my real name and my real story but worried that if they knew my truth they would no longer want me. The Sisters of Charity brainwashed us to forget our sorry pasts and move forward as God so graciously wanted for us. I froze that part of myself in time, numbed my feelings and tried to look forward, but it still haunted me at night.

Edna promised that nothing from my past could change the love they already felt for me, and that my history would only endear me to them more. They also told me it was my choice how much I wanted to share with them; they understood some stories were too painful to be recounted. They didn't tell me then but later I realized they must have been frightened for the life Scotty had lived before now as well. Come to think of it, I didn't know the life Scotty lived before the stoop in the Five Points either.

Edna and Pap agreed I could help Scotty for one afternoon a week and he could come to our house for a few hours on Sundays after church. I was delighted by this agreement and couldn't wait to see and smell the farm where Scotty lived.

When he showed me his bunk after school, I was humbled. Scotty lived in the hayloft directly above the horses along with two older lads who did not attend school. At the moment, they were in the field, which was why he could sneak me in and show me around. The room was clean enough but it lacked color and life. The animal stench was bearable, fresh hay was piled in the corner by his pallet, which helped mask the smell of manure; luckily he said it wasn't his job to muck the stalls. He had a brown woolen blanket neatly folded at the foot of his cot and on the cot was the Bible he received from the sisters nearly a year ago. A rug sat beside his bed for his boots and he had a nail in a wood beam for his trousers and nightclothes. Aside from a small washbasin the boys shared, that was all they had. He never complained either and felt lucky to have a place to hang his hat.

"Except that you don't have a hat," I said teasing him.

"Well, it's good enough for me, now let me show you the grounds and fences that need repair," he said without delay.

"Okay, but first can I see the horses?" I missed Oliver at that moment.

"I had a horse named Oliver once, he was a beauty." I was struck with the memory of feeding him apples and carrots and the way my da would heft me up onto his back and lead us in a slow jaunt around the fields.

We climbed down from Scotty's quarters toward the stalls where a chestnut pony caught my eye. The pony swished a midge with his tail and went back to eating. "This one here looks a little like Olly, as a matter of fact."

"Gosh, I never took you for a cowgirl, Red." Scotty chewed a piece of straw and did a goofy side step dance that made me laugh.

"I wasn't a cowgirl, but I did love the farm." I ruminated some more on how peaceful our farm routine was and described the scene to my friend. "My da was up before the rooster's crow to milk the cows and muck Olly's stall as well as the pigpen. He sprinkled grains in the chicken house, but let me collect the eggs. I was real quiet and slow about collecting the eggs because Harriet, our hen, was fanatical about anyone in her house. She would squawk and nip and bite me until I left. Mama schooled me in my letters and at night, da would teach me my numbers. Our place was real nice and quiet, we were a happy family."

"That sounds real nice," Scotty said and encouraged me to go on with my story.

"Then da fell off the ladder in the hayloft one morning before chores and he died instantly. Mama stayed in bed for two days straight. A few neighbors stopped over to check on us and some offered to help as well but mama declined any charity. Luckily, the women brought casseroles so we had something substantial to eat while mama put her plan together. The first plan was that we would work the farm just like my da did. We tended to the livestock and harvested crops that were then shipped via the Sound to New York City but when it came time to plow the fields for planting, the work was too difficult and our neighbors were busy with their own fields. Mama made the decision to sell the animals and move us closer to the city where she could take in work as a laundress. We didn't have any family nearby so this was the best and only solution."

I saw that I still held Scotty's interest so I continued. "The cows were getting on in age so we didn't fetch more than a few dollars apiece for them. The butcher bought the sows and our neighbor took the hens. We hired a coach and brought our table, mattress, hand-woven rugs, pots and pans, and clothes with us when we moved. If we needed anything else we would have to dip into our shallow savings and buy it."

"What happened to Oliver?" Scotty asked.

"Shucks, I am not sure if I know. All I remember is feeding him apples one day and the next he was gone." A tear escaped and ran down my cheek; Scotty reached in and wiped it away.

"What happened to you and your mama then? I am sorry I never asked before."

"Mama found us an apartment in a tenement building in the Five Points. She didn't want to live there but it's all we could afford. Our place had its own window in the peak of the roof line that let us look out into the city. Initially, we shared one bedroom and had our own small kitchen area and enough space for our table and the matching chairs that my da made. We spread our most colorful rug under the table to catch the crumbs and keep the dirt less noticeable. We put our lighter rug next to our mattress so that in the morning when our feet hit the floor they weren't met with the cold." I thought about how much mama and I missed my da then. I was grateful my mama was smart and strong and not afraid of hard work.

Scotty never interrupted my story so I continued. "We went from store to store and introduced ourselves around town and down on the docks to anyone we saw. We told them we would do their laundry and that we would do it better and cheaper than anyone else in town. We had a few dollars saved in our hidden pouch and could rely on the kindness of folks at the Mission if we became desperate. But mama didn't want to beg or be in anyone's debt. We did laundry for strangers, we worked hard at it too because we had to be the best in town. That's about all, you know the rest. My mama died from her teeth problems and then fate brought me to you." We stared hard at each other for a moment, searching for something to say.

Finally, Scotty broke the silence. "Wow, I didn't know your mama had such big cahones! It takes guts to do what she did, moving with you to the city and working without a man." Scotty rudely grabbed himself and I punched him in the arm, warning him not to be so crude.

"Don't need no man to get along, we got along fine, though we missed da."

"Oh yeah, Red? Don't need no man, well, how you gonna get along without the likes of these two?" And with that he rolled up his sleeves and flexed his muscles at me, which made me laugh and feel better.

That's what I liked best about Scotty, he always knew how to lighten the mood. He could make me feel better instantly and I had to admit, his muscles were impressive.

Scotty and I spent Mondays working the farm together, we put out fresh hay for the cows that stood around us, ankles caked in mud as they browsed for tender shoots. When that chore was complete, we spent time white washing the fading fence that surrounded the pasture. Edna lent me a pair of Pap's old gray trousers and I wore suspenders to keep them up. We worked well together, Scotty on one side of the fence and I on the other. We painted and chanted our letters and rules such as, "I before E, except after C." After our allotted time, Scotty would walk me the two miles to town and Edna would meet me and exchange niceties with Scotty before we all went back home. On Sundays, Scotty worked with Edna on his schoolwork and then he and I had a little time to enjoy playing before he had to get back to the farm for the afternoon milking. We always included Eddie in on our fun, which included bubble-blowing competitions, kick the can, or tag. We always let Eddie win or he would spend the afternoon sulking.

One Sunday afternoon after Edna tutored Scotty, she took notice of how he strained to focus on the written words in front of him. She asked him if he would be willing to go for an eye exam with her. He agreed and low and behold, he was nearly blind in one eye. This explained at least some of his reading difficulties. He was fitted for a pair of glasses and suddenly everything was clear and precise.

"How can I repay you, Miss Edna?" he asked, offering his allowance of twenty-five cents per week.

"This is my gift to you; you are very special to Mary and I am more than happy to help." Edna took Scotty's glasses and folded them before placing them in their case.

Edna asked me how much I knew about Scotty's upbringing, but I was honest and told her I knew very little, except that he had been alone a long time and for that, I thought he was very brave.

CHAPTER 6

❧

SCOTTY'S STORY: NEW YORK CITY

Autumn in New York City was putrid. The cold rain pelting my skin, sinking into my bones was bad enough, but the streets were littered with shit and piss and the rain watered it down, making all the crap thin out and run in torrents through the streets. Rabid dogs ran wild and crapped anywhere they pleased, horses were tied to banisters where they stood in inches of sludge. Rats got tangled under your feet and the city smelled like a cesspool. At night, we had to huddle close under our stoop on Mulberry Street or else the drunks would splatter us with their vomit. Bars got out late, brawls happened in the streets, there were shoot outs, and people lay dead or passed out in ditches. The daytime was better; we all had morning jobs and then hid out in one old factory, brewery, or another. I inhabited the stoop with Karen and Tommy.

Gangs in Five Points were deadly and had taken to fighting for amusement. They would rally chickens and starve them in separate cages before setting them loose in a pit where they would peck each other to death. They did the same with rats and the half-starved dogs that wandered the streets, enticing them with scraps of food into a caged ring where they were forced to fight for their lives. The animals were kicked, whipped, abused, and neglected by gang members who soon grew bored and looked for more authentic cage fights. Pretty soon the members offered themselves up for fights in order to make a profit.

I watched a few fights while hiding behind crates in the brewery. I spent my days off the streets hiding in order to avoid trouble but now it seemed trouble had found me.

"What do we have here?" A scraggly young man with three earrings and long strands of greasy hair grabbed me by the back of my shirt lifting me up off my feet.

"He asked who you were," a second punk with few teeth hacked a blood-tinged loogie right at my feet.

"I'm Scotty," I said, and then tried to make a run for it. The second gangster caught me and held me against the wall.

"What are you doing here, Scotty? Are you spying on us for them Dead Rabbits?" The guy with the greasy hair started pushing me and taunting me and was egged on by his mate.

"Nnno, I just didn't have anywhere to go," I stammered.

The boys looked me over and after witnessing my state of poverty, they took me to Pauli. Pauli, they said, would know what to do with me.

"What's your story, kid?" Pauli looked me over and rubbed his tired eyes.

"I got no story," I told him, trying not to make eye contact.

"Where do you work, kid? You gotta eat, how do you earn a living?"

"I sell the newspaper on Sunday morning and steal the rest." I was scanning the exits and looking for an escape route as I spoke.

"So what are you doing here in this old place, huh? This is our territory, are you spying on us? Who are you really working for?" Pauli spun the pistol that sat on top of his desk and when it stopped, the barrel of the gun was pointing right at me. His tattoo appeared to be getting bigger as he flexed his muscles in anger, spittle ran down his chin, but he didn't wipe it away.

"I don't work for nobody, sir. I told you, I sell papers and hide out, that's all." Besides watch you guys abuse and torture animals, I thought to myself.

"Well, Scotty, you put me in a bad position I'm afraid. If I believe you and let you go, you could go back where you came from and report everything you've seen. On the other hand, you could prove to be useful to me. How long have you been hiding here?"

"I've been hiding here during the daytime for a few weeks now. I haven't seen anything though, I swear." This wasn't entirely true, I had seen plenty but said I spent the days sleeping so I could stay awake at night to protect myself.

"So you have been here for two weeks and we didn't notice you until now?" Pauli rubbed his whiskers, noticing the spittle finally and wiping it with the back of his hand. "I have a proposition for you. I am going to believe you; you're too stupid to lie because you know if you did we would have to punish you, right?" Pauli shuffled the papers in front of him and stacked them neatly in the corner of his desk as he spoke.

"Right," I said, answering his taunt, even though I hated being threatened.

"You're going to work for me now. You're gonna spy on the Dead Rabbits and tell us who they got over there training to fight. See, I need to know who to put up against them, gotta know who to get ready, who to feed and who to keep hungry."

Pauli laid out a plan for me starting with quitting my paper sales job. I was to report to him every afternoon and in return, he would give me dinner. If I didn't show up, they would come after me. I had to find the Dead Rabbits' hide-out and then weasel my way in.

My first day on the job for Pauli I didn't find anything. I checked the paper warehouse, the mill, and the grocer's warehouse but found nothing of interest. I was terrified to report back to Pauli without any news.

"You may have to go farther across town, kid; the Dead Rabbits know we inhabit this turf so I doubt they'd be anywhere close by. Try the shoe factory and the building on Second Street that looks like it's collapsing."

Pauli gave me half his sandwich and I ate it in two bites. I was scared to death of what I would find in the morning when I made my way across town.

First, I sauntered around the shoe factory; the back portion was closed off but I noted that for its size it could easily fit a gang of a dozen or so men training to fight. I made my way through a side entrance and snuck through the building, everything was quiet. I sat in a corner behind scraps of material used for making shoes and waited. There was a round table in the room and cards were littered on the floor. More than likely, this place was used for illegal gambling. I waited some more but by mid-day no one had come into the factory to train. I decided it was early enough that I still had time to check out the dilapidated building on Second Street.

In this section of town, only the poorest of the poor remained. The building was in ruins, partially collapsed from sewage and farm run-off. Tenants living in this section were riddled with disease from the unclean quarters they lived in. The smell alone could knock someone off his feet.

I pinched my nose and entered the building, terrified it would collapse on top of me, or that I would catch a disease while I was inside. First, I walked the narrow perimeter hallways and neither heard nor saw anything that led me to believe the Dead Rabbits were here. But as I made my way closer to the interior of the building, the smell changed from sewage and filth to pungent body odor. I followed my nose and came upon a makeshift gym. There were several squares partitioned off with rope and piled in the corner were rolls of hand tape. There were jump ropes and free weights, as well as a punching bag. The bag was attached to the ceiling with a clamp and thick links of chain that I thought looked heavy enough that they could bring the entire building down on itself.

My stomach growled but I had to stay put and see what exactly happened in this gym so I could report to Pauli.

Several hours later, a group of gangly kids who had been picked off the streets were paraded into the gym and taunted by much bigger, fit-looking kids. The ruffians were lined up and put into rows according to size. The warm-up included a stretching routine followed by high knees and punching the air above their heads while holding weights. If they let up and dropped their arms or the weights from exhaustion, they were met with a swift punch to the gut. Following the initial warm-up routine, the kids were separated, some went to work on the boxing bag while others grabbed jump ropes. Still others were taken to the center ring where they met with trainers and worked on impressive combinations. I could hear the trainers yelling, "upper cut, jab, right hook, left hook" and watched as the fighters put movement with the words. I noted the foot placement for each punch and heard the trainers yelling, "Proper foot placement gives your punch more power."

I was terrified that I would be found. I sank deeper into the corner in the rafters but still had a decent bird's-eye view of the scene below. I counted fifteen scrawny kids that were presumably being taught to fight. They seemed to range in age anywhere from six to sixteen. There were five trainers, each worked with their own group of kids. Some trainers were better at floor work, while others excelled at head and body movement. Others worked strictly on punch combinations; all together they were a formidable opponent for Pauli.

I thought about hiding out here from now on. Pauli would never come here to find me. It would be too dangerous for the Roaches to enter this side of town. My stomach growled again and I began to feel sick from hunger; of course, this reminded me where my meal was coming from tonight.

After the kids finished their training, they dried off with towels and left. What intrigued me the most was that the trainers stayed behind. The five of them got into the ring with each other and sparred. They went for two-minute rounds, no protective head gear, no gloves, just themselves and their body weight. No one held back. They fought hard in two minutes using footwork and combinations to score points. Blood flowed freely out of one fighter's nose down his chest, causing me to gag. When the two-minute bell rang, the fighters shook hands and the one with the bloody nose shoved cotton up his nostrils and carried on. Two different trainers entered the ring and fought. This continued until each individual had sparred with one another for two minutes. Blood from smashed faces pooled in puddles on the floor, knuckles were split open and bleeding, the fighters glistened with sweat, but none appeared to be winded, unlike the kids earlier who tired easily. These young men were in the best shape of their lives. They knew what they were doing and it made me fearful for my life. I shrunk further into the corner and closed my eyes, hoping if I couldn't see them that the reverse would be true as well. After another hour or so of jumping ropes and lifting weights, the five trainers finally left the gym area. I was reluctant to get down from the hiding spot and sneak out of the building and risk being caught. I had no idea what time it was and was unsure what to do.

I thought of Karen and Tommy then. I wished I could go back to them without putting them in danger of the Roaches who would look for me if and when I didn't show up. I wondered if they were safe and feared that if Tommy was caught by these thugs and forced to fight he would surely lose. Tommy was all talk; inside he was just a fearful kid trying to get by one day at a time like the rest of us.

I climbed down, taking my time and finding my way out of the now dark but still dank building. I made my way across town and finally found the brewery that housed the Roaches and went directly to Pauli's office.

"Where the hell were you? Huh, you fucking punk?" The greasy guy who helped Pauli was raving mad.

"I asked you a question, you little shit, you better speak up." He had crossed the room in a few long strides and grabbed me by the shirt collar.

"Jesus, Squid, you're gonna scare the shit out of the kid, let him go," Pauli interjected.

"I found them." As soon as I said that the goon released me and was sent away to get me some grub. After I ate, I recounted everything I saw right down to the blood-stained floors.

"Come with me, kid." Pauli led me to a section of the factory that I hadn't been in before.

He pushed open a large metal door and I was hit immediately by the stench of body odor and blood. I looked around and saw a gym that was similar to the one the Rabbits used to train. This gym had a punching bag and another smaller bag that I later learned was a speed bag. Two squares were taped off on the floor and free weights, jump ropes, and other pieces of equipment I didn't recognize sat in piles.

Fighters were in the midst of training. It was a smaller number of kids, but because this gym also had five trainers, the boys got more personal attention. Here they not only focused on offensive training but on defensive training, ducking the punch, bobbing and weaving, and dancing around the floor. These fighters looked lighter on their feet, although I was no expert.

"Tell me what you see. What are the differences between their gym and mine?" Pauli nudged me forward to get a closer look.

"I think you have more stuff, like that small bag over there, they don't have that." I looked around for more differences.

"That's called a speed bag. It helps develop your rhythm and give you quick hands."

"You have fewer rings, they have four marked off. You only have two." I wasn't sure if that mattered but it was a difference.

"You also have fewer kids in training but the ones you have seem stronger. Their kids look like they're hungry, I don't mean hungry to win, I mean they are skin and bones. I swear I could count their ribs if I were close enough."

"Hmmm, they must have a new group fresh off the streets. They round up kids and offer them protection if they'll fight. Then they feed them when they win and starve them when they don't."

"If I had to place a bet I would wager that your guys would win, that's if the fight were right now." I hesitated to tell him what I was thinking.

"Go on, kid," Pauli encouraged me to be honest.

"Well, they have five trainers and they are tough, they never even looked tired after sparring. I think they might be in better shape than some of your trainers."

Pauli looked around the room and took note of his trainers. Several of them had gone soft and were carrying extra weight around the middle. That ended today.

"Okay, kid, here's what you're going to do. You're going to make a list of all my guys and trainers and tomorrow you're going back over there."

I flinched at the thought and Pauli noticed my hesitation.

"I only need you to spy once in a while, before a big fight. I have a lot riding on our next fight. It's in ten weeks and we stand to either make a lot of money or lose a lot of money, understand?"

"What am I supposed to do over there?" I asked, fumbling with my coat button.

"I want you to take our list and make some physical notations about each of their guys, are they lefties, do they have a strong right, how is the defense, who is quick, who is slow, who could knock us out in one punch. Got it?" he asked, waiting for my reply.

"I think so. But, Pauli, how does this help you?" I wondered out loud.

"You leave that to me, kid, once I know their strengths and weaknesses I can better prepare my team."

Pauli had softened toward me a bit, he told me I did good job and set me up with a cot and blanket in a room far away from the gambling scene.

In the morning, I woke and pissed off the window ledge before heading to the other side of town. I took my time, checked my back often to make sure no one was following me, when finally the collapsing building was in view. I watched the building for activity before sneaking toward the entrance. No one was in sight; it was quiet. I snuck in and made my way through the narrow hallway until I reached the rafters. I hunkered down and waited. I waited for hours until anything happened and my stomach was already growling. I didn't get breakfast from Pauli because he was still asleep when I left. I wasn't able to beg any on my way over, and when I checked inside a garbage can for food, all I found was last night's vomit. I had lost my appetite then and made my way there.

After several hours of sitting crouched in the rafters, several kids came into the gym. They were already sweating and it appeared they had been running. A few of them were holding their stomachs as if they had cramps and one was puking in a bucket.

"Damn, five miles before noon. That's harsh, man." It was the red-headed kid who puked and complained. He was scrawny, but tall, five feet eight inches, maybe a buck ten.

"Quit your complaining, you ninny, before I get you a skirt." A short, dark-skinned kid who I didn't recognize from last night whipped him with a towel. The group stood around waiting and finally one of last night's trainers walked in.

"Time to spar, fellas." He matched the boys into pairs and had them going in two of the four rings.

The red-headed kid was lanky and his arms had a long reach. He didn't look strong but when he punched his opponent with his left, the kid stumbled. I wrote this down.

The boy with the darker skin was slow. He had no footwork and kept his hands up in a defensive position, exposing his body. I wrote this down too.

The ink from the steel pen Pauli gave me tickled my nose. I stifled a sneeze but before I could stop myself, I let out another one. All the fighters stopped what they were doing and looked around. I shrunk even further into the corner and prayed.

The trainer looked around the gym and gathered the boys closer to him. They all dispersed and I thought maybe I got lucky. Then I realized the trainer had sent the boys to investigate the sneeze. I heard footsteps climbing the rafters and pissed myself.

"Gotcha." The red-headed boy pulled me up from my crouch and dragged me down the short set of stairs, throwing me in front of his trainer.

"Well, well. What do we have here? Search him boys." The boys patted me down and found nothing. I was smart enough to hide my notes under a wooden slat in my hide-out.

"Who are you and what the fuck are you doing here?" The trainer asked, and like Pauli, he spit when he talked.

"I just didn't have anywhere else to go." I hoped my prior excuse with Pauli would hold up.

"You really expect me to believe that shit, kid? Someone's

been feeding you. My guess is you're spying." He wiped the sweat beads off his brow.

"No, I swear, I am not spying. I don't know where to go to be safe. The gangs, they are getting bad. I found the building and snuck in, that's all." Before I could continue, the trainer started using me as a punching bag.

"Well, as long as you're here now, I guess we'll just have to use you as our punching bag for practice today." He started on my body with jabs and hooks; after a few solid punches, I was already bending over.

Then the red-headed boy stepped in and the trainer watched as he lunged at my face. I ducked several of his upper cuts, but with his friends cheering him on he went at me hard. He landed several uppercuts to my chin, and busted my lip wide open. I doubled over in pain but the boy didn't stop. He had no mercy, instead he went after me even harder, he went for my ribs, and after a few punches, I fell to the floor.

Next up, a scrawny little kid, maybe six or seven, started kicking my back numerous times before stepping over my body and kicking me right in the balls. I was nauseous instantly. He had absolutely no remorse either and I thought if any of them would have, it would be him given his young age. The rest of the boys all got their turn with me. I stood back up and tried against one or two of them. They laughed at me and my piss stain. I had no training and was not in shape. I could taste my blood and for a minute, I felt vengeful and attacked with flailing arms but this only made them laugh harder at me. The next thing I knew, I was in the middle of the ring with four kids bouncing me between them, and then it was lights out.

I was in and out of consciousness all night; when I finally came to I was petrified. I didn't recognize where I was but it was inside someone's house. I could hear snoring and the place reeked of booze. I tried to stand up but it hurt just to breathe. I was sure I had several broken ribs, among other things. I forced myself to sit upright and stripped the sheet off the bed, tied it around my waist for support and stood up. I wobbled and struggled to get my balance.

Out of nowhere I heard someone say, "Where the fuck do you think you're going, ace?"

I must have been knocked out again because when I woke up next the five trainers were staring me down.

They pulled me up and out of bed against my protests. I had dried blood everywhere from my mouth, to my ears, to my nose. My balls were even swollen and walking was nearly impossible. They dragged me back to the gym I was all too familiar with and centered me among them.

"Now, you're going to tell us what the fuck you're doing here, aren't you?" One trainer with bulging biceps stepped forward and punched me so hard in the gut that it knocked the wind out of me and I landed on the floor.

"Stop, please," I cried like a baby while I begged for mercy.

"We don't stop until you tell the truth." Trainer number two stepped up and landed a right hook to my jaw that sent several of my teeth flying along with blood and spit.

They tied my hands behind my back and kept on going, taking their turn landing punches over my already broken body.

"Tell us, who are you protecting?" someone asked.

I refused to give in. They could kill me if they wanted but I knew if I told them about Pauli I was as good as dead anyway.

My eyes were swollen shut and I could no longer see. I fell to the ground so they took turns holding me up while the others continued to beat me. I passed out and woke up while a new group of kids, some scrawny, some well into their training, began to assault me all over again. I was a lesson for them against mercy.

I was dragged unconscious to the bed I slept in the night before and again woke to the smell of my own piss and a group of trainers peering over me.

"What are we gonna do with you, huh?"

"We could just beat you to death, I suppose," another answered with a throaty laugh.

"Just to be fair, we'll give you one more chance." The trainer held up a knife, presumably for inspiration. I thought for sure he was going to take off my ears.

My mouth felt like it was stuffed with cotton balls. I hadn't had anything to eat or drink in two days and blood pooled and drained into my stomach making me nauseous.

"Need a drink?" One of the trainers held out a glass of water and I felt a flicker of gratitude, until he splashed the contents into my face, and I realized the glass was full of salt water. I jerked back and winced in pain.

They dragged me back to the gym and repeated the beatings; I passed out numerous times because the pain was unbearable. Everything felt broken, everything but my spirit. I went to a place in my mind, a square-shaped room that was quiet and red and had a metal chair in the corner. I sat in that chair and plotted my revenge. I listened to the sounds of the assailants' voices as they pummeled me and I committed them to memory. I noted their accents and what they called each other. This quiet place was mine. They could hit me over and over but it was still there and they weren't able to take it from me. I sat in my corner; I took the punches, the kicks, the broken bones, the gushing blood, the pus, and gunk that pooled in the corners of my mouth and eyes. I listened. I took it and I waited.

The next time I woke, I tried desperately to sit up and gather myself. Although I hadn't had any nourishment or drink in days, I had to piss. It nearly killed me to sit up and I let out a yelp.

"Hey, kid, sit back down." It was Pauli's voice I heard.

I sat back down and tried to open my eyes but they were still swollen shut. I tried to talk but my jaw wasn't working and I felt metal in my mouth.

"Let me do the talking for now, kid. You're damn lucky to be alive, you know that?" Pauli sat next to the bed, his voice sounded tired and worried.

"Remember Squid? The guy who found you lurking in the brewery? Well he found you near death in a ditch across town. He was out recruiting and I'll be damned if I know how, but he recognized you. He ran all the way back here and swore you were breathing so we sent out our guys and they brought you back. That was three days ago."

I tried to mumble a reply but it was no good.

"All you're going to do right now is heal. My wife is looking after you." I could hardly believe Pauli had a wife.

"She is good at this, so let her okay?" Pauli patted my leg gently and left.

I slept for the better part of the day but woke up when I felt a warm cloth pressed against my forehead.

"You were screaming in your sleep and we don't want the wires to come out. The woman continued to sooth me with soft strokes across my head and then placed the cloth over my eyes.

"Your jaw was broken in several places. We had it wired shut so it will heal faster. I am going to try giving you liquids later, doctor's orders." She left my side and returned with a freshly rung cloth.

"My name is Candy, by the way. Well, it's Candice, but everyone calls me Candy." I winced when she leaned across me and the bed moved slightly.

She kept heading south with the cloth and I was mortified that she might be giving me a sponge bath on my privates. I instinctively moved my legs closer together and she gave a little chuckle, sensing my distress.

"Oh, honey, I've seen it all!" Candy laughed as she placed an ice pack on my scrotum to help reduce the swelling.

"In a few days you will be able to open your eyes and eat liquids without my help. Soon the swelling will go down on your fists, arms, and legs. You were really battered. You have several broken ribs, which is why you have tape around your chest.

Candy sniffled a bit but quickly regained her composure. "Now is a good time to rest," she rubbed my hair once more and then left the room.

I went back to the quiet place in my mind, the walls were still red and the same chair sat in the corner with me in it. I plotted and thought of all the ways I would have my revenge, starting with becoming a Roach Guard.

As the days went by the swelling did go down and I could finally see my surroundings. I was in a room off the gym and apparently, all the guys had sworn revenge in my honor. The first day I was up and around with Candy's help, she walked me to the gym and the guys cheered when they saw me.

I was anxious to get the metal out of my mouth and could feel the gap where I had several teeth knocked out. I started writing Candy notes; I asked when the metal was coming out, what day it was, how she met Pauli? If only I could meet someone like Candy one day. She was patient and kind and had a gentle touch.

The following week, I went back to the surgeon's and he doused me with something that put me out in seconds. When I woke up the wire was out of my jaw. I was afraid to talk at first, afraid that any movement of my jaw would cause tremendous pain. Because I was so young, the healing took place quickly and I was talking and eating within weeks.

Pauli sat me down and apologized to me profusely. Then he asked me to recall what I could from the incident.

I told him exactly what happened and described the beatings in detail. He winced and even cried at one point when I told him about the quiet place in my mind.

"Thank you, Pauli. You saved my life," I said.

"No, I put your life in danger when I sent you over there in the first place. Candy will never forgive me for that. She is right, you were too young and I put you in harm's way."

"But you found me. You didn't know if I was spying on you first but you decided to have faith in me. You saved me."

I didn't quite know how to ask to become a member of one of the most notorious gangs in New York but that was all I could think about now.

Pauli caught me staring at his tattoo and said, "Don't even think about it, kid. Candy would kill me."

"I need my revenge." I cracked my knuckles and paced his office floor.

"I want to kill those mother fuckers for what they did to me. Do you know that after they beat me, they took turns pissing on me?" I looked Pauli directly in the eye even though I was ashamed to admit this. "They spat on me, threw booze in to my fresh wounds, and laughed when I winced. I need to find a way to settle this; I will never forgive myself if I don't. I want to settle it in the ring." I had thought about it long and hard. I could train and learn to fight; I was light on my feet and was strong for my age and size.

"So you want to be a fighter, huh?" Pauli was hardly surprised by my determination.

"Yes. I want to fight." I was adamant.

"You'll start tomorrow. Now get a good night's sleep." He held the door open for me and I left the office with nothing but revenge and blood lust on my mind.

Later, I heard Pauli and Candy arguing about me. Candy said I was too young for the fight scene, but Pauli understood vengeance and the visceral need to get even.

Training was physically challenging, but my body was healing and growing stronger by the day. I was expected to run daily. I ate a diet of lean meats and vegetables. I lifted weights and could practically feel my muscles ripping and mending with each curl. I studied the trainers' movements, their foot placement, and the way they pivoted to get the most power.

"Stick and move, Scotty." The trainers for the Roaches drilled this into my head.

I worked relentlessly on the speed bag, finding my own rhythm, developing confidence. Within weeks, I was ready to spar, propelled forward in my training from my ordeal; I did well in the ring. I learned how to duck any punch and come back with a one-two combination of my own. I learned defensive tactics but it was the offensive moves that got me the most excited. I loved fighting. It was a release for me and Pauli said I was a natural. I fought with everything I had. I released the anger I had pent up for being left to fend for myself by my neglectful parents. I fought against the grueling, poverty-stricken city I lived in. I fought for all the kids who were bullied, but more than anything, I fought to prepare for my revenge. I was suddenly full of hatred and the anger in me fed me and kept me alive. Without my vengeance, I was just a kid sweeping storefronts and scraping for food on the street corner.

The fights were scheduled and the gym was buzzing with excitement and testosterone. Our fighters encouraged each other with slaps to the back when someone exhibited skill, and we always helped each other improve too.

I didn't understand how these gangs that hated each other so much could even bear to be in the same room without killing each other. Pauli explained the rules, which were set in stone. No weapons were allowed in the arena, and if anyone started a scuffle, they were thrown out at once. Judges were not necessary because the fights went until knockout or forfeit. They were scheduled on neutral territory and were not announced until the day of the fight to keep the police away. A boy from one team would go into the ring and anyone could challenge him to fight. The fights weren't previously matched up. Fighters used only bare knuckles, no gloves or tape, just raw power.

"Yo, kid," one of the trainers called over to me later one afternoon, "Pauli wants to see you in his office."

"How are you doing, Scotty?" Pauli was sincere in his concern for me.

"I'm ready." Maybe I was overconfident but I didn't need moves when I had so much venom pulsing through my veins.

"You know, kid, the boys that tormented you might not even be at the fight. You saw them months ago; who knows what may have happened to them during that time. You might be fighting complete strangers, you still sure about this?" I noticed Pauli's scuffed dress shoes and thought about the tough guy image he presented to everyone besides me and Candy.

"I am doing this for me, putting them to shame no matter who it is. Match me up with their best fighter, I don't care. I'll rip him to shreds." My anger was palpable.

"Yeah, and what if he rips you to shreds? I can't stop the fight. You know that, right? It's rule number three."

"You won't need to, Pauli, I got this. After I win, I want in." I stared right into his eyes when I said this.

"You want in what, kid?" Pauli raised his eyebrows in question.

"I want in the Roaches. You saved me from the streets and saved my life when you could have left me in that ditch to die. I don't have any family, I don't have any place to go, this is my life now."

I thought Pauli was going to launch into a lecture about the Roaches' history as well as the other notorious gangs in the Five Points, but he decided to trust me instead.

"You got sand, kid. You know that? I've been thinking, can you keep a secret?"

"Sure, Pauli, what is it?" I asked intrigued.

"Well, Candy and I are expecting a baby." Pauli's smile was huge, showing off his pearly white teeth.

"Wow, Pauli, that's great news. Congratulations. You're going to be a father." I could hardly believe what I was hearing; good news was scarce nowadays.

"Yes, I am. Candy and I don't want the baby growing up here, in all of this." He motioned to his surroundings. The brewery they lived and trained in was notorious for gambling and prostitution, it had saloons and brothels as well. In fact, I had my suspicions that Candy was once a prostitute herself.

"This is no place for a kid. We are going to hit the road after the fights; we'll take our winnings and head west. We have discussed it, kid, and we'd like you to come with us." Pauli kept his plan simple, they would steal away in the middle of the night and no one would ever know what happened to them. It was Candy's idea and he opposed it initially because of his loyalty to his brotherhood. After thought and contemplation, along with some careful planning, they decided to make a go of it. They had been putting money aside ever since and knew the night of the fight was the best time to leave. Numerous members would be hurt if not dead from fighting and that would take the attention away from them.

"Really? You guys want me to come with you?" I couldn't believe my luck.

"We do, but it's our secret. The Roaches wouldn't let me out that easy. Once you swear your oath to them kid, it's for life.

That's why they can't know." He looked worried and a crease formed between his eyebrows.

"I swear I won't tell a soul, just like I never told those jackass Rabbits about you."

"I know you wouldn't, that's why I trust you to do well in the ring. If you get hurt, you could jeopardize our plans. Scotty, one more thing, I am hoping after this fight you can just go back to being a kid. This baby will need a big brother. Too much anger is not a good thing, got it?"

I knew anger had taken over my life but I didn't realize that Pauli could see into me like that.

≈

With the fight day approaching I anticipated my new life with Pauli and Candy, would the baby be a boy or girl? Would I really be considered his or her big brother? It was all so exciting but I had to put it out of my mind for now. Now I had to focus on training.

The day of the highly anticipated fights arrived. I learned that the Dead Rabbits actually split off from the Roach Guards last year because of too many differences. The Roaches supported the primary liquor sellers and the Rabbits opposed this; fighting ensued within the gang until it was unanimous they separate. The Rabbits went on to become political sluggers, thieves, and thugs earning a reputation for being deadly criminals. The only thing the two gangs still had in common was their mutual hatred for the Bowery Boys who ran the lower east side of the city. The Bowery Boys were made of Native Americans who became butchers and mechanics, or who were bouncers at either the saloons or dance salons. They abhorred the Irish immigrants and any other foreigners and fought fiercely in gang fights on account of their burly strength.

Pauli warmed me up and then kept me calm before my fight by rubbing my shoulders. He wiped petroleum jelly across my cheeks and nose in hopes my opponent's fist would slip off my face if it ever made contact. Then he rubbed me down with oil so I was more difficult to grip. I wore nothing but a pair of pants cut off at the knees for mobility. I was ready.

The first fight ended with a deadly blow to the Rabbits' fighter. One of our trainers had him in the ring for six rounds and was tired of playing with him; in the seventh round, he knocked him out cold.

The second and third fights were even bouts; one win went to us and the other to the Rabbits. I searched the crowd for the red-headed kid who nearly killed me but hadn't seen him yet.

The reason I hadn't seen him was because he wasn't in the crowd that gathered to place wages. He had stepped into the ring. I pulled on Pauli's shirt and said, "This fight is mine."

I didn't bother to wait for his reply before making my way to the ring. He was taller and had more reach than I remembered, he had filled out more too. He looked more intimidating now than he had when he beat me and yet I had all the confidence in the world, that even though he was looming over me, I would win. The crowd booed the fight before it began, knowing it was a sure win for the Rabbits. I had a strategy in mind. I was going to make him dance, tire him out for a few rounds and then I'd let him have it. I was a patient fighter and would use it to my advantage. This kid had arms that were longer than my legs, so I had no choice but to go inside to cause him damage. I was seething with hatred, my blood boiled and I waited for my moment.

"Remember me?" I taunted.

"Sure don't," he replied, messing with my head. Fighting was as much a psychological game as it was physical. I had to erase his remark immediately.

Round one he got a little too close a few times, I used my slip and punch to avoid his long arms and strong left hook. I used the bump to get back at him when I could. It was the third round when I started loosening up and was able to release myself. I let my hatred take over and I went inside doing damage to my opponent's torso. He could barely breathe because of all the body shots. When he got his hands down to protect his kidneys, I threw uppercuts to his jaw, spit mixed with blood went flying over my shoulder but I kept going. I pummeled him, losing my form and control. He came back at me with a hard right that knocked me off balance but brought me back to the moment. This kid was tired and hurting. A few more body shots and I had him. He was protecting himself, his hands were positioned right in front of his body so he could deflect my shots. I had to split the guard. I was on the offensive, light on my feet, throwing jab fakes and making him work the floor. My moment came and I lunged in, he was expecting a strong right so I hit him with a left and he went down. I threw my arms up in astonishment and stood over him before spitting in his face.

"Remember me now, dickhead?" I wiped the beads of sweat from my brow and left the ring to cheers of the onlookers and bookies who won big time for betting on me.

Before I made it to Pauli's side, we all turned toward the sound of police horns and whistles. They found out about the fights and meant to take every one of us in for lock up. There had to be one hundred uniformed officers. Pauli mouthed for me to "run!" before I was attacked. I turned and booked out of the facility. I ran and ran for miles, until I was sure no one was following me. I took shelter in the hallway of a tenement complex, having no idea where I was. All I knew was that I had won my fight. I had exacted revenge. I didn't get my chance with the small scrappy kid who kicked the shit out of me, or the dark-skinned kid who never held back, but I won against the redhead who found me and ratted me out.

I must have fallen asleep because the next morning there was an old biddy shooing me away from the hallway with her broom. The sunlight hurt my eyes; I looked around to get my bearings but was in unfamiliar territory. I walked for a while and finally recognized a street corner that would lead me back to Pauli. Only Pauli wasn't at the brewery, no one was. Everyone had scattered and I wasn't aware of any secret meeting place. I bet Pauli and Candy took this opportunity to take off and start their life outside of New York City.

I sauntered around the building before entering it from behind. Once I was inside I found my way to the training room, everything looked exactly like it did yesterday, except no one was around. There was always someone in the gym lifting or shadow boxing, but not today. I checked Pauli's office hoping to find a note or something, anything that would lead me to them. Everyone simply vacated the premises. I was alone again.

I spent the day walking around the city, trying to decide what to do now. The brewery had been abandoned, that was clear. I could go back to the stoop with Karen and Tommy, but then what? I would figure that out later I supposed.

That night I stole food from a restaurant. I walked right into the kitchen and grabbed bread and cheese and ran until I reached Mulberry Street, home of my old stoop.

"Where the hell have you been, Scotty?" Tommy shook my hand and pulled me in for an embrace.

"Oh man, you wouldn't believe me if I told you." I shook my head, it had been months since I had seen my old friends.

I told them what happened the day I was found hiding in the brewery and how I was forced to spy on the Rabbits. Karen cried when I told them I was nearly beaten to death. They both listened intently when I talked about my training and revenge. They sat in silent awe when I recounted my fight, blow by blow. I had been through hell and back and they both agreed they were happy I was back, especially since I had fighting skills now.

The following night, after a long day of searching for work and food, scoping out the brewery and trying to find any news I could about the bust, I settled into the stoop. I was surprised to find a skinny little girl already there. Her knees were pulled up tightly to her chest and she had fear in her eyes.

"I'm Tabitha," she stuttered.

CHAPTER 7

❧

EDMUND SUFFERING

I was fourteen years old and had been living with the Whitmores for nearly ten years when I almost met my maker. It was the holiday season, my favorite time of year. Christmas trees decorated with tinsel and mercury glass ornaments filled the house with a fresh pine scent. The pine mingled with but did not overpower the aromas emanating from the kitchen, cinnamon, peppermint, nutmeg, and vanilla. I favored the snickerdoodles over any other confection that my mom and Aunt Edna made. Lord knows they made dozens of batches for our table as well as to package and give as gifts. Stockings hung from our mantle, which was decorated for the season with greenery and sprigs of holly. Gifts in glorious wrappings sat under the tree in the hearth room making it hard for me to resist touching them in order to guess what was inside.

Our family had little downtime during the Christmas holiday. We dashed from one tree trimming to another for weeks on end, and then the holiday house parties began. Invitations for galas and fundraisers had been coming in for months along with dressmakers and tailors. It was inevitable then that one of us should fall ill from exhaustion and exposure. My mother, Sarah, was the first hit with the flu. She stayed in bed with a high fever for a week, tended by Edna and Mary. The ladies alternated caring for her but by the fourth day of her illness, my dad began feeling sick. His limbs ached and he tired easily. He forced himself to take time off from work at the bank and joined my mother in bed. They slept for hours on end, only waking when Edna insisted they have a drink. I thought I had escaped the nasty virus but just as my folks were starting to feel better, I became grievously ill. The flu not only brought my fever to a body-shivering one hundred and six degrees, causing dehydration, but it also riddled my frail lungs with phlegm. I coughed from my toes; the deep burning pain that accompanied it felt like a stoker poking my chest. Sarah and Mary applied a eucalyptus tincture to my chest hoping that the vapors would open my airways but there was too much mucus. I felt like I was drowning but I didn't have the energy to care. I was placed in a tub of ice, which produced shivers enough to rouse me but not enough to decrease my temperature substantially; I was too ill to stay home and was admitted to the hospital.

I developed pneumonia as a complication to the flu and was treated with opium and quinine without the results the doctors had hoped for. The doctor overseeing my case decided I needed to be bled. He lacerated the skin on the underside of my forearm and let it drip. For eight weeks, I lay in my thin hospital bed, my breath barely audible, with loose skin falling off my bones. Mary never relented in taking my health and well-being upon her shoulders. She stayed with me daily and throughout many nights. She would pound my back with cupped hands and catch my green mucus in a tin pan, which she then dumped and cleaned herself. She bathed me with comfrey to bring down my fever and whispered into my ear that I had to live.

I believe I left the world for a moment, however brief. I recall being lulled by a feeling of peace and serenity, it washed over me, pulling me toward a bright yellow light. It was Mary who pulled me back to this world, crying, "Eddie, don't leave me." Her cry was the only sound I heard.

I opened my eyes to the sight of Mary, leaning over me, her face was blotchy and tear stained from grief. She thought she'd lost me. I never saw a more pitiful or beautiful sight and knew I must find the will to live. The weeks of bloodletting continued and miraculously by the sixty-fourth day, I felt hunger pains. My wheeze was less taxing and my lungs felt more open. My fever hovered in the ninety-nine degree range but with Mary and Sarah's dedication to my health, I was released and allowed to go home at last. I would regain my strength over the next several weeks, beginning with short walks to the front hall, then around the yard, and finally up and down the tree-lined street.

I was in debt to Mary. She was the love of my life; she didn't know it and I doubted she felt the same. I couldn't help my feelings any more than I could have controlled contracting the flu.

Because of the asthma I suffered with as a child, I spent the majority of my youth indoors learning to master chess while the other boys my age were playing stick ball and enjoying running around outdoors. While they went fishing, I went to the library. When they swam in ponds, I studied law books and trial cases.

Hence, it was my greatest desire to become a lawyer and then, when the time was right, to ask Mary to be my wife. Edna and Pap, and my folks, might balk at first, but eventually it will all make sense. Mary and I are destined to be together. I don't remember my life before Mary nor would I want to. It was fate that brought us together ten years ago and destiny that encouraged and guided two sisters to adopt us so that we could continue to be close to each other.

I vaguely remember the train; most of my images are rendered from Mary's retelling. She laughed when she told me how I would pretend to be the conductor, yelling "all aboard!" and then bring my fists to my mouth to blow a loud whistle sound that mimicked the great engine. She told me that I was taken from her for a spell, I had been adopted by a family from Ohio, but by the time our train arrived in Iowa, I was returned. The mother was overwhelmed by my constant crying, and my longing for Mary made her anxious. Mary was loyal to me as well, when Edna first addressed her and discussed adoption she refused because she didn't want to leave me. That is how I came to live with Sarah and Samuel, who have been wonderful and nurturing parents. Mary was then and is now my savior.

The only stumbling block in my way is Scotty. He is Mary's "friend" from before the train; they met in New York City and were reacquainted in Binghamton. I detested Scotty from the first moment I laid eyes on him. He had filth under his fingernails and he smelled like a farm, which made me nauseous. He took Mary away from me. In years past whenever he came around, she indulged him instead of me. As children, they would let me tag along and win at games but I knew when I was unwanted. None of that mattered now; soon enough Mary would see the reason that I was better for her. I would be a lawyer with my own firm. I would be wealthy and would build her a home anywhere she wanted. Scotty could offer her very little in comparison.

After my illness, I had a fresh outlook on things. Mary needed me as much as I needed her. I had no cause to worry about Scotty.

Years ago, I went to great lengths to set Scotty up. I did such elementary things as steal chalk from the teacher's desk, swipe lunch pails from hooks, and scratch profanity in desk tops. When the teacher asked who was to blame and Scotty was reproached, I admit I felt a tad guilty. Mary was full of spit and vinegar knowing full well Scotty was not responsible for the shenanigans; however, no one would listen to her reasoning. Instead, the teacher and school board cast out the disheveled farm hand as opposed to any other respectable student from the town's prominent families. Scotty and Mary stayed after school sanding desks to their virgin state and wondered out loud who the real culprit was.

I played along, saying things like, "We'll just have to keep our eyes peeled for anyone sneaking around," or "Golly, I hate seeing you get your knuckles whacked, that must sting like the devil."

Before long, Edna and Pap, along with my folks, got wind of what was happening at school and learned that Scotty was expelled. They called a family meeting at once to discuss the consequences.

Mary and I sat on the couch in Edna's parlor, all the adults sat in front of us, but it was Pap who spoke up first. "Children, we've heard about the trouble Scotty is causing at school and we're worried about the influence he has on you. You are both exceptional students and we are concerned about your association with him." The other adults nodded in agreement while he spoke.

I was internally thrilled at this development, but for Mary I had to act just as defensive of Scotty. What I didn't want was to see Mary in pain.

"It's not true! I can't imagine Scotty would steal, well not anymore anyways." Mary was mad and defending her friend. She could barely contain herself as she spoke.

"Mom, pop, Scotty would never do such things. You can't take us away from him!" I blubbered into my handkerchief and stole a glance at Mary, who was doing the same.

Edna stood up, cleared her throat, and spoke. "Until this case is settled at school and we know who is causing the havoc, Scotty will not be welcome here on Sundays anymore. Mary, you are no longer permitted to help him on Mondays at the farm either." Edna looked distressed when she took her seat.

Mary cried and wiped her nose. "That's not fair!" Mary, to whom justice was important, stomped away to her room and slammed her door hard enough that it shook the house and made Pap flinch.

I dried my eyes, it was amazing that I could force myself to cry at will, and then I went to sit on my mom's lap. "I'll do what you want, mom and pop," I said and laid my head against Sarah's ample bosom. She stroked my curls and said, "That's my good boy."

Edna and Pap were pillars of society and they would simply not allow their daughter to communicate with a farm hand who lacked a higher education and had questionable ethics. My plan worked, or so I thought.

Mary and Scotty rarely spent time together anymore, she was not allowed at the farm and he was too busy with his work to come to town. What I didn't know was that they had been sneaking out for years at night.

I made extra cash by delivering Sunday morning's paper across town; it had been months since my illness and I was finally up to the task once more. I missed my early mornings spent delivering the paper, and looked forward to the quiet that came with the dark predawn sky. Watching the sunrise was another perk I had missed.

I was delivering Edna's paper when I saw something moving out of the corner of my eye. I investigated the motion and found Scotty and Mary involved in a familiar tryst behind the knuckled oak. Scotty was cupping Mary's breasts and she was kissing him passionately, both of them were so caught up in the moment that they didn't see me. It was highly improper and I was shocked by Mary's behavior.

That night, I did what all men do, after the dinner hour I poured myself a brandy and swallowed it down even though it burned my throat. Then I poured another, and another. My folks were out at a dinner engagement so I allowed myself to get good and drunk so that I could wallow in my misery. I hadn't been drunk before and felt as if I could take on the world. I had bounds of energy and ran through town, singing and sloshing about. It started to rain and the torrent came at such an angle that it wet my collar straight through, seeing as I wasn't in my right mind I started to strip. A girl, about my age, who was new to town, was watching my antics. I hadn't met her, yet she grabbed my hand and ran with me through the puddles. We ran past the tavern and up a staircase to a lonely room where she lived. Mary was all but forgotten.

CHAPTER 8

GERT:
A DIFFERENT KIND OF EDUCATION

I spent my childhood chewing my hair to keep quiet. I sucked the salty ends and chewed them, twirling the wad into circles and making nests in my mouth, never swallowing, just chewing and sucking. From behind the closet doors, I could hear the men talking with my mother at first, and then there were hushed sounds of laughter, bed squeaks, and my mother's groaning and grunting. I soon realized I could watch from between the slats if I angled myself just right, and from then on, this is what I did.

Mother told me to get in the closet as soon as we heard a rap on the door. Once she knew I was settled, she fluffed her hair and the satin pillows on her bed, pinched color into her cheeks, and then opened the door and welcomed her client. The clients varied, some were rugged outdoor-type men, and others were men who barely spoke English but who were always respectful. Some were older and wealthy, as apparent by their shoes. The wealthy men had shiny shoes with pretty tassels, the farmers and laborers had boots. If the boots had mud or muck on them, mother gently asked the men to take them off at the door; once they became regular customers, this was routine.

She often locked eyes with me while I watched and she motioned with one finger to her lips for me to keep quiet. No one ever knew I existed; in this room, it was just my mother and her men.

For thirteen years, I observed and learned the ways of a man by watching my mother "entertain them," as she called it. It provided us with a room and board and I rarely remember feeling hungry. Her work was a means to an end, nothing more.

Mother was a self-possessed beauty; she had dark almond-shaped eyes with long come-hither lashes. Her skin was soft and supple because she bathed regularly with rose water, The remains of which she put in her black, silky hair, so she always smelled nice. She cared very much about her appearance and keeping herself looking youthful. We often took long walks around the city to take in the fresh air but also to stay trim. Mother handed out note cards on these occasions and I realized this was how she developed her clientele. Her card read, "Sarah's Sweet Delights" on the first line, followed by, "no appointment needed," and then she penciled in our address below. It looked to me like she was advertising a bakery and that's what she wanted any non-interested parties to think. Some men were just too dense, she said.

Men came at all hours of the day and night to have my mother's company. She lounged in her silken robes all afternoon waiting for a client to call. I couldn't tell whether or not she liked what she did, the way she moaned underneath a man made me wonder if she was happy or in pain. During those times, I wanted to burst out of the closet and help her out from under the hunk of flesh crushing her, but she said that if she was moaning it meant she was enjoying herself. Why then didn't she moan all the time, I asked? She explained that different clients liked different things. Some liked her loud and others liked her to be quiet and keep still. Still, others had to know she was receiving pleasure in order for them to find their own release. These were the "real" men she said, the ones who gave a damn.

I had even seen my mother take a colored man to bed on occasion. With him, she really seemed to be enjoying herself. I wondered if it was real or if it was a show for him so he would finish sooner. I asked her when he left and she said, "Gert, if you are ever so lucky to have a black man who wants you, take him to bed, you won't be sorry."

One particular evening a man we didn't know came knocking at our door. He was not a regular and my mother didn't remember giving him an invitation. He smelled like booze, which was always cause for alarm. She told him he must be at the wrong address and said her husband would be home any second. He crossed the doorway anyway and said he knew he was in the right place, he had been watching men come and go all week and was determined to see what was so special.

The man caught sight of me because I didn't have enough time to hide, my foot was exposed and he laughed. It was an ugly laugh that got caught in his throat on the way up, forcing a cough.

"Now I see why the men are whistling when they leave. Come here, little darlin'. Don't you play coy with me." His grin revealed his missing teeth and the rest were so yellow I could hardly imagine what he smelled like up close. He motioned me to come toward him but my mother stepped right between us.

"She is not part of the bargain, but I promise, if you'll let me, I will show you a fine time." Mother was as demure as I had ever seen her, sweet talking this poor excuse of a man.

She never scrunched her face at his vile smell although I could barely breathe it was so rotten. He unclothed right in front of us and his repulsive body gagged me. Mother, on the other hand, walked toward him like she was impressed and made a fuss over his muscles. All I saw was a fat and smelly dirty old man.

She reached for him, and brought him toward her bed, she made him forget all about me. Before long he was moaning and groaning and she was coaxing him by saying, "Yes, that's right, ooh you like that, don't you?" She disappeared under the covers for a moment and stared into the man's eyes when she reappeared, daring him to do anything but think of her. She let him think he was in control, but she and I both knew that she had him right where she wanted him.

The man laughed while he dressed, stumbling as he tried to pull his pants on. He was a fool, a drunk, and the whole place needed a laundering and scrubbing now.

We didn't mention the man the following day, but we stripped the bedsheets and washed them in scalding water along with the coverlets and pillowcases. Soon enough the room smelled fresh again and we went out for a nice walk. We silently prayed he wouldn't be back and he wasn't for a long time.

‮ಎ‬

Mother carried on with her regulars, a few more caught glimpses of me because I was growing and it was harder to stay quiet while hidden in the tight closet. Many men liked having me watch and offered big money for me. Mother said no, she told the men I was not ready; I hadn't even had my monthlies yet and wasn't considered a woman.

"Tomorrow is your golden birthday, Gert!" my mother exclaimed one afternoon.

"My golden birthday? What does that mean?" I asked.

"Well, you are turning thirteen on the thirteenth of the month, the numbers coincide, and that only happens once in a lifetime. Let's do something special." She sat on the bed next to me and bounced on the mattress.

"Maybe we can get ice cream?" I asked.

"Surely we can get ice cream, with jimmies too. Maybe we can even shop for a new dress and pair of shoes for you."

We settled in for the night but were woken by a loud knock at eight in the morning. The knock was impatient and loud. Mother hushed me and I went into the closet before she opened the door. It was the rotten man. It had been nearly a year since our episode with him and we prayed that he was too drunk to remember where we lived. Not so. He barged into our apartment and demanded to see me.

"Get away, you old hag!" he pushed my mother across the room and she stifled a sob.

I could hear him approach the closet and tried to nestle myself under a coat, but he simply pulled it off me and grabbed my arm and pulled me up. He looked me over and started to undress, his pants were at his ankles in seconds and he had me in his grip before his pants were off his feet.

"Your turn, sweetheart," he demanded, nuzzling my neck, and fondling my buds beneath my clothes. My mother was on her feet begging him to take her and not me.

"She is a virgin; surely you don't want someone who has no idea how to pleasure a man." Mother used her sultry voice and grabbed his privates.

He pushed her away with one hand and pulled me onto the bed, placing me beneath him. Instead of fumbling with my dress he pulled up my skirts and began ripping away my underwear.

I was sweating and couldn't breathe under his weight. I tried to slither out from under him but he was too strong and this time he wasn't drunk or easily swayed. I scratched his arms, and kicked and bucked with all my might.

"I love a feisty one," he laughed out loud, then started kissing my mouth.

I bit his wandering tongue and drew blood, he was about to strike me but my mother hit him over the head with our cast iron pan. His eyes rolled backwards in his head and he fell off the bed.

"Gert, run!"

"Mother, no, not without you!" I pleaded.

"It's time you take the money and get away from here. Go far away and don't ever come back. It's too dangerous for you here now." She motioned toward the coffee jar that held our savings. I grabbed a few dollars and promised to come back after the dust settled.

I took one last look at my mom, hugged her tightly, and started to leave, but not before she whacked the man again on his head and I saw blood trickling from his mouth. I ran out of the building, past the section of city I was familiar with and quickly became lost. When I saw a church, I ran for it. We had never gone to mass but I thought it was the best place for me to lay low for a little while.

Inside it was peaceful. I sat in a pew and stared at the figure of Jesus before me, blood dripped from his wrists, but it didn't startle me. I was in awe of my surroundings. The stained glassed windows were cut to form pictures, the beeswax candles and red velvet draperies were all so lush and beautiful. I laid my head onto a cushioned pew and fell fast asleep. When I woke up I was greeted by a woman in a black dress and funny white hat. She introduced herself to me as Sister Agnes.

She reached toward me with loving arms and brought me to a powder room where I took a bath and washed away my sorrows. She held up several dresses until she found one that fit properly and then outfitted me with stockings, shoes, and a shawl. She asked about my family and, when I was reluctant to respond, she asked about my future. She talked about orphan trains and all the promise they offered someone like me. She sent word to my mother that I was under her care; we waited the appropriate ten days but my mother never came to claim me. I went to our apartment across town and found it vacant. How could my own mother abandon me like this? I had no choice but to give in and agree to ride the train.

I sat on the train, staring out the window, sucking my hair until it was wadded in knots, thinking of my mother. Whether or not it was true or imagined, I thought she was losing weight and looking gaunt. Her skin was dry and flaky and her hair was falling out in clumps. I made up a disease, an awful disease that would take her in her sleep. The nameless disease ravaged her mind and body, causing tremors and delirium, forcing her to forget she ever had a daughter. This was the only way I could bear the thought of her apart from me. I imagined she died, and it was a quick death followed by peace. I imagined her light shining above me in the brightest star, one day we would meet again, of this I was sure. For now she had sent me on my way with her last penny, saving me from a life of poverty and prostitution, it was her last gift and I was grateful.

I wanted to get off the train at the first stop. The whiny children were too much for me to handle. My thoughts were focused on my survival; I had frozen the image and memory of my mother, the murderess, and kept it hidden in an imaginary box. I had to find work and I knew of only one way to make money. I ran from the platform where we orphan train riders were being paraded into the city in search of my first client.

I lied about my age; the dark charcoal around my eyes helped make me look older than I really was. I took a job as a barmaid at a tavern called the Ale House in Binghamton, New York. I cleared and cleaned dirty dishes, made drinks when necessary, and kept refilling them as directed by my boss. I earned my keep with this work, and as far as the townsfolk knew this was the only way I earned a living. The job came with a room above the bar that had been outfitted with a bed and bath, plus a small vanity. It was perfect. I would be very discreet about my real money maker; the only people who knew I was a prostitute were my clients. Given their place in society, I doubted they would snitch. I used the mirror to practice my many provocative looks as well as to apply charcoal around my eyes and balm to my lips. I studied my gait and practiced swaying my hips when I walked until I felt certain it was sexy. I fluffed my hair so it appeared more voluminous and as soon as I had acclimated myself to the city, I earned enough wages to buy rose oil and begin my business.

I chose my clients, they did not choose me. If I saw someone dapper, or wealthy at the tavern, I gave him his bill along with an invitation to join me later for a nightcap. At first, the men were startled, but those who took me up on my proposition realized that regardless of my young age, I was worth the money. Besides, I lied, telling my clients I was sixteen when in reality I was thirteen.

My first client was young and drunk. He kept muttering something about a girl named Mary. He might have been a virgin himself, he fumbled so much between the sheets. I became impatient with his lack of experience and did the work, sticking him in me for the thirty seconds it took for him to finish. He apologized profusely before passing out on top of me.

"If they were all this quick it wouldn't be so bad," I thought to myself. Edmund became a regular. He was a pretty lad to look at; he had black, thick, curly hair and eyelashes that were longer than mine. He was lean and had a fragile quality, the smoothness of his hands indicated he had never known a hard day's work.

His shoes had tassels and were always shined and free of scuffs. He showed up at odd hours and sometimes only wanted to be held. He never asked about me but always left a large tip and therefore I decided he could use my time anyway he pleased.

My clients varied as much as my mother's did. The difference was that I controlled who I invited and I asked for complete anonymity. I also had my men make appointments. I wanted gentlemen because they were far less likely to discuss me with their comrades or business partners. By my fourteenth year, I could pleasure a man and have him begging for more within the half hour. I loved the power I possessed and was certain that I would be in riches soon enough. I dreamed about a house high on a hilltop with goats and chickens running across the lawn. Among the animals were several curly haired children laughing and playing chase. I dreamed of a man who came home and embraced me, carrying flowers in one hand and candy in the other. The man on top of the hill loved me, not because I could pleasure him, but because of who I was inside.

CHAPTER 9

❧

MARY: IN LOVE, 1867

"Mary, the Ladies of the Literary Society would like to invite you to attend our monthly meetings," my teacher and mentor, Miss Kate, had informed me. "We think you will enhance our discussions and learn a great deal from the orations and debates."

"I would be honored," I proclaimed. I soaked up books such as *Emma* and *The Scarlet Letter*, and was left with many questions about love and life. I wanted to discuss these books and others with like-minded women, prompting my invitation to the club. Miss Kate suggested that because of my enthusiasm for learning I matriculate and become a teacher upon my graduation this year. She explained that reforms had taken place across the country during the war, causing a rise in the demand for publicly funded schools. As more men were becoming soldiers or entering the labor force, women were prevalently seen and accepted in the classroom as both students and teachers. After the war ended, the trend of female teachers continued. Miss Kate was independent and I admired her character greatly. She encouraged me to help the younger children and praised my work with them, telling me often that I had the patience of a saint whether I was helping them with their shoelaces or their penmanship and arithmetic. I truly enjoyed working with them, and my dream of becoming a teacher was planted. I set my sights on teaching in a public school system rather than use my talents as a tutor or governess for the wealthy.

Often, the children I helped brought me gifts to say thank you. Sometimes I found a shiny red apple on my desk beside Miss Kate's, other times I was given loaves of homemade banana nut bread, or slices of peach cobbler. I was delighted when Samantha, a six-year-old student who I often helped, brought me a bright yellow ribbon for my hair. My hair was shoulder length and hung in soft waves around my face. It was auburn colored and the ribbon would complement it perfectly. I thanked her with a giant hug, noting that Edmund was immediately by my side to see what happened.

When I wasn't reading, I was usually outdoors studying the foliage or fishing and swimming. I baited my own hooks and often dissected my catch to learn more about the anatomy of a fish. I found sewing to be painstaking and my stitches were crooked and my finishes lazy, although I liked cooking. Cooking was not only fun but it was a necessary skill as well. This was the reason I de-scaled and de-boned the fish I caught and chopped off their heads to fry for Edna and Pap.

I rarely, if ever, fussed over my hair. The other females lucky enough to attend school went to great lengths to brush and style their locks; it baffled me because they wore bonnets for the better part of the day. I thought Edna would keel over when I took her kitchen scissors one scorching afternoon and cut my curls right off to my chin. It was so relieving to be rid of its weight and it was far cooler too. Edna walked into the kitchen just as I was sweeping the tendrils and taking them out to spread across the garden as fertilizer. Edna wasn't cross; but it was hard for her to understand why I would do such a thing. I had precious few female friends and when I wasn't helping Miss Kate at recess I spent time playing marbles or stick ball with the lads. I had been called a tomboy since I was young and wore the badge with honor.

Unfortunately for me, Scotty was no longer enrolled in school so I had no one but Edmund to keep me company on my long walks home. Scotty's workload on the farm had increased over the years, and that coupled with the ruthless injustice he faced when he was accused of theft, cemented his decision to drop out. He enjoyed his work and didn't miss the scrutiny of his classmates whatsoever.

I was lucky enough to be alone with Scotty after the incident that placed him before the board of education so long ago.

"You have to believe me," Scotty said, taking my hands in his and pulling me from the path we were on, behind a tree. He looked directly into my eyes and swore he didn't do it. "I would never risk losing my place on the farm; if my employers got wind that someone thought I was stealing I would be back on the streets again." He dropped my hands and hung his head, kicking pebbles and making scuff marks in the dirt.

"I believe you, Scotty. I truly do," I said with fierce loyalty to my friend. "Why would Edmund lie and claim to have seen you in the act? It's so peculiar. We have to catch the real thief is all and then we'll set everyone straight." I smiled at Scotty and rubbed his back in a circle for encouragement. I felt the friction between his soft cotton shirt and my fingers. If Edna saw me doing this she would probably scold me for being improper, but I had spent countless nights with this lad under a stoop in New York City and felt that if he could keep me warm while we slept, surely there was no harm in patting his back, even if I did linger. I often saw my own mama and da touching one another in this comforting way, so it felt right.

"It's going to be alright," he said. Here Scotty was the one being treated unjustly and yet he was comforting me. The tears flowed freely down my cheeks and he wiped them away.

"When will I see you?" I asked pathetically. I knew Edna and Pap wanted to put distance between us until the dust cleared.

"I'll sneak down to you at night, when you hear a tapping sound at your window, that's me. You'll have to be quiet when you sneak out or you'll get in deep trouble." Scotty put his hands on my shoulders and gave them a gentle squeeze.

"I don't like being deceitful, but if it's the only way we can see each other, then we have no other choice."

The first night I heard the ping pang sound of the tiny pebbles pelting the glass, I sat straight up in bed. I smoothed my hair, which was peculiar since I never cared about my hair. I tightened my robe and took off my slippers, but before heading out I stuffed my bed with extra pillows to make it appear as if I were asleep. It was the ultimate betrayal to Edna and Pap, but I couldn't see any way around it. I carefully made my way past Edna's room and avoided any stairs that squeaked, treading quietly through the kitchen until I was at the back door. I saw Scotty in the distance and ran to him. We grabbed hands and ran through the back yard not stopping until we were in the fields behind my house. In the beginning, our meetings were brief and never in the same place twice. Our fear of being caught consumed our time together. Later, we became less fearful and were willing to take risks in order to see each other.

It was unfair that he had to decide between work and a proper education, and I hated that he was accused unjustly. On the first night I met him, this was our main topic of conversation. To our disappointment, nothing we said or did rectified the situation. I tried reasoning with the teacher and with Edna and Pap, but it was all for naught.

Scotty was resigned to the fact that he wouldn't matriculate and would instead continue his days on the farm as a worker. This bewildered me because he was intelligent; he had more than street smarts. So math wasn't his best subject and he often got his letters confused, he had an uncanny ability to work puzzles and analyze problems in a logical way that couldn't be taught. He also had an innate sense of direction and geography. I wanted him to continue to learn alongside me, so often at night, I filled his mind with historical facts and scientific findings that I knew would be of interest to him. I taught him astronomy and together we gazed at the sky, making wishes whenever we were lucky enough to see a shooting star.

More often than not, we just enjoyed being together. We would run through the fields dodging cow patties, we played hide and seek, climbed trees, or just spent hours talking. He was the one person I could relax with; because of our shared history, there were no pretenses.

On one occasion, I asked Scotty about his memories of New York City, and I inquired about his family as well. It was a bone of contention for him, but I was unaware of this because he came across as being self-assured and content at all times. He carried no ill will toward the woman who was supposed to take care of him, but rather for the situation as a whole. His mother did nothing but lay around in bed all day. He was scraping for food for as long as he could remember. He had younger siblings who were taken or given away, he wasn't sure which, but he did remember a brother named Eli. Eli was a blond lad, just a toddler, who was always crying from hunger. Scotty did his best to provide for him but he was just a child himself. When I asked Scotty how many siblings he had, I was surprised to learn he had six or seven. It was hard to imagine being alone in the world, especially in New York City when you had sisters and brothers.

Scotty told me that his mother only spoke German, that she found it hard to get along in this country, and that his father was a mean bastard, which added to her suffering. I asked if his father spoke English and he explained that his mother was an immigrant who lost her entire family during her passage to America. She married the first man who showed her any kindness when she landed, and that man was his father. Scotty's father came home drunk and beat his mother regularly, always reaching out to whack a kid, too. Scotty did his best to shield and protect the younger ones, and often took the brunt of his father's vengeance on himself. It was a sorry situation, he never felt love within his family, except for the affinity he felt for Eli. His sisters were dirty and whiny, clinging to their mother in her bedsheets, trying to coax her up. Scotty was more apt to fend for himself than rely on anyone else.

We talked about looking for Eli one day, and Scotty said he would really like that.

Scotty anchored me to time and place. He didn't pretend around me and never wavered in who he was. He was a hard-working, loyal friend. He liked me with long or short hair, was not intimidated by my smarts or the fact that I studied hard and loved books. To him my intelligence was as much a part of me as the bridge of freckles that ran across my nose. Often at night, after running wild through the woods and fields, we would find a tree and nuzzle against it together. His arm would drape casually across my shoulders and I would listen to the steady rhythm of his heart. Sometimes I twirled my fingers through his curly hair and studied his profile. He was not handsome in a traditional way, but his features were symmetrical and manly. He was muscular from his work on the farm and he was rugged. He often spit chew in front of me or swore like a ruffian, a gentleman would never be so brazen in front of a lady. But I wasn't easily offended and Scotty was the one person who treated me like I wouldn't break. Perhaps that's what drew me to him.

One night, after staring up at the stars and making wishes on the brightest one, I listened to his heartbeat; it was not its steady self but fluttered wildly. He released his arm from behind my head and without pause, he leaned in and kissed me. His lips were soft and slightly moist and he had stubble that scratched my skin, but I didn't mind.

After he kissed me, he studied my face as if he were looking for a reply. He laughed nervously, but then I reached out for him and pulled him toward me until our lips were pressing once again. We fumbled a bit until we found our rhythm and laughed when our lips became chapped. The first time our tongues touched we both flinched with excitement from the new sensation.

After that night, everything changed. I found Scotty's kisses to be entrancing and thought of little else. They brought forth a longing from me as well as a neediness from him. If he wasn't able to make it down to my house in town more than a few times a week, I became moody and sullen. I feared the worst; that I had done something wrong or that he didn't like the way I kissed. I worried he didn't want to be with me anymore. Perhaps he thought I was too bold, or maybe I had sour breath.

I was wrong on all accounts. He felt the longing too, and it distracted him from his farm work. He was infatuated by my mind as well as my body, and told me this in both spoken and written words. His letters professed his love simply but beautifully. He struggled with writing, but the fact he took the time to write me love notes enthralled me all the more.

Scotty was very complimentary, he always made me feel beautiful and he acknowledged that I was now a young woman.

"Mary, I declare you have the most beautiful smile I have ever seen, it lights up your whole face." He admired my eyes and told me how soft my skin was too. But it wasn't just my physical attributes that drew him to me; he often remarked on my spirit, telling me that I was strong and brave, he also liked the genuine kindness I showed others and the confident way that I carried myself. We shared an odd sense of humor as well, we both found certain bodily functions to be hilarious. Any other young lady would exclaim to be repulsed whenever Scotty burped or farted, but I laughed out loud thinking of the Canter boys. If it wasn't one, it was another tooting and burping all day long.

One special night, Scotty gave me a gift. It was an oval-shaped locket with an engraving of a meadow etched on it. He had been saving his allowance since he started work and wanted to buy something special for me.

"It's for the photo of you and your mother," he said as he lifted my hair out of the way and attached the clasp. It was the loveliest and most thoughtful gift I had ever received. I promised him that I would treasure it and wear it always.

I was unable to sleep at night and spent the daytime in a sleepy daze. Scotty filled my heart and soul. He was my friend and my confidant, was this love? If so it was very different from the love I felt toward Edna and Pap. I had a feeling in my stomach that reminded me of butterflies whenever I ran to meet him. His embrace secured me; it felt like home whenever I was in his arms. His kisses aroused the woman in me and as we became older, our bodies responded with an urgency to one another. We spent many nights in the grass kissing and guiding each other with what little skill we had, fumbling as we learned.

In the winter months, our meetings were scarce and we grew feverish from want. When we finally had the opportunity to meet our sense of desire was so strong that we cast all propriety and fear of consequence aside. We lay down in snow banks, haylofts, outcrops, anywhere we knew we wouldn't be discovered. I inhaled his mingling scent of farm and masculinity. He told me that I smelled of "home."

I was overcome with feelings and needs that were unquenchable. One night we were both so tired from our tryst that we fell asleep in each other's arms. We didn't wake up until sunrise and panicked that we would be found out. I ran home and as soon as I stepped inside, I put on the morning's tea. Edna was surprised to see me up and about so early, but I told her it was high time I spoiled her for once and made her sit down and let me make breakfast as well. She was delighted by my thoughtfulness and I was sickened by my lie.

We continued like this in secret because Edna and Pap didn't feel Scotty was a good suitor for me. He dropped out of school and had no means of providing for a wife and family. They paraded me in front of their friends' children, setting up would-be matches with older boys who were to become law students, pharmacists, bankers, and the like. I was always pleasant and did my part to carry on a conversation; this way Edna and Pap weren't suspicious and had no knowledge that I was already deeply in love. I didn't care what kind of money my love had, but rather how he treated me. I was going to be a teacher anyway and could support myself if I had to. Scotty asked my opinion on matters, we talked philosophically, and he wasn't at all put out that I wanted to work. Many of the suitors I attended teas with deferred to Pap for my opinion on political issues, religion, business, and even personal matters. The men, several who I went to school with, and who called me tomboy, were just as uncomfortable with me as I was with them. Other young suitors were far too dapper and full of pretense; they didn't suit me well at all. I wasn't one for velvet collars and stiff white dress shirts with flaming cravats, I preferred soft worn work shirts and suspenders. Some of my suitors put more time and care into the way they dressed than I did for heaven's sake. In fact, Edna was always laying out my dresses for me, so I hardly put any energy into my attire at all.

One particular morning while Edmund was out throwing papers onto sidewalks, he managed to catch me at four-thirty a.m. as I stumbled, hair tousled, lips chapped, toward the door. He had seen our passion-filled embrace, and fondling, and although he was merely a boy, he was enraged and full of jealousy.

"What in the world were you doing outside with him?" he whispered to me in the dark, his voice was imposing and full of hatred.

"It's not what you think, Edmund!" His anger startled and confused me. I had never seen him this way.

"Well then, explain it to me," Eddie threatened.

"I love him, nothing else matters," I said.

Edmund's eyes seethed with hatred, his hands remained clenched in tight fists and for a brief moment I was afraid he was going to hit me. When he raised his hands and I flinched, it startled him.

"Do you think for one second that I would hit you? Don't you know that the reason I am so mad is because I love you? That you are all that matters to me? That I think about you day and night, and nothing else?" he took steps toward me, his eyes were locked on mine.

"I don't know what to say, Edmund, I am sorry. I don't return your feelings. I love Scotty. I love you too, just not the same way."

"How could you let him grope you like that? It's disgusting; I ought to have him arrested," he spit.

"Edmund, no. I am willing, we wish to marry..." I begged him to keep the matter between us.

"It seems he has no respect for you, if he is sneaking around with you at night and pawing at you like a common wench." Edmund stepped closer to me and grabbed my wrists before continuing, "He is wrong for you, he is nothing but a farmhand, and you are educated and beautiful..."

"Edmund, let go. You're hurting me." I had to keep my wits about me, but this was all wrong. He grasped my wrists tighter, pulled me toward him, and kissed my lips. He pushed me against the wall and forced his tongue down my throat.

I pulled away and slapped him hard across the face. "Never do that again." With that, I turned and left, climbed the staircase quietly and locked the bedroom door behind me. Edmund was only a child in a man's body. He didn't own me or possess me, but certainly acted like he did.

Edmund confided the matter to Sarah who then discussed it with Edna. I was forbidden from ever seeing Scotty again.

"You can't tell me what to do! You aren't even my real parents. I will leave then, I am nearly old enough to teach and earn a living anyway." I was overcome with fear of losing Scotty and eager to hurt my guardians in any way possible. How could they possibly understand what he meant to me when they never had anything taken away from them?

I became forlorn; I withdrew from everyone and everything except my studies. I refused to discuss the situation. Edna tried to talk to me, or soften me with new yarns and fabrics for clothing. She even tried tempting me with new poetry books by female authors. As much as I wanted the books, I refused them. I would not let her buy me with tokens such as these. No. I lost weight and stopped caring for my hair. I let it grow and hang in greasy untended curls against my face. I went to bed early and woke to face the day with just enough time to walk to school. I skipped breakfast and lunch, and ignored the hunger pangs that pressed against my belly. I walked with my head down; I refused to look anyone in the eye. They were all traitors. Taking us in and telling us we would be welcomed, yet at the first sign of trouble they cast Scotty out. It bothered folks in town that Scotty and I were different. We didn't belong here and we both knew it. We had a hard edge to us, and were skeptical. We constantly worried about our next meal, even though it was provided for us now, the fear of going hungry never goes away.

When Edmund came to see me, I ignored him completely. It was his fault anyway. It was creepy the way he always showed up at my side and I was wary of his motives. The kiss and the unusual threatening demeanor he displayed when he found me with Scotty frightened me. I wanted my own life, and felt it was up to me to decide who I loved.

"Go away, Edmund!" I yelled at him more than once, sick of his looming presence. There had to be a way around this and I would find it even if it meant running away.

I desperately missed my parents, sometimes I even wished for my own death so that I could be near them again. I had forgotten the sound of my da's voice long ago and my mother's was fading. I cried and felt sorry for myself; I found it difficult to be happy. Everything I loved was taken from me and I was tired with grief.

CHAPTER 10

❧

SCOTTY: THE WRIGHT FARM

Ours was a private affair that carried on for years before we were discovered by Edmund, who ratted us out. Finding ways to see one another after that was difficult. As a last resort, we were forced to communicate through letters that we hid in between the rocks on the farmer's wall that lined the fields behind her house. For a long time, Pap slept sentry on the davenport, making sneaking out impossible. Often our only opportunity to see each other was during the daytime. We would meet in the hayloft at the Wright Farm, where at least there we had privacy. Mary would claim she had a tutoring session or was in the library studying, she hated to lie but we decided that nothing and no one would keep us apart.

I was twenty-one and Mary was turning nineteen, which meant we could begin courting in public. We couldn't wait until we no longer had to sneak around. The time we spent entwined brought us close in ways unimaginable and I feared we wouldn't be able to keep ourselves from making love soon. We had experienced passion and pleasure at the hands of one another and confessed our deepest love. We longed for each other when we weren't together and at times I found myself milking a cow dry, I was so lost in thoughts of Mary.

Her round, gray eyes sparkled and spoke to me in a way that didn't require words. Her hair was past her shoulders and hung in soft auburn waves; she often braided it at night, which was good because it kept out of our way. I knew what made her tingle and how to pleasure her until she was exhausted from the experience and could only collapse, spent, in my arms. We talked about getting married and about waiting to make love; we had so many dreams and nothing was off limits. We discussed where we wanted to live, how many kids we would have and what their names should be. We even talked about our honeymoon.

Mary was a beautiful young woman and sometimes I was afraid I would burst the moment she touched me.

My plan was to ask Pap for his permission to court Mary and then ask for her hand in marriage; surely he would see that Mary and I belonged together. It made perfect sense given our history. I could only hope he had put the mishaps at school and with sneaking out, years ago, behind him as we had, letting bygones be just that.

I spent several nights birthing calves with Mr. Wright; one was difficult because she was turned sideways. We had to apply pressure to the stomach and try to move it with our hands. Finally, Mr. Wright asked me to scrub up. I had to go inside the heifer and attempt to turn the calf internally. I had blood and insides caked up to my shoulders, the work was more physically taxing than anything else I had encountered on the farm. I suddenly thought of my fights; they were challenging but in a different way. This heifer depended on me now and with that thought I broke out into a full sweat. I didn't want to hurt the heifer, she was in enough pain and her demeanor told me that she was giving up. I found a hoof and scrawny leg, grabbed hold, and started to pull. I pulled with all my might and whispered for the mother to stay with me. Finally, after hours of gently nudging and pulling, the calf turned. It was born alive and, although the heifer died, it was considered a successful birth because we saved the newborn.

My employers wanted to celebrate with me and asked me to spiff up and join them in town for dinner.

I was surprised and honored. In all the years of working for them, they had never asked me to join them for dinner.

We went in their carriage to a tavern in town that purchased our beef. I became nervous on the ride, because I had never eaten in a proper establishment before. I was self-conscious, but once we were seated, my nerves subsided. The atmosphere was comfortable and the people around us were engrossed in their own conversations.

Our waitress was energetic and overly attentive. She spilled soda on my lap and grabbed tonic to mop my breeches much to my embarrassment. She left with a wink and nodded for me to come toward her in the back room. I wasn't leaving my company on her account and stayed right where I was, thank you very much.

Boy, you did well today. You birthed that calf with the skill of a true farmer. You made us proud, and we thought it was only right to thank you." Mr. Wright patted his wife's hand and they both smiled at me and held up their drinks in congratulations.

I was going to say something but he continued.

"You're a man now, which means that you can leave us any time you'd like. You don't have to work for your board, in truth we need to begin paying you for your time. You can stay in the barn if you want for a small rental fee, but we have another idea to run past you." Mr. Wright drummed his fingers on the table making a rat-a-tat sound.

"The Mrs. and I are getting on in age and we are plum tuckered out. We are thinking of selling the farm. It's just too much work for us anymore. Our boys don't want to buy in and we don't want to sell our property to just anybody. We think highly of you, you never complain and are very competent. So, I suppose we want to know if you are interested?" Mr. Wright wiped his mustache with his napkin and put it back on his lap while he waited for my response.

"Yes! I am interested. I have to say that I've really come to enjoy working the farm. But I certainly don't have enough money to buy it outright. I'm just not sure how to make it work." I was perplexed, but Mr. Wright had some ideas and we began talking them over.

When dinner was done and Mr. and Mrs. Wright had gone home, I ran to Mary's house. I summoned all my courage and knocked on the front door, hoping to speak with Pap. He answered immediately but had a scowl on his face when he saw that it was me.

"Sir," I said nervously, "I want to start seeing Mary formally, but thought it would be in her best interest if I asked you for permission to take her out on a date."

"Boy, it seems to me that you should have thought about that a long time ago. Before you started sneaking out with my daughter and treating her like a common wench instead of a lady."

"Sir, I am buying the Wright Farm, the paperwork is being put together now. I can offer her a good life, I promise. You must know that I love her, she is the only one I have ever loved." I pleaded with Pap, but I wasn't surprised when he threw my past in my face.

"So, you want Mary to be a farmer's wife? Hmmm, I wonder how long that will last? She is educated and used to the finer things in life. No, boy, if you really love her then you would want the best for her and you aren't it. Not only are you a farmer, but you are also a thief." He blew air out his mouth and his neck was turning red. "Now get out of here before you embarrass yourself." He slammed the door before I could utter another word.

The defeat I felt was worse than the beatings I suffered from as a boy in New York by the hands of the Rabbits. Surely this is not what Mary would want. She loved me for who I was and our conversations were never lacking just because I wasn't educated, were they?

I went home to plot this out, but when I reached the barn, I knew something was horribly wrong. Dozens of cows were out to pasture and it was far too late for them to be outdoors. The horses were stirring and Mr. and Mrs. Wright were pacing and crying.

"What happened?" I cried as I ran toward them.

"You tell us. Maybe you know something we don't." Mr. Wright looked forlorn and wiped a tear from his eye.

I walked into the barn and found the new calf dead on the ground, as well as several other heifers. They were killed, intestines and blood were splattered across the hay and on the stall doors. I ran toward the calf, and dropped to her side. I put my head beside her mouth and listened for breath; she wasn't nearly as bloody as the other animals and upon closer inspecting didn't appear to be gutted. I began chest compressions and Mr. Wright came in to stop me.

"It's too late. She's gone, Scotty." He usually just called me boy, because he knew I hated Matthew, but today he used my given name as he had heard Mary refer to me, and it gave me the encouragement I needed to save the calf.

"She can't be, I have to try." I pushed him away and continued to compress her chest and blow into her mouth. After several trials, she still hadn't budged, but I was a fighter and I willed her to live. I continued the life-saving work, and finally when time seemed to stop, I gave it up to God. Then low and behold, she opened her eyes and mooed.

"She's alive!" I yelled. Mr. And Mrs. Wright joined me in my frenzy to get her up and moving around so that we could get a more thorough look at her. We moved her from her location to the second barn where there was already a fresh mound of hay.

None of us could begin to imagine what happened in the few short hours we were gone, but we knew one thing for certain, the work was nothing short of evil.

⚘

I had to go to Mary; several days had passed since the animals were so brutally murdered and it had been over a week since we last saw each other. I can't imagine who would be so cruel and heartless; these were supposed to be my cows, living on my farm. I didn't even get a chance to tell her this exciting news yet. Pap probably told her I was worthless, I knew he was filling her head with punishing thoughts about me.

It was mid-summer and the windows were open to allow the breeze to stir the air and cool things down. Mary's lace curtains flapped silently so clearly the pebbles wouldn't work. I couldn't risk leaving a note that anyone, namely Edmund, could find. I had a strange feeling that he had been following us and spying on us; it was unnerving to say the least. Somehow I had to get in the house. I knew where the spare key was kept and I found it easily enough. I unlocked the latch and panicked when I dropped the key and it clattered to the ground. No one stirred and I continued my way to the stairs. I held my breath and prayed I wasn't caught because I knew full well that if I were I'd be sent to jail. I was trespassing and Pap wouldn't hesitate to press charges.

I stepped lightly into Mary's room and closed the door behind me. I watched her sleep for a moment and then I covered her mouth with my hand and tapped her arm gently to rouse her.

"Mary, wake up," I whispered in her ear and shook her ever so gently.

She jerked straight up, frightened by the intrusion. She couldn't see me in the dark, but she could hear my voice.

"It's me, Scotty." I told her not to scream. She threw her arms around me in a tight embrace and I noted her pungent smell. She had grease layering her hair and she looked as awful as I'd ever seen her.

"You've lost weight, what's wrong? Please tell me." Her cheeks looked hollow and her eyes held so much pain, I could see her by the moonlight now that my pupils had adjusted.

"I was forbidden from seeing you ever again. Pap refuses to let us court, but they can't take you away from me, Scotty, they can't!" I held her as she cried. She loved me, that much was clear, but she loved Edna and Pap too.

"Listen, we don't have long. I have to tell you something." I wanted her to focus so that I could fill her on what had been happening and we could make a plan.

I told her about my visit to Pap and how he rebuked my desire to court her and then become engaged. I told her about my dinner and the possibility of buying the farm. I hesitated, but I had to tell her about the animal murders at the farm. I needed to leave town until the dust settled. We talked about who was setting me up and why, but nothing made sense.

I could sense her desperation and it unnerved me. She had unraveled during our time apart. It was as if she abandoned herself when she felt overwhelming despair, she went inward, to her safe place just like I did.

I wiped her brow, pushing her hair off her face and then kissed her tears as they fell one by one onto her cheeks.

"I love you, Tabitha." It was the first time I spoke her true name since the stoop in the city. I wanted her to know that I loved all of her, the frightened little girl who was my friend years ago and the young woman with scraggly unwashed hair who was my lover now.

She lifted the covers and invited me under. We talked in whispers about the murders and why I needed to leave. I promised to send word to her through Mrs. Wright. They were the ones encouraging me to leave for a while because they knew I was innocent. They had seen me fight to bring that calf into the world and then fight to save its life a second time. They suggested that my absence would make room for the real culprit to be found. I had my own suspicions but didn't want to point fingers, yet.

They also agreed to postpone the paperwork for the sale of the farm for a little while and promised that they would let Mary know when they heard from me.

"We can run away, we can leave tonight. I only need a few things," Mary begged to come with me.

"Then we'll both look suspicious, and we don't want that. I need you to stay here, keep your eyes open for anything unusual. Okay?" I told her that I had a strange feeling about Edmund, I thought he was following me and I wanted her to be careful around him. I also needed to know that she was going to take care of herself so that I could do what I had to do without worrying about her.

"Where will you go?" Mary searched my eyes for an answer.

"I plan to go back to the city and look for Pauli and Candy. I have a brother or sister out there somewhere that I'd like to meet. I will start in my old stomping grounds and ask around. My sibling would be almost ten years old now, even though we aren't related by blood, I know I'll love him."

"Do you really think they might still be there? It's been so long."

"I don't have any idea, but hopefully somebody will have information. I will get a job and find a temporary place to live. But you have to decide what you want in the future. You have worked so hard and accomplished so much. It might be a year or so before I can come back here and buy the farm. Even then, we have to decide if we want to come back to a place that hasn't always been kind. Everyone thought I was a liar and cheat, and now some people think I may have had something to do with the animal killings, it's no way to live."

"But you aren't a suspect, are you?" She begged me to stay, and felt certain the real perpetrator would be found.

"I am not a suspect, yet, but I am a person they are watching."

"The only thing I would stay in Binghamton for is Edna, she has been more than kind and generous to me. It just makes me so mad they think they can dictate who I love."

"I know, but Edna is being protective of you, just like your mother would be. She is looking out for your best interest." Edna agreed with Pap that someone of Mary's stature needed an educated suitor.

"But how can they know what's best for me? Why would they think I would be happier and better off with a banker or lawyer than with you? The men that call on me don't care about my feelings, or my thoughts, they just want a wife to run a household. They want a woman that remains quiet, gives them children, and doesn't complain or ask about money."

"You've had callers?"

"Don't worry; they are all so pompous it's ridiculous. I only speak with them to appease Edna." Mary nestled in closer to me then, her breasts brushing up against my shirt.

"I want to marry you, Mary. I love you. You know that, right?"

"I do know that. I want to marry you too. I want to spend the rest of my life with you, wherever that is. As long as we are together we will be okay. My mama used to say that all the time, but it's true. I feel stronger with you, and lost without you."

"Even if that means you'll be the wife of a farmer?" I asked.

"Especially if it means being the wife of a farmer!" she whispered.

"How will you cope if I am gone for a year? What if they force you to get engaged, or to marry someone else in the meantime?" I panicked at the thought. Would Mary continue to let herself go, or would she rise to the occasion and take care of herself physically and emotionally again?

"Let's make a promise right now. I promise to love you and only you, to wait for you as long as it takes." Mary held me close and stared directly into my eyes when she spoke.

"I promise to love you and only you, and to wait for you as long as it takes before making you my wife. But I need you to be brave, okay?" We clung to each other as we thought about our future.

"But what about Edna and Pap, they don't approve of me and that means you will have to go against their wishes," I stammered.

"We'll worry about that later, a lot can happen in a year." Mary ran her fingers through my curls.

"One more thing, Mary, happy birthday." Mary was turning nineteen years old tomorrow and I wouldn't be here to celebrate with her.

Our kiss goodbye and movements under the covers said all we had in our hearts. The intimacy we shared was ours alone, no one could take that from us. It was more than passion, it was grief and mourning, anger and confusion, culminating with worry and love. We missed each other already and we hadn't even parted yet. We became one before dawn, then said a tear-filled goodbye and I left the way I came in.

CHAPTER 11

❧

GERT: THE CLIENT LIST

I soaked a sponge with vinegar before my next client appeared. But when it was Edmund who knocked on my door without an appointment I went back in my bathroom and retrieved it. Edmund was a well-dressed young man with a trim physique and broad shoulders. He was five foot nine, a good height for his age. He had money and opportunity, and could have any woman he chose, yet he spent his free time with me. He wanted to learn, he said. So I taught him and in return, he taught me. I had never allowed myself to release with a client, but Edmund took such bliss from my pleasure and such care in bringing it to me that I allowed him to kiss my mouth and use my name. He never penetrated me, except for the first time, when he was drunk. He was saving himself for someone special, he said, so we employed every other method and enjoyed our shared experiences.

Edmund was gentle and nurturing. He always brought me flowers or perfumes, or some other knick-knack that he thought I would like. He didn't like my room, he thought it was far too sparse and needed to be decorated. I didn't want to personalize my space and allow my clients to see the real woman I was becoming.

I adored the floral scents he brought as well as the moisturizers and facial creams. I kept a small treasure box under my bed and used these special items for my favorite clients.

Edmund begged to take me out to dinner and shows, or for simple strolls in the park along the water's edge. I told him I wouldn't want to risk running into a client while I was out with him because that would put his reputation at stake. Edmund wasn't the least bit worried about his reputation, but I assured him that with my client list, he would want secrecy.

I was nothing more than a prostitute and what was worse, I was a liar. I was not someone's lover. I had to rein myself in and object to Edmund's fussing over me, but the man-child insisted and didn't relent.

"It's such a lovely day out, you are always holed up in this room, or the tavern, let's get out and enjoy some fresh air." Edmund pleaded with me and I admitted that fresh air would do me a world of good.

Finally I agreed. I primped and fussed over my appearance and finally I allowed him to take my arm as we strolled from the tavern, across town, past the grocers where I saw Josiah stacking potted plants for sale.

"Do you know him?" Edmund directed my elbow as we stepped off a curb.

"Do you really want the answer?" I asked.

"Yes, yes, I do," Edmund said, flabbergasted.

"He is a client as well as a friend. He is actually one of the nicest men in town."

"Golly, what do you do with him?" Edmund asked.

"Why, that's none of your business! What Josiah and I do during our time together is between us." Edmund was so distraught at the thought of me with a colored man that I laughed.

We walked past the edge of town and ventured toward the ice cream parlor, passing the police station and town court on the way. Mr. Carey had stepped outside for a smoke and nodded his head at us when we walked past.

"I suppose you know him too, huh?"

"Edmund, if you are going to behave like this then we should just turn around now. Yes, I know the town judge; he comes the first Friday of every month. He is a kinky bastard, but he treats me well and I like him."

"He is kinky, what the heck does that mean?"

"God, you are such a prude," I laughed.

"Well, explain what makes someone kinky. Let me in on the secret."

"Let's just say that the justice likes to play dress up now and then. He also likes to implement toys during our time together. He usually brings a sack of dress ups and we take on different roles. It can be pretty fun actually." Edmund's jaw dropped, and he shook the images from his head.

"This is all new to me, I guess I need to find a robe and gavel so that we can play some games too. It sounds intriguing."

"Yes, sometimes he has me dress up like a school boy and other times he wants me to be a nun. Sometimes, though, he wants me just as I am, a prostitute. He calls me his dirty little wench and slaps my ass, but it's funny because he is finished faster than you! The man salivates from the moment he walks in to my room and starts withdrawing his toys."

"Wow, I don't even know what to say, Judge Carey, municipal by day, pervert by night."

The day had taken a delightful turn; Edmund continued to be interested in my clients and I decided rather than use it against him I would use my individual experiences as teaching tools. We bought ice cream and fed the ducks our cones while we sat on the grass and watched children playing across the pond. They had handmade boats and were having sailing contests.

"Now that man can't be one of your clients." Across the water, sharing a picnic and looking very content, was a man, his wife, and their children.

"Actually, he comes every Wednesday afternoon." I debated divulging this but it was true and it was good for Edmund to see that even the happily married men had lapses in judgment.

"What?" Edmund protested, "I don't believe it. He looks so happy and he must have five or six children."

"That's precisely why he comes to me. The Mrs. doesn't want any more children and has turned him away from her bed. He is hornier than you are! One time he couldn't even make it to my bed; he jumped me with his pants on." I laughed at the memory, poor guy.

"I suppose it's quicker that way." Edmund muttered, not knowing what else to say.

"It is, and he always pays me for the full session even though he only stays twenty minutes or so. Sometimes he likes it twice, but that depends if he can get aroused again." I winked.

"This is all very eye opening. Please, please tell me that you have never entertained my dad or my uncle? I couldn't live if I thought you had been with either of them."

"No, I haven't. Most of the men in town are upstanding, I have propositioned many with invitations, but I have only twenty or so regular clients who keep me in room and board."

"Does Mr. Smith know? He owns the tavern, right?"

"Of course he knows, he is one of my best customers. I don't mind being with him because he takes care of his hygiene and he doesn't have a woman he leaves to come see me. It pains him that I do this for a living, and he wishes he could pay me more to serve, but money is tight."

"So far we have black, horny, and kinky...how would you classify me?" Edmund asked.

"You are by far my best student." I gave Edmund a peck on the cheek and checked my watch for the time. I had to be back by two-thirty. When Edmund asked why, I scolded him and made sure he understood that if he wanted us to be friends, he had to let certain things rest. He didn't need to know every detail of my day or it would drive him mad.

"Okay, but I do have one more question. How do you keep from becoming with child? Does that ever worry you?"

"I soak a sponge in vinegar and take a tonic every day. It worked for my mother, I was the only child she ever became pregnant with, and she had far more clients than I do." My monthlies came regularly now, but I was unconcerned with becoming in the family way; the men often pulled out in fear of just that. Besides, the tonic I took was said to be very potent and I drank it faithfully even though it was bitter and left a sour aftertaste in my mouth.

Edmund grabbed my hand and pulled me beside him on a bench. "Gert, please don't do this anymore. Let me help you somehow. You are so young and beautiful; you claim to be sixteen but I don't believe that. I know if you let me we could find some other way for you to make a living."

"Who says I want anything else? Who do you think you are anyway, my savior?" Edmund looked at me differently now. I was on my own and doing my best to survive; I wish he would just leave it be.

"No, I certainly don't think I am anyone's savior but I still wish I could help you."

"I don't need help and I don't want your judgment. The only time I feel ashamed is when I am being judged, and that's what you are doing right now." I stood up, brushed the wrinkles from my skirt, and took my leave.

"Wait, it's just that I want you for myself. Can you understand that?" he pleaded.

"I understand that you are a jealous fool who I thought was my friend. I was wrong. If you want to spend time with me then take me as I am and don't try to change me. Nothing makes me feel worse than someone who wants to save me."

Edmund followed. "I am jealous, okay? I am jealous of any man who lays his hands on you. I know it's what you do, it's how you survive, but Jesus, Gert, you must want more from life?"

I smacked him hard across the face and hoped it left a mark that he would have to explain to his precious Sarah. What a bastard, trying to change me.

"Fuck you. The last thing I need is a martyr in my bed." I stormed away and never looked back.

※

I was ready for my three o'clock appointment but the door flew open at two and a deputy sheriff stood before me. He had a baton in his hand and tapped it against his leg while he surveyed the room. What on earth was happening? I was scared I was about to be arrested and wondered who ratted me out; all my clients were on the up and up.

"Settle down, little lady," the wormy man said as he edged his way further into my room and closed the door behind him before locking it. "You see, I have been watching you for a while now. I find it quite interesting that there are so many comings and goings from this room."

I couldn't think of a single excuse, so I just stammered gibberish.

"It seemed to me I should investigate and see what all the fuss was about." The deputy moved closer toward me and removed his shirt. He admired me from afar, holding me in his smarmy gaze while blocking the door so I couldn't escape.

"I'm sorry, sir, but you have the wrong idea about me. I don't know what you think happens up here, but I work as a barmaid and that's all. Please leave." I moved to the far side of my bed, flashbacks of my mom's apartment filling my mind with dread.

"Uh huh, I see. You're just a poor barmaid. How about you give up the charade and give me a little something that will help me keep my mouth shut and keep you from the slammer? Does that sound like a good idea to you?"

The heathen was upon me, taking off my shirt and ripping my skirt. He didn't even try to undo my buttons.

"You're quite the beauty; I see why the men like you. Nice size bosoms, not too fat around the middle, you even smell nice." He murmured under his breath.

I was shaking in his presence. he pinched my breasts and my middle, then rubbed his hands up and down my legs, circling and appraising me.

"Yes, you'll do just fine."

The man had caught me off guard and I scrambled to think what to do. He was smothering my mouth with his sweaty hand so I couldn't scream. I noticed he was soft until he slammed my head against my bedframe. Then he grew a tad, but still not enough. I had time and I looked around the room for something, anything that I could whack him with. But he was too strong. He threw me up against the bed and straddled me, holding me down with one arm and working on himself with the other.

"Ha! You are pathetic, can't even get it up," I said, and spit in his face.

He hit me hard across the cheekbone; I felt the bones in my upper jaw crack and my lips split. I tasted the salty brine from the blood that spilled from my nose. He was hard now and began his assault on me immediately. He kept one hand across my mouth and the other he used to fondle my breasts. He kissed me across my neck, even lapping the blood that was running down my chin from my split cheek.

"Nice girl, pretty girl, be quiet, that's right." I knew he was coaxing me, because I could feel him softening again.

I smirked and he hit me with his fist this time. My eyes rolled backwards into my head and I lost all sense of time and place. His grunting brought me back; I kicked and bucked and tried desperately to get him off me. The more I bucked and fought, the rougher he became and the more he liked it. He flipped me over onto my stomach, exposing my buttocks, parting my cheeks he assaulted me from the backside. I stifled a scream into my pillow. He tore my insides but I had to focus. If I let him have his way with me, he would grow soft again. He knew this too, so he taunted me. "You're just a no-good slut, aren't you? A little slut without a mommy and daddy, huh? Well, you're my little slut now. I'll have you any way I want and you'll take it."

He hit me again and pulled my hair from behind. He bent me in an awkward position and thrust deeper into me. "I said you'll be my little slut, isn't that right, wench? Finally he finished and he wiped the sweat from his brow. I got a good look at him and took note of the scarring he had across his chest.

"Oh, you like that? Good, because you're about to get some scars of your own. You're just a slut and now you need redemption for your sins." He pulled his belt loose from the pants that he draped across my chair and held it over me. To my surprise, he turned it so he held the leather stripping in one hand and the metal buckle was on the ground. He cracked it in the air and proceeded to whip himself across his chest several times, drawing blood. Then he turned it on me.

"See, we are just a bunch of lazy sinners here in this room. We need to repent and beg for forgiveness. Maybe if you ask nicely, I'll go easy on you this time."

I cried my heart out to him. "Please leave, I promise I will go to confession. I'll do anything you want, just leave me alone." I suddenly thought about Edmund's offer to help.

The deputy whipped me over and over across my breasts. My nipples bled, my skin tore open, and then again he turned the buckle on himself. He whipped his member over and over and flipped me on my stomach once again. He put the belt to my bottom, whipping me and then himself in turn. I didn't plead anymore, I just closed my eyes and begged to die.

"Open your eyes, girl. I said open your eyes, God damn it," he was hovering over me. "That's right, when you see me on the streets, and you will, you don't know me, understand? I gave you thirty lashings this time, but I can promise you that's nothing compared to what you'll get if anyone finds out about this. I mean anyone, not even the pretty boy, Edmund. So you just go on and tell everyone you're sick until you feel better."

His face haunted me, his eyes had no mercy or empathy. I forced my eyes to remain open and refused to let him steal what little dignity I had left. I could hardly breathe from the pain and knew he was suffering too. He beat himself as savagely as he beat me, blood pooled at his feet and he had to dress carefully. Once dressed, he walked slowly, using the furniture I had as a support to hold onto. He finally left the room and that's all I remember until I heard the echoes of someone pounding on my door. Everything was so far away, I tried opening my eyes, but it was next to impossible. When I woke up, I was in a hospital.

CHAPTER 12

EDMUND: SAVING GERT

"Eddie, dear, someone is at the door for you." Sarah called to me through the house.

"Won't you please come in, sir? I am sorry, I didn't catch your name." Sarah was polite even if this was the first black man to approach her door.

I rounded the corner to find Josiah standing in the entryway speaking with Sarah; he had his cap across his chest and was politely refusing a glass of lemonade.

"Hi, do I know you?" I asked, quietly solicitous.

"Edmund, don't be so rude. This kind man came asking for you; take him to the sitting room." Sarah pointed the way and left us alone to converse.

"Come in, Josiah, is it?" I led him to the room, curiosity quietly getting the better of me. We settled ourselves across from one another rather awkwardly.

"What can I do for you, Josiah?" I asked.

"Sir, we have a problem," he stammered as he spoke.

"I don't even know you, how can we have a problem?" I asked, baffled.

"It's Miss Gert, she has been badly hurt. We have to go to her right now." His expression was full of anguish and I knew it must be bad if he came all the way here to fetch me.

"Okay, okay, just a minute," I said. "Mom, I am heading into town for a little while to give Josiah a hand with some work. I will be home for supper."

We took my carriage into town and tied the horses to the tavern posts. We used the back steps and took them two at a time to Gert's room. What I saw when I opened the door was horrifying. Gert was in a puddle of blood; she had been ravaged, beaten, raped, and tormented. She was unconscious, but alive.

"What the hell? Who did this?" I ran to her bedside and held her in my arms, begging her to wake up. "Gert, Gert, sweetheart, wake up!"

"I came for my three o'clock appointment and found her like this," Josiah looked everywhere but at Gert when he spoke.

"Did you see who came in or out before you?"

"No, I only saw you with her earlier today when you was out walking together."

"Jesus Christ. We have to get her to the hospital, now. Let's keep her on the mattress. Quick, you take the top and I'll grab the bottom." This was a crisis and I didn't care one iota who witnessed the spectacle. However, because Gert was naked, I took off my jacket and covered her frail body with it. The mattress wouldn't fit down the narrow staircase so I scooped her into my arms and carried her downstairs, placing her gently in the carriage. I climbed in beside her and positioned her across my lap, giving Josiah the reins. My shirt was saturated with her blood and it covered my hands too.

Once we were at the hospital and had Gert settled into a room, we both scratched our heads and tried to understand why someone would do something so horrible. Josiah and I knew Gert saw clients by appointments and invitation only. I told him about the few I clients I knew to be on her list and he shared what he knew.

"We need to call the sheriff. Whoever did this to her has to be caught," Josiah said with urgency.

"I have an idea. Can you stay here for a little while longer?" When Josiah agreed to stay with Gert, I left the hospital and made my way back through town, stopping at the courthouse.

"Excuse me, may I please see Mr. Carey, it's a rather urgent matter," I told the receptionist.

"He's unavailable at the moment; perhaps you can leave your calling card, or make an appointment," the woman said, although she barely acknowledged me when she spoke.

I slammed my fists on the table. "No, that won't do, I need to see him immediately."

The judge heard the noise and opened his door to see what the racket was. When he did, I rushed toward him. "Sir, we have a rather sensitive problem. Perhaps we can talk in your room?" I pleaded.

"What on earth is this all about, son? Who are you?" The judge was taller and more intimidating than I previously imagined. I thought of him wearing his wigs and lipstick, playing games with Gert and would have had to stifle a laugh if this weren't so serious.

"My name is Edmund, sir. I have come about Gert."

The judge took a step back. First he pretended not to know anyone by that name, but I assured him that I would not besmirch his good name.

"She has been badly beaten, she might die. She is at the hospital now."

"I see. How disturbing. Come with me, son." The judge straightened his wide necktie and grabbed his top hat, leaving word with his secretary that he would be gone for the rest of the day. We took my carriage back to the hospital and found Josiah straight away. There had been no updates. Gert was still unconscious. A few moments later, when the doctor noticed the judge, he took a moment to tell us in more detail how she was hurt.

"It appears the young lady was raped. She was whipped with a studded belt across her breast, abdomen, and pelvis. She was then flipped over and flogged again. She has open wounds on her back that start at her shoulders and end just below her buttocks. We can try to repair the physical damage if we take her into surgery right now, of course it depends upon how much blood she has lost and what we find when we get in the operating room. It's her state of mind that concerns me the most; after a beating like this she may never be the same again. She will need in-home care for a long time as well," the doctor said, searching our eyes.

I wondered if she had any doctors on her client list. It would be helpful if she did.

"Before I can take her into surgery, and, please pardon me for asking, but does she have the means to pay?"

"Consider it paid for, doctor. I will see to it personally." Judge Carey had an affinity for Gert, we all did.

The doctor and nurse may have guessed what really happened to Gert; she was a young orphan girl, presumably in her teens, living alone in a big city. She worked as a barmaid and had little money to support herself. Regardless, we all agreed she didn't deserve to be beaten and left to die. Several nurses entered Gert's room and prepared her for surgery; when they wheeled her past us, I bowed my head in prayer.

CHAPTER 13

❧

MARY: UNEXPECTED JOYS

I felt the baby move in my fourteenth week. So far, I had hidden the pregnancy from everyone. I had lost so much weight when I was forbidden from courting Scotty that, to everyone around me, I finally looked healthy again. I resumed my normal schedule, which consisted of going to school and then to the library to study. I ate supper with the family and tutored several elementary aged children every day. I stayed on top of my chores as well. I worried though, because sometime in the next month or so I was bound to start showing.

I prayed with all my might that I would hear from Scotty soon. Mrs. Wright promised to pass along any information she received but so far, nothing had come.

I was woozy early on in my pregnancy. Certain smells made me ill and sleeping was more and more difficult. One morning I came downstairs for breakfast, but as soon as I smelled the frying bacon, I passed out.

I woke up as tiny droplets of water were being sprinkled on my face. Edna was panic stricken. I assured her there was nothing to worry about. I told her I was dizzy because I hadn't eaten since lunch time the day before and I was just hungry. She over-fed me all day and, although I wanted to purge, I had to keep things down so she didn't become suspicious.

That night in bed, feeling the baby move, I thanked God for this blessing. He or she would be loved by a mother and father, and God willing, his grandparents wouldn't shun us. I was terrified of their reaction to the pregnancy. Scotty and I had discussed having children one day, but certainly not until we were wed. It was all so overwhelming now, but we had sensibilities on how to survive. The days of our furtive embraces were behind us now.

CHAPTER 14

✤

BARTHOLOMEW: OBSERVATIONS

I had observed the comings and goings of the Ale House wench for a month while I ate my lunch and supper at the tavern. I sat in the back corner of the restaurant facing the bar. I was able to see the back staircase by angling my body adjacent to the mirror that hung straight across the top shelf liquor, allowing me to see both the reflection and identities of those who defiled the sanctity of the establishment. The black man came weekly for service; he always looked around like a weasel that was afraid of his own shadow, then he gulped down a stout before slinking up the back stairs to her room. The tavern owner took his turn as well, spending more time than the others with her. He made her grunt and groan the loudest. Gentlemen I had yet to become acquainted with came to see her as if they were on a mission, not bothering with the pretense of eating in the tavern. They walked straight through the front door, past the bar and up the back staircase. Then there was the judge. He carried a case with him whenever he came; the case was fairly large so obviously it didn't contain paperwork. I snuck up after him and listened at the door. I felt like a Peeping Tom as I listened to the slut and her master play games. He liked to dress her up as a queen and he would be the jester, or he would be a cowboy and she a cowgirl, lassos and fake guns were all a part of the game. I heard her gasp when he pulled out handcuffs, but the clicking and locking sounds of them stiffened me right away and I took care of myself, spilling on to the carpet of her front door. Younger lads as well as those old and gray came to visit Gert, but the young man with the dark curly hair that flowed freely beneath his cap captured my attention the most. He was not a fully grown man, yet he visited Gert daily. I stood at their door listening while they laughed and grunted playfully, enjoying every moment they shared in her bed. It sickened me. All of these folks were sinners, and I was the worst.

I had lost control once again. I allowed myself to think about the man-child with the curly hair. The boy was petite and well-manicured, I wanted to tug at and feel his soft curls. I lusted for him, thought of him endlessly, and dreamed about him as well. My evil line of thinking had to be cured. It was unnatural, ungodly, and I must pay the price for my sins. I flogged myself with my switch for my impure thoughts in the early morning hours when I woke up with wet sheets. Later in the afternoon, when I saw the man-child accompany the harlot through town, I had had enough. She held his arm at the crook of his elbow and they waltzed through town without remorse or guilt. They fed the ducks, ate ice cream, and even held hands a time or two.

If one more person comes out of that conniving wench's room today I will be forced to go up there and make her repent. Sure enough, an older, wrinkly gent walked down the staircase; he adjusted himself at the bottom step before sitting at the bar and ordering a meat pie and beer to wash it down. I knew the hours between one and two were always busy in the tavern, making it harder to discern between Gert's customers and the tavern's. I had yet to see anyone go to her at this hour and decided it was time for me to make my move. I had my rod with me, and I had purposefully put on my metal-studded belt when I dressed this morning.

She was shocked when she opened the door to find me outside. She even feigned an illness and told me to go away. Now why in the world would she service dozens of men, but not me? This made me mad and curious. I pushed my way into her room, observing the pungent smell of sweat mixed with sex and roses. The combination was musty and tangy and made me hard at once. I had unnerved her, good. She wasn't used to playing rough, but after today she would be begging for it. I pushed her toward the bed, banged her head on the frame, and watched the blood trickle from her temple. The sight of it made me stiffen. I forced her legs open, but she fought me, kicking me with all her might. I was not delusional; I knew what games she played in this room, now she was going to be subject to my punishment. I was the law in this town and could just as easily take her to jail for questioning, but the sheriff was too busy for such nonsense. Instead, I would teach her a thing or two, like how it felt to be entered by a real man.

The harlot spit in my face and bit my mouth when I kissed her. She bucked wildly beneath me to get me off her, but I enjoyed her coy act. As soon as she gave in and became still, I shrunk.

"Beg for forgiveness and I will take mercy on you for your sins." I demanded.

"For my sins? What about yours?" she grunted.

"You question me?" I followed the retort with a swift backhand to her pretty little face and maybe now it wouldn't be so pretty and her clients would lose interest in her services.

"You're hurting me, get off!" Gert screamed and punched me with her little balled up fists, she almost managed to get out from under me too, but then I flipped her over and took her from behind. If she refused to beg for mercy then she would pay.

When I was through with her, I shimmied my belt from my trousers and began my bodily penance in front of her. I lost control and needed redemption. I felt guilt for having succumbed to this weaker side of me. My body was pure evil and needed controlling, pain was the only thing I responded to. I subjected the wench to my belt for punishment as well. I quoted the Bible to her the entire time I drew blood, pleading with her to ask for forgiveness, but she refused. I left her alive, this time. If I ever saw the man-child enter her room again she wouldn't be so lucky.

I sat quietly and dutifully behind my desk in the sheriff's office doing paperwork. Droplets of blood threatened to seep through my trousers. Walking was near impossible in my current state. Pissing was out of the question, so I wasn't able to take in any fluids. Bodily penance was necessary to show remorse for my sins. My member was swollen beyond recognition, and the open wounds on my thighs rubbed against the material on my pants, causing great pain, which I deserved since my thoughts were impure.

I wanted to defile and disgrace every man who walked through the tavern doors up the back steps to Gert's room, starting with the boy. I would begin my search for him, Edmund, and he'd be my first. Then, I'd defile the black man. Before I could do that, I needed to heal. I prayed for forgiveness for being so weak, I begged for mercy and strength to do what was right. The voice that spoke to me and whispered in my ear said, "God wants you to kill them all."

CHAPTER 15

༺ༀ༻

GERT: AMNESIA

I woke to the sound of birds chirping. Their melodic song was long and drawn out, one bird calling to its companion in order to deliver a message. Looking at my surroundings, I had no idea where I was. I felt overwhelmed and distressed by the lack of recognition of everything in this room and felt hives welling up and spreading out across my neck. Anxiety and panic set in; I scanned the room desperately, willing myself to remember it. I focused first on the large volume of butterflies organized by class and displayed within a handsome shadow box on the wall I faced. Viceroys, Admirals, Emperors, Snouts, Swallowtails, and Skippers with magnificent markings and impressive wingspans stared at me with their eyespots. I settled on the Blue Morpho butterfly, her metallic turquoise blue wings were stunning. I made her my point of focus whenever my panic felt overwhelming. Staring at her dull brown underside, I counted her eyespots and estimated her wingspan somewhere between five and six inches. Then I closed my eyes, imagining this lovely creature among a field of flowers, lilies, larkspur, and roses. I was far more relaxed after this exercise and used it to calm myself.

In the far corner of the room sat a leather chair, draped across it was a cabled ivory afghan. Beside the chair there was a Bombay-style, stone-top walnut dresser that was elegantly carved with a leaf motif. Its matching side table was to my right and held a decanter of water, presumably for me. Flowered taffeta draperies flanked the windows and the colorful braided rug indicated to me that this was the home of a woman. Her decor was stylish as well as sensible.

I poured myself a glass of water from the decanter and took a sip, my throat throbbed and swallowing was difficult but not impossible.

A woman I didn't recognize entered the room and once again my fingers tingled with anxiety. I was so nervous that I dropped the glass.

"Where am I?" I asked, my voice shook as I spoke.

"There, there, child, you will be alright. We are taking very good care of you. Edmund and the judge wouldn't have it any other way."

"Edmund, who is that?" I didn't know anyone by the name Edmund; as for the judge, did this mean I was in trouble?'

"Edmund is my son, as well as your friend. The judge is also a friend, no need to be afraid. Edmund found you and asked if we could care for you while you recovered.

Speaking was difficult because of the wounds in my throat. The woman gentled me with her hand, pulled the cabled afghan from its home on the chair, and laid it across my lap. She put me in a sitting position and began to wet a clean white towel in the basin beside me. Its warmth felt nice and her gentle demeanor put me at ease. She hummed a tune I didn't recognize as she proceeded to give me a sponge bath, starting with my face and neck. When she reached my torso, she searched my eyes for permission before continuing.

"Gert, darling, you were badly hurt. If it is too painful for you to see yet, please just close your eyes and let me tend your wounds. I have experience with this and promise to be gentle."

The first wrapping this woman pulled off my chest was painless, but those that followed had me wincing. I wanted to look at my body and therefore, opened my eyes. I was covered in gaping wounds, although they appeared to be healing, which, this woman said, was the reason they itched. There were no active bleeds and after she cleansed them, she administered a salve that was thick and gooey. She bathed me for half an hour, explaining she would allow me to get some rest before she returned to do my back.

My back? Was my back full of gouges as well? I couldn't imagine what happened, but she called me Gert, and somehow I remembered that as my name. I remember the crisp way the "t" rolled off my tongue, cementing my name.

I searched my memory for anything else having to do with me, a bedroom perhaps, a family, personal effects, but it was all in vain.

Hopeless, I closed my eyes and let exhaustion seep into my bones.

CHAPTER 16

❧

EDMUND: MEN ARE BASTARDS

"Mother, father, please I beg you to let Gert stay with us for her follow-up care."

"Who is she, Edmund? How are the two of you acquainted?" They were suspicious of our relationship.

"She is nothing more than a close friend who has fallen on hard times recently; she has lost both of her parents and works at the Ale House tavern in town." The less I confessed the better.

"How in heaven's name has she been providing for herself? Where does she live?" mother asked.

"The tavern provides her with room and board. She would be too vulnerable there now, mother. She isn't safe. We have to let her stay here, in the guest room, at least until she gets her memory and strength back."

"Didn't the judge offer to take care of her?" father asked.

"Yes, father, he did, but I thought with mother's hand's-on experience as a hospital volunteer that she would be better off here. Besides, we have the space."

When they asked more questions about the nature of my friendship with Gert I lied. I stated that I tutored her occasionally because her job no longer permitted her to attend school. My mother and father consulted in private on the matter and decided it would be Christian and charitable to take on such a case. They permitted Gert to use our guest room and took on the responsibility of her care. Whether or not they suspected Gert's secondary occupation as a prostitute, they never mentioned it; however, to them that would make their undertaking even more Christian.

The woman I loved lay stripped of her dignity and was near death in the room right beside mine. I could hear her crying out in pain at night and whimpering during the day. Her torment was both physical and psychological. I wanted to go to her, to slide in bed beside her and wrap her in my embrace. I wanted to kiss her worries away. Some would say I am too young for such intense feelings, but regardless of my age, my heart was breaking. It was visceral, this feeling of protection and agitation for Gert all at the same time. If only she'd let me help her when I offered. If she'd understood that I didn't look at her as charity, I just couldn't stand to see her spreading her legs and servicing men aside from me any longer. She told me more than once that if it bothered me we could no longer be friends. It did bother me, but rather than part ways and lose her influence in my life, I tolerated what she did. Now that she spent her days in and out of consciousness, torn and confused, I wish I had been more insistent and less tolerant. If I could have gotten her to quit prostituting herself, I could have saved her from this harm.

We had a doctor who specialized in trauma come to the house and assess Gert. We hoped after his examination that he would help us understand what her future looked like. He called her condition "amnestic syndrome" or amnesia. Her case of amnesia was "retrograde," meaning she had an impaired ability to recall past events or any information that was previously familiar. It was possible she could recall childhood experiences that had been deeply ingrained in her memories; however, her brain blocked anything recent due to the physical and emotional trauma she experienced. The doctor explained that her memory loss was isolated, but that it wouldn't change Gert's intelligence or her awareness and personality. He went on to say that seizures, tremors, and difficulty with small motor movements were possible side effects and that we should be on the lookout for them.

"Mother, she needs me. May I please spend some time with her?" I begged.

"Son, she needs time to recover for a few days first. She doesn't remember anything at all, only her name." Sarah feared that my presence would set her back and, because she was already so anxious, she thought it was best if I waited. Aunt Edna helped as well; tending to her while she used the bathroom was a particular challenge.

"What if she doesn't remember me?" I cast the thought aside; she had to remember me.

I spent my time deciphering who among Gert's clients would have any vendetta with her. Who would beat her so savagely and why; she never hurt anyone. I loved her. I knew this now. It took me a little while to recognize this feeling, the tingling in the pit of my stomach, the longing and then breaking of my heart when I saw her lying beaten and unconscious. I used to think my feelings were for Mary; I obsessed over her nonstop. In fact, Mary was the reason I went to Gert in the first place. I was sexually frustrated and took it upon myself to find help. I also wanted lessons in order to be a better man for Mary, who I had imagined as my future wife.

Gert obliged me in every way. She allowed me to kiss her, something most of her clients weren't permitted to do. Our kisses were full of tenderness and something else. She taught me to use gentle sweeps of my lips and to keep them moist at all times. She taught me the art of massage, beginning with warm, scented rose oil that she infused herself. I started at the base of her skull, taking my time and working my way down her muscles with soothing, tapping, and kneading strokes. She instructed me to use my thumbs and fingertips, working them in deep circles into the thickest part of her muscles for the best relief of tension. I followed by flattening my hands across her back and shaking rapidly, loosening the blood, getting it flowing and creating energy.

When she returned the favor, I was in heaven, except for the smelling like roses part.

This woman was strong and uncommonly brave; she had been on her own for nearly a year, creating a life and supporting herself. Granted, I hated what she did and how she earned a living. I refused to be a martyr, as she accused me on one occasion when I asked her to let me help her.

"But, Gert, there is so much more that you can do to earn a living." I had pleaded with her to find another way before she got hurt or contracted syphilis, but I was unable to get through to her. I suspected she was younger than the age she proclaimed to be but wasn't going to press the issue with her now.

An investigation was underway. The sheriff had been contacted and was meeting with the judge today. I had an appointment with him after lunch to see what, if any, progress had been made.

Josiah and I walked the streets, looking for anyone new in town. We asked the tavern owner if he had seen anyone new in or out and, except for the deputy sheriff who had moved here in the last few months, everyone was a regular. The owner did try to look out for Gert, fearing the worst. He said she was naive and when he found out what happened to her, he was speechless.

Surely the sheriff would be speaking with all of his deputies and they would continue the search until the rapist was found.

They assured us they would do everything possible and we believed them.

Until then, I had to find Gert a new home. I've even considered asking for her hand in marriage. I love her and would suggest that we not delay but get engaged at once. We could then get married in three and a half years when I turned eighteen. I counted my money and had more than enough between allowance and stocks for a down payment on a suitable ring. I normally would be asking her for an opinion on such a topic, but because she was unavailable, I needed to seek Mary's advice.

"Good day, Aunt Edna!" I chimed in through the window, catching Edna kneading her famous beer bread dough.

"Eddie, come in, sit down. Let me get you a drink," she wiped her hands on her apron and went to pour me a lemonade.

"Don't go to any trouble for me, Aunt Edna, I just came to get some advice from Mary. Is she home?" I looked around the tidy home but there was no sign of Mary downstairs.

"She is upstairs studying, go on up," she nodded in the direction of the stairs.

I approached Mary's room, knocked lightly, but when she didn't answer, I opened her door a crack and peered in. What I saw was shocking. Mary was staring at her profile in the looking glass' her hand was gently pressed on her belly, which looked swollen.

She stammered and shuddered when she realized I saw her. I was afraid she was going to holler at me again, which is all she seemed to do lately. I had really gotten on her nerves, she was more apt to tell me to get lost these days than to invite me in for a chat.

"I'm terribly sorry," I started to say but then she ran to me and pulled me into her room.

She looked down and shook her head. "What am I going to do?" It appeared as she had been walking small lately, hunching over and keeping her arms tight by her sides. I read her body language incorrectly, what I took as insecurity was really her way of protecting her secret. Seeing her nearly naked, with her shift pulled up and over her budding belly, it was impossible not to notice.

"So it's true, then, or was I just imagining that you looked pregnant?"

"It's true." Mary looked embarrassed and refused to meet my gaze.

"How far along are you?" I asked sternly.

"Seventeen weeks to the day."

"I presume Scotty is the father of the child?"

"Yes."

"Does he know?"

"No. He left right after our first time; actually it was our only time."

I was fuming mad. What was with the men in this godforsaken town? One brutally beating the woman I love and the other impregnating my cousin, whom I had thought I loved.

"That bastard. He had no right to do this to you. Was it forced? We will find him and have him arrested at once."

"God, Eddie, no! I wanted this. I told you, I love him. I invited him into my bed and not only allowed it but asked for it. Besides, I am not a child anymore. I am nineteen years old, I can make my own decisions now."

I swallowed back the bile that rose in my throat. "He should have known better, he is a man; he knows how to protect you from such things. Where is he? I will find him and bring him here at once." The starch from my cravat was irritating my nose something awful and forced me to sneeze.

"Eddie, listen to me. He left town after the animals were murdered."

"I'll bet he did," I said, stepping lightly around the subject, hoping Mary didn't sense my unease.

"I realize that Scotty isn't as refined and dapper as you are," she assessed my fine clothing, from the velvet collar on my frock to the turned up sleeves on my crisp white dress shirt, which was tucked into a bold plaid trouser pant, "but he is no murderer. He actually birthed one of the calves, then revived it when they thought it was dead. Mr. and Mrs. Wright sent him away until the dust settles. They believe him and so do I."

"Hmm, well it doesn't matter, the most important thing right now is the baby. Unless..." I was pensive for a moment.

"Unless, what, Edmund?" Mary asked eagerly.

"Unless, Mary, you would marry me?" I got down on one knee in front of Mary and offered my hand in marriage. I would do anything to save her from shaming herself and her family. I didn't love her like I once thought I did, and now I wanted to spend my life with Gert, but I would do this. It would be a small sacrifice for all the love and care she bestowed upon me when she took me under her wing so long ago. It was ironic, though, that I came here to ask for her help in choosing a ring for Gert.

"Marry you?" she fondled the ruching on her sleeves' inseams nervously, and said, "Eddie, you are so dear to me. I love you for asking and for being willing to take another man's child as your own to protect me. But I love Scotty and furthermore, you and I are cousins. We are more like brother and sister and it wouldn't be right. Besides, Edmund, you are still a child yourself."

I felt the truth of her words sting like the slap she lashed me with when I forced a kiss on her. However, several points were debatable.

"First of all, we aren't biologically related; secondly, we could be very happy, Mary. I have proved to have a knack for making money, I am accelerated in all of my courses and plan to graduate a year early. My ultimate goal is to attend law school and have my own practice someday. Furthermore, I take insult to your calling me a child. I'll have you know I am a man now." I cleared my throat upon my admission and let her mind wander until she knew exactly what I referenced. I was nearly fifteen, I was as tall as Pap and behaved more like a man than half the idiots in this town.

We sat in silence on the bed, each of us lost in thought. I thought about my intimacy with Gert and shook my head in distress because of her current state.

"After what we both went through as children, above all else the priority is that this baby has two loving parents and a home." Whenever I thought about the orphan train, it was with angst. At least Mary remembered her family. I didn't, although in recent years I found out that my mother died from either typhoid or yellow fever. My father was still unknown. I took off my frock, adjusted my cravat, and took Mary's hands.

"How are you feeling? Have you had morning sickness?" Now that I really looked her over, I could see that her breasts were swollen and that her usually flat belly was protruding slightly. Her secret wouldn't be safe for much longer.

"I had morning sickness for a few weeks, it was challenging with Edna hovering over me all the time. I told her it was a stomach bug and luckily she believed me. Now I do feel better, my energy is back, and the baby is even moving. Want to feel it?"

Mary took my hand before I could say no and placed it directly on her belly, sure enough the baby kicked.

"Ha! I felt that!" How strange! Perhaps this was a cause for celebration instead of worry and angst. I told Mary, but she was too afraid to share the news with Edna and Pap and besmirch their good name.

"They don't like Scotty as it is, which is not fair. So he doesn't dress all fancy or have a college degree, that doesn't make him any less of a man. Eddie, he is a truly good man, I swear it. If he knew I was with child he would be right by my side helping me through it."

"It seems that trouble follows him wherever he goes though, doesn't it? Are you sure you won't change your mind about this?"

"I am sure. I wanted this, I love this child already and I love Scotty more than I ever thought possible."

"Then I will go and find him for you. I will convince my folks I have business for the paper. Do you have any idea where he might be?"

"He went back to the city, the last place you want to go. They won't believe you anyway about having business for the paper, nor would they let you go back to the city unchaperoned. They think you are just a boy."

"You're right. I never wanted to go back to that rotten place, but trust me, I'll find a way. I have to come up with a story that's convincing enough...then they'll see that I'm not just a boy anymore. I wish you'd stop thinking of me that way too, I am a man now," I said, puffing out my chest. "What I don't understand is why Scotty would go back to the city, what's there for him?"

"He planned to search for Pauli and Candy."

Mary told me about Pauli and his wife Candy, and in this one conversation, I learned more about Scotty than ever before. He was no different from Mary or myself, or even Gert. We were all survivors. All of us were orphaned for various reasons, with a legacy no less.

"I have a delicate situation at home, did you hear about my friend Gert?" I asked and then proceeded to tell Mary about my trysts with Gert. It appeared that neither one of us was so perfect after all. Mary was devastated that something so horrible would happen in our small town. No matter what, she would see to it that Gert was taken care of in my absence. She would volunteer to help with her care while I was away and I trusted her completely. If and when I leave, I know Gert will be in the best hands, hands of the three women I was lucky enough to call my family.

I rose early the following morning, my bags were packed but I still needed to come up with a reason for my departure. Perhaps if I told Sarah that seeing Gert like this was causing me so much distress that I just needed to go somewhere where I could be alone. Mary was right, she wouldn't buy the story that the newspaper wanted to send me.

Before I finished contemplating this, Sarah was bustling down the hallway toward Gert's room. She stopped on her way past my room and popped her head in to say good morning. She had a note that she said Mary dropped off earlier when on her way to tutor a student before class.

The note read:

My Dearest Eddie,
I simply cannot let you go to New York City; it is no place for a young lad such as yourself. I remember the streets well and am certain that I will find my love and be home soon. Please do not concern yourself with me, remember that I survived the streets alone as a very young child and surely I can do so now. I have taken my allowance with me and will secure a room in a decent hotel. It will feel strange to board a train once more without you in my arms for security. I will miss you. I left Edna and Pap a note, telling them of my predicament. I hope they can find it in their hearts to make room for my child, and forgiveness for me. I have to follow my heart...for I no longer have only myself to think of.
Love Forever,
Mary

I folded the note in fours and tucked it under my mattress, "Oh, Mary, what have you done?"

CHAPTER 17

᪥

SCOTTY: THE FIGHT CIRCUIT

Anger pulsed through my veins with such velocity it was difficult to sit still on the train ride from Binghamton to New York City. I closed my eyes, but the screeching sound made by the train as it wound its way along the curving tracks sparked the memory of my last ride. The scenery out my window was not as desolate as it was years ago, that was for certain. Babies cried and people mingled in dining cars, the primary difference between now and my last ride was the destination. Today, passengers had specific places they were headed for business or pleasure.

I didn't think this trip would be so burdensome, forcing me to think about what I left behind both in Binghamton now, and in the city all those years ago. I thought about my siblings, little Eli would be a teenager now if he were still alive. Guilt nagged at my insides and made me nauseous. I couldn't erase the vision of Eli as a teenager, begging for work on a corner, or worse, being part of a gang. I thought about my mother and father briefly, but didn't want old memories to interfere with my current frustrated mental state. Such thoughts would threaten to pull me down further into my self-pity, forcing me to wallow even more about all that had happened and how much I missed Mary.

When I arrived, I took note of the city and saw that it hadn't changed much since I left. The fast-moving current of people disregarded the putrid stench of piss and shit that assaulted my nose once again. There were wall-to-wall people milling about in the Five Points, speaking hundreds of different languages. Abandoned children still ran through the streets and picked through garbage or begged for money. The scene was nothing short of pathetic. I was overcome that I was once a child on the streets; had I really looked so tiny and ragged? I spent many years begging, sweeping, and then fighting, quite literally, for my life. It was more obvious to me now than ever before, had I stayed here and not gone on the orphan train, I would surely be dead.

I desperately wanted to help the children I saw, I wanted to put them on the trains that were still in operation and send them toward a chance for a better life. I empathized with their plight and struggle just to stay alive. Pauli helped provide me with food and shelter for a time, but more often than not, I was left to my own devices, getting into trouble, fighting for survival, stealing and begging just like thousands of kids did now.

I had to find Pauli and meet the child he and Candy shared, my sibling. He may be able to help me find work and keep my mind from worrying too much about Mary. If they aren't here I will bide my time, help as many orphans as possible before going back to Binghamton.

I desperately missed Mary and promised to send word to her, but that was challenging. So far I hadn't found anything but trouble in the city. Employment was next to impossible. The more I looked for work the more bereft I became. My money was dwindling fast. Mr. Wright sent me with fifty dollars, but after spending several nights in a decent hotel and paying for meals I was nearly broke again. What was it about this place that made me feel so incompetent? It was impossible to get ahead.

I saw posters for "world champion fights" on nearly every street corner. "Vladimir the Victor" was going to fight an Irish immigrant named Patrick Kelley tonight. I had to be there; if Pauli was anywhere in this dump, it would be at the fight.

I shuffled through the throngs of people to the arena on Anthony Street early, donned my old spy hat, and slipped unnoticed behind the scenes of each team. Trainers were on hand as well as one or two doctors per team. Back when I fought, there was no doctor, just Pauli. If you broke your nose, he straightened it, and if you were bleeding you taped it. Broken ribs you suffered through but no one ever required a doctor. This must be one hell of a match up. Vladimir wore faux leather shorts with fur trim; he was an enormous showboat, getting the crowd riled up by yelling taunts and jeers at his opponent's country. His shoulders were the size of cantaloupes and were just as hairy as the rest of him. He was physically imposing, and when in the ring facing his opponent, he gave him a death glare, his stone face didn't so much as twitch. Patrick Kelley bravely entered the ring wearing green shorts to represent his country; the crowd cheered for him. The opening bell rang and Patrick held his own for the first three rounds, using interesting combinations and a fantastic straight punch, but then pain and exhaustion set in. He had taken too many hits to the gut and was no match for Vladimir. He went down ten seconds into the fourth round, when Vladimir searched the crowd, looking for someone else to fight. I met his eyes. I wasn't up to the challenge, yet.

I talked with the bookies after the fight and asked what type of money was involved if someone beat Vladimir. I also asked how many people had tried. I watched the crowd mingling all around me trying to find someone strong enough to take on Vladimir. I could train a strong contender and take a percentage of the winnings to help me get by for the time being. I remembered my skills, had honed them regularly to keep in shape. I also scanned the crowd for Pauli.

The fight atmosphere tickled my blood; I felt a surge of adrenaline watching the following match ups. Fighting had been a part of my life and once it's in your blood, it's hard not to get sucked back in. I could practically feel myself in the ring throwing punches and ducking jabs. In the ring, you took matters into your own hands. No one made decisions for you, or told you what to do.

I spent several more days searching high and low for Pauli and Candy in the Five Points. I was flat broke now and would have to walk everywhere I went now, I had decided to head further up town and have a look around.

I was smitten with the Broadway theater notices and posters that lined the streets advertising operettas and pantomimes, and I even felt tempted to have a look inside the museums that recently opened. However, the more I searched the hungrier I got, and the more dire my circumstances became. I had checked the brewery and every other factory and gambling hall in town, now I needed to decide whether or not to stay or to head home and confront my problems. Home, that was an unusual word coming from an orphaned child, now farm boy, particularly one suspected of heinous crimes.

I went back to the arena where the fights were held and asked around once more for Pauli and Candy. I got to talking to a trainer and he offered me one hundred dollars in an amateur bout the next week. He said I could use the facilities to train and was welcome to eat with their team. They called themselves the "Gutter Boys."

The Gutter Boys grew up in the dregs of the Five Points and were often pitted against one another anyway; they put together a team of ruffians willing to fight and so far they had done surprisingly well. They made money because most people bet against them. They were scrappy and smaller than most of their opponents but they were a tough bunch.

I agreed to fight. One hundred dollars would get me home and give me some money left over that I could start a bank account with.

I started my training immediately, greeting the day with a mixture of hope and fear. I broke my fast with a plate of eggs, fried chicken, plenty of fruit, and toast. I ate so fast that the team made fun of me for treating it like my last meal.

It might not have been a smart move but it was going to earn me much needed money and I had no other choice.

CHAPTER 18

※

MARY: MEETING SONYA

Bereft of emotion while traversing the countryside from Binghamton to New York, I pushed away thoughts of Sister Agnes in her black habit and the hand-whittled wooden cross she wore dangling from a shoestring around her neck. The other chaperones, Mr. and Mrs. Porter, on our train ride west so long ago threatened to cloud my mind as well. No matter how hard I tried it was impossible not to have flashbacks, the stale smell of the train and the feel of the stiff wooden seats catapulted me back in time. The ride west was long and lonely; siblings were ripped apart and fostered or adopted. Uprooted and afraid, the remaining kids on the train cried nonstop. It was my job to wipe runny noses and comfort the neglected children. It was a miserable, gut-wrenching position to feel unwanted by society and then to be ripped apart from the only anchor you had intact. I remembered when Edmund was taken from me, the agony of losing him brought on tremors and night terrors; I was alone again just as I am this very moment, but if there was one thing I knew how to do it was take care of myself.

I closed my eyes in concentration when I thought about my biological parents, as well as Edmund's. I had spoken with Sister Agnes on his behalf and found out that his mother had been sick from typhoid fever. A neighbor brought him to the sisters for care before his mother passed away. Typhoid was abundant in New York City because of the sewage and sludge contaminating the drinking water and food supply. Eddie's father remained a mystery and we never uncovered his mother's occupation. Was she a stripper, a dancer, and did she get pregnant accidentally? Or did she and Eddie's father love each other? Was he a hero fighting in the war, was he a deputy attempting to keep order at a time when New York was experiencing its largest-ever influx of immigrants? Was he murdered? Was he an addict of some sort, or did he in fact hold a responsible job, but die in an accident? We would never know the answers, yet the questions we had about our families consumed us and poisoned our minds with what ifs.

Luckily this would be a short trip; I would only be stuck on the train for four hours and then would arrive at my destination. I had more than enough time to formulate a plan. I was feeling a tad woozy and clenched my belly, promising my unborn child that we would find its father. I called on my inner strength and was determined to accomplish two things during my trip. One, I would find Scotty and bring him home with me, and two, I would find Sister Agnes. She was instrumental in turning my life around for the better and I couldn't wait to visit with her and thank her properly.

I would start looking for Scotty in the Five Points, more specifically in Paradise Square. When the train lurched to a halt at Grand Central Station, I stumbled off the platform, looking around my surroundings expectantly for him. It was wishful thinking, but Scotty was not there. Several men did approach me, seeing a single woman unaccompanied in the city left me open for a wide variety of sinister propositions. Men asked where I was staying, they whistled at me and called me a "star-gazer." Some even offered to carry my bag, but I declined because I wasn't born yesterday. I remembered the stories about the street thugs who appeared out of nowhere and promised to be helpful when what they really wanted was my wallet, or my virtue, neither of which they would get. It was a lawless, corrupt city and my former self, that scrappy little girl who kicked, hit, and lashed out at strangers, came out to protect me. I walked with my head held high along the grimy city streets, checking my back until I reached my hotel and checked my bags. I had never stayed overnight at a hotel alone before, but I would manage. I ordered a carriage and set out to Walton Street.

I didn't have a photo of Scotty, or of Pauli or Candy, in fact I had never met them, but I felt I would recognize them right away if I crossed them on the street. Scotty gave me a very detailed description of the pair, who sounded like a couple of characters. Walking along Walton Street I saw so much destitution and felt an overwhelming need to intercede on behalf of the dozens of orphans I saw. I forgot myself and my mission and stopped to talk to several of the children. A young girl in rags approached me and stared longingly at my food. I shared my sandwich with her on a street bench and watched her gulp down the bread and its meaty center in a few bites. She had dark brown eyes, long lashes, and was covered in filth. Her outfit was threadbare, and many sizes too small. She didn't have any shoes and told me that her name was Sonya. I inquired about her family and home, but she shrugged her little shoulders in answer. She was painfully shy but was managing and fending for herself on the streets. She became my shadow and followed me all around the city, her bare feet slapping the mud as she walked. I went everywhere I could think of in my search for Scotty. I checked the shipping docks thinking he may have picked up work there. When I didn't find him there I went to numerous newspaper stands, storefronts, and even hotels, but he was nowhere to be found. Scotty was either currently at work or still in search of it; maybe he had even left the city altogether. I hadn't heard from him in nearly four months and was suddenly panicked and felt very much alone. What if I never found him? I would have to go home with my tail between my legs and face Edna and Pap, Sarah and Uncle Sam, as well as Edmund, alone. What would they think of me, now that I was a no-good hussy? That I was a loose, wanton woman who was willing to give up a bright future as schoolteacher for one quick tumble with a farm boy? It wasn't like that, and if I had to go back alone I would make sure that they knew how much I loved Scotty. I would swear to them that he didn't take my virtue but that I gave it to him willingly, with great love. I summoned my courage as I thought about raising a baby and then held my head high and resumed my search.

I changed my course of action and went to several homes for unwed mothers where I inquired about Candy. I described her in as much detail as I could, providing dates and explaining my predicament. However, no one had any record of Candy staying with them or giving birth there.

As I continued to search, I took note that Sonya was still on my tail. I was feeling parched and hungry and the baby's weight was tugging at my belly in a curious way. I had not been on my feet this much in several months and knew my body was taxed. I sat on a corner bench under a blossoming maple, taking in the sights and sounds of the city. I wished I had remembered to bring a bonnet to shield my eyes from the day's bright sun, but in my haste, I had forgot to pack one. I closed my eyes and imagined it was 1860. The hustle and bustle sounded the same, people came and went in and out of shops, vendors sold papers and candy, boys offered shoeshines on every corner, and the clip clop of horse hooves echoed between the buildings. The smell was no better now than in the past, in fact the sewage issue seemed more pronounced. Sludge was everywhere and I had to lift my dress so that it didn't ruin my hemline. My shoes were covered in slop. I would make a point to clean them properly in my hotel room, and I promised to be grateful that I had a proper bed to sleep in and warm water to bathe in.

I beckoned Sonya out from behind the maple and asked her to sit with me and keep me company. Together we watched a black-and-white finch, no bigger than the palm of my hand, flutter about building a nest in the treetops. Sonya was missing several of her teeth and I guessed she was six or seven years old. She spoke very little, but she did seem to understand everything I said to her. I decided she would become my companion for the time being, she lived here now among the corruption and knew more about the city's underworld than I did. I hated to admit it but I was thinking about the fight circuit. If Scotty had been unable to find work, or his family, my gut feeling was that he would either enter a fight himself, or at the very least he would bet on a few.

It was getting late and I knew the hotel wouldn't let Sonya inside in her current state. We found a running fountain and I used my under garments as a washcloth and cleaned her face and arms free of weeks of filth and grime. I had money to spare so we found a store that sold second hand clothing for children and ducked inside. The outfits and signs in the windows promised they had the best prices in town. I took Sonya by the hand and we looked for a dress that fit her properly. I wanted to find her something practical that was made from a durable fabric that wouldn't wear out easily. But when she pointed to a pink gingham checked dress with starched white collar, I couldn't resist. I let her try it on and then bought it for her when we saw that it fit; we threw away her old rags and went to find shoes to match.

It was nearly dusk when the two of us walked back to the hotel. I invited Sonya to stay with me for the night and she was more than happy to accompany me. She and I slept comfortably in an over-sized bed; I wondered if she had ever been in a real bed before now. The child stole my heart; I covered her with the down comforter and watched her sleep. I felt my own baby moving inside me and thought my circumstance was most peculiar. I didn't want to give Sonya any false hope by doting on her, but now I couldn't stand the thought of her living alone on the streets once I left the city and went back home to my comfortable bed and loving family.

In the morning when I woke up, I could hear Sonya humming a sweet tune. She played with my auburn hair and her fingers drew on my back. She had the most contagious smile and I felt a strong sense of purpose fill me. We indulged in room service and then took turns bathing; I spent the better part of an hour on Sonya's hair. It was tangled and hung in knots from lack of washing and brushing. When it was dry, I gave her a middle part and gave her two French braids that attached in the back and formed a bun at the nape of her neck. It was going to be another hot day today and this hairdo would help keep her cool. She looked precious and what's more, she felt giddy as a result of the new clothes and hairdo. Sonya was so undernourished that she could barely eat an entire pancake. I encouraged her to drink her orange juice and then we stacked our plates outside the door. The only thing that unnerved me about Sonya was how trusting she was. I would never harm her, but what if someone else did? I realize I had started to fuss over her like a mother hen.

We walked the swollen streets from uptown Manhattan to the more gruesome and fearful Five Points, crossing from Baynard to Leonard before seeing Paradise Place in our sights once again. Sonya held my hand as we went, leading me toward a ramshackle arena of sorts. There was a fight scheduled in a few days and we studied the posters to see who was competing. A giant man by the name of Vladimir had posters everywhere, encouraging people to bet on him. There were others too, Patrick Kelley, Bill O'Malley, Brian O'Donnelly, all these lads were Irish. My guess was that they had immigrated here recently and when they found America, the Promised Land, to be lacking in job opportunities, they had no choice but to fight.

We searched the benches of the arena, only finding scraps of garbage and old ticket stubs. When Sonya picked up food from the ground and put it to her mouth, I told her no and she dropped it immediately. We bought a warm bag of roasted nuts to share and sat enjoying the salty morsels while we watched workers set up the event all around us. There was no sign of Scotty, Pauli, or Candy anywhere. Exhaustion overwhelmed me and I needed to sit a while longer, so we lingered longer than we should have.

On my fourth day in New York, I decided to change pace. Instead of looking for Scotty, I would embark on finding Sister Agnes. She was a beacon for me and the thought of seeing her brought tears to my eyes.

Sure enough, Sister Agnes was still placing orphans from the roughest parts of the city on orphan trains and sending them west. She had great success in placing the children because she was diligent about placing ads in all the newspapers a week before the train stopped in a designated area along the route. She looked the same, she was slightly more plump in her cheeks and chin, but otherwise she had the same wooden cross and glasses.

"Sister Agnes?" I said from behind.

She turned at once and immediately remembered me, even though I was one of thousands of children that she took care of over the years.

"Mary! It is so wonderful to see you!" she clasped her hands in prayer and walked toward me. She embraced me just like she did so many years ago and I felt a sense of peace wash over me.

"Who do we have here?" she asked, nodding to Sonya who was hiding behind me, clutching my dress.

"Why, this is my friend, Sonya. She has become my shadow this week, I am afraid she is living on the streets and I was hoping when my journey here is over that I can bring her to you for assistance?"

"Of course. Do you know anything about her?" Sister Agnes asked, looking at the girl with warm, welcoming eyes.

"She is very shy, I found her all alone, she was scraggly and threadbare, she is a waif, is she not?" We exchanged a knowing glance and sister directed her next comment to Sonya. "Guten tag, Sonya." Sonya beamed and began talking a blue streak in a language I was unfamiliar with.

"Oh my goodness, sister, how did you know?"

"Sonya is a common name for those of German decent; we have thousands and thousands of German immigrants in the streets now."

Sister Agnes continued to converse with Sonya in German and I did my best to use context and follow along.

It was incredibly exciting to have a breakthrough with this child. Now that we had a means to communicate, we were able to learn all about her. Her story was pitiful, she was on a boat with her family crossing the ocean when everyone started getting sick. Sadly, her entire family died and were disposed of by being dumped overboard into the sea. Sonya finished the crossing alone.

"I will see to it that she goes to a good German home. Now tell me, Mary, what brings you back to New York?"

I confided in Sister Agnes, telling her about my pregnancy. She vaguely remembered Scotty who was given the name

Matthew when put on an orphan train. I told her that we were in love, but that he came back to the city for work. I didn't go into detail beyond that. He didn't know about the baby and I needed to find him and tell him. Sister didn't judge me; she only listened and held my hand while I spoke. When I was done, she asked about Edmund. I felt guilt leak from my pores because I hadn't spent much quality time with him lately, he was more reclusive these days, he spent hours upon hours studying law books and trials. He worked numerous odd jobs unlike other boys his age who played ball to fill their time.

The clock struck noon and Sister Agnes had many children to prepare for their upcoming journeys. I wished I had been more diligent in my correspondence with her over the years, but time got the better of me.

Sister Agnes shined her light over anyone she befriended and I was glad to call her my friend.

CHAPTER 19

❧

SCOTTY: PLACE YOUR BETS

For a fleeting instant, I could have sworn I saw Mary on Cross Street today. Cross Street is catty corner to Paradise Square and I was having lunch at the Oyster Shack. After all these years, the restaurant still served up the best seafood in the Five Points. You could get a juicy crab roll for a mere seven cents; it was a bargain given the sandwich's large size, and tender meat. Some people questioned the authenticity of the ingredients, but I gulped it down, grateful for a full stomach.

I did a double take when I saw a woman that resembled Mary walk across the street holding the hand of a little girl, her daughter I presumed. I was seeing her silhouette everywhere I went, she occupied my dreams at night, and now I was imagining her here in the city. Just the thought of her being in the city caused me to panic. It had been several months since I last saw her and I prayed she was taking better care of herself now. Our last moments together were full of tenderness and sorrow. I was haunted by her frail appearance, hollowed eyes, and greasy hair. She looked how I felt, which was miserable. She was vulnerable and wore her heart on her sleeve, one of the reasons I loved her so intensely. She gave me the courage I needed to get back in the ring.

I had to win my fight tomorrow. The prize was one hundred dollars split two ways, seventy to thirty in my favor for the win. If it went well I would consider picking up a few more matches; it would be ideal to earn enough for a down payment on a farm, preferably the Wright's. I wanted to buy Mary an engagement ring, and still have money left over for proper furnishings and necessities.

The sale price for the farm was two thousand dollars, which included the buildings, equipment, and the animals. There were currently fifty head of cattle, eleven horses, countless chickens, three or four billy goats, several feral barn cats, which didn't concern me, and two retrievers that I assumed would go wherever their masters went. The red barns that housed the animals were satisfactory for the time being, there were only minimal leaks in the roofs and the haylofts operated smoothly enough. The issue with the fencing was ongoing, as was the case at every farm. Boards rotted and were replaced; white washing was a chore that could easily be managed. I learned over the years that all of this was a normal part of farm life.

The barn that housed the tools, carriages, and any spare parts did, however, need to be torn down and rebuilt. As it stood now, it was only one good storm away from collapse. I figured that would cost a good two hundred or more to build with the cost of materials and hired help.

Two thousand dollars, plus the additional money for the barn, furniture, and food for the animals, was a serious amount of money. But I wanted this more than anything in the world. I needed it actually; I needed something tangible that belonged to me. I would take pleasure in working hard and reaping the benefits. Nothing else compared to the feeling of birthing a calf or breaking a foal. Perhaps we could even add pigs to the mix for slaughter purposes. This would be a very reliable source of income and wouldn't add too much to my costs. If I could get enough money to purchase a few initially, they would breed quickly. The dollar signs were adding up, causing me to have indigestion. I had to focus instead on tomorrow's fight. If I won this bout, I would advance.

My workout requirements for the day included the psychological aspects of training. I was in good physical shape, now I had to focus on getting into my opponent's head. I asked around to find out who I was fighting, and after a good amount of investigation, I learned I was matched up against a black kid from the Sixth Ward. He was shorter and stockier than I was, but I heard he was very muscular and strong. People said he could deliver a punch that would knock me right out. I would have to work on my jabs to keep him away while I tired him out.

"I will win this, I will win this, I will win this," I repeated. I was convinced I would be victorious, I could feel the money in my hands already. I was confident that I had what it took to win, I wasn't being cocky, there was a difference. I had great respect for my opponent; clearly he was training as hard, if not harder, than I was. I could bet he wouldn't get a seventy to thirty cut of his winnings either due to his color. The blacks always got ripped off.

Bets were already being placed and the arena buzzed with excitement. Vladimir was back to decimate another poor soul. Anyone willing to get in the ring with him got one hundred and fifty dollars, no split. It was tempting but not worth my life. The man was enormous, his thighs were the size of watermelons, I guessed he was somewhere around three hundred pounds of muscle. He was imposing and I intended to stay clear of him.

CHAPTER 20

❧

PAULI: AFTER ALL THESE YEARS

"It's been almost ten years."

"I know, love. A lot has happened over the years, why, just look at us! It's hard to believe we are shop owners with property we can call our own. You with your thinning salty hair and me all fat and happy," Candy glanced around their bright and cheery home that burst with live plants, amused by all that she had accomplished and gained over the years. She twirled in her pajamas and still looked as beautiful to me now, despite the weight she gained around her middle and bum. She collected plants the way some women collect jewelry. We had spider plants that trailed from the ceiling to the floor, strawberry plants that produced fruit, we had several kinds of jades, cacti and asparagus ferns with feathery fronds, but Candy's favorite was the purple orchid and she tended it like it was a baby.

We both thought back to our time spent holed up in the old brewery in Paradise Park, home to the Roach Guards. The deadly gang profited from the brothel they owned upstairs and the gambling hall below. Candy herself was a prostitute until I laid eyes on her and forbade her to continue. We have been together ever since. Girls came and went in the brewery and many were my pet for a time, but none stole my heart at first glance like Candy did. We made love our first night, it was not just an act, as she performed many times before; this was real. We fell madly in love with each other and became inseparable. She took the position of nursemaid among the Roach Guards, and was very skilled at it. She proved this time and again, but especially when a small boy who was full of spit and vinegar came into our lives.

"I remember it like yesterday, when Lenny pulled a scrappy little thing into my office, the kid was filthy dirty and terrified for his life. Yet he stood before me with the courage of a lion, head up, shoulders back, looking me right in the eye. What a piece of work. If there is one thing I am sure of, it's that vengeance keeps a man alive, and Scotty had plenty of that. He is out there, somewhere."

"Amen to that. I hope he has moved on and found love. But I remember how angry he was. He wore a grimace all the time, and frankly, why wouldn't he after he was beaten and left to die?"

"You nursed him back to health, my love, and I thank God for that every day."

Candy came toward me and sat in my lap, knowing how hard it was for me to admit that Scotty was lost to us. We looked for him day and night for three weeks straight, but then we had to focus on the baby. Candy had started to feel sick, she was in her first trimester but started to spot. I had to get her out of the city and to a place that felt safe so she could get the rest she needed. We left the city limits and went to New Jersey, the move cost us all our savings. We summoned a doctor at the hotel where we were staying but before he even arrived, Candy started to bleed profusely. She had a miscarriage, no doubt caused by the stress of our squalid living conditions and lifestyle.

"It wasn't meant to be," Candy assured me, giving me strength when it was her body that betrayed her.

"It's my fault, I should have insisted we leave sooner. Five Points is no place for a pregnant woman to live, let alone raise a family."

"What's done is done, baby, we will try again."

That was the worst month I can remember, not only did we lose our baby but we also lost Scotty, the boy we fell in love with on first sight. He had a fighting spirit and clung to us in a way that made us feel needed.

"I'm sorry I haven't been able to give you any children, my love," Candy kissed my forehead and fussed with my hair.

"Darling, it's I who am sorry, I know how desperately you wanted a family. If only I had found you sooner." My voice trailed off as I remembered the youth that approached me twelve years earlier, asking if I needed any favors. She was a star-gazer, she had silky blond hair and wore a low cut blue gown that showed off her ample bosom. It was enticing, but I took one look in the harlot's eyes and felt a connection that warranted more than just a favor.

"You saved me, Pauli. Thank God I found you when I did, and thank God you weren't like all the other men." Tears rolled down her cheeks as they always did when she recounted her days as a prostitute, servicing men in any manner they chose. Dancing a strip tease for them or blowing them before and after the bedding took place. It was purely humiliating.

"I fell in love with you immediately, and I wouldn't change a thing between us, kids or no kids. I love you more today than ever before." I put my dishes in the sink and hugged her, holding her tighter than usual. "Well, I better go and open the store, we have a new shipment coming in today. Do you think you'll be out soon?" I asked.

"Yes, let me just freshen up and take care of my hair. I'll be there shortly."

I knew she wasn't just setting her hair in curlers but gathering herself; whenever we talked about the child we lost and the children we never had, Candy became emotional. Luckily, we had the store to focus on. Neither of us liked New Jersey and both were hopeful that someday we would find Scotty again in New York, so we moved back. We took a few boxes of top hats and gloves, belts and cravats that we stole along the way. It was our last crime and it enabled us to establish the Mr. and Mrs. Shoppe in Lower Manhattan.

We opened a store midway between uptown and downtown so our customers were a mix of the very well to do and those not so well off. Initially there were ups and downs, but now the business thrived due to a solid clientele who liked our merchandise. We carried everything from pre-fabricated to custom-made men's wear that included hats, caps, shirts, coats, frocks, cravats, belts, socks and shoes. For the women we had aprons, dresses, bonnets, parasols, and gloves in the display case. Candy even embellished a few of the aprons herself and they always sold out right away. We considered our lives blessed because we had a flourishing business and a safe place to sleep at night.

The bell we dangled from the door rang indicating our first customer of the day; she was a lady who kept a studious eye on the child outside the shops door. The child seemed to have become enthralled with a stray dog and sat scratching it behind the ears. The woman was in search of a parasol to shield her from the sun, she was pale and obviously with child.

When she looked up and met my eyes, she swooned and fainted.

"Candy! Get out here at once, I need you!" I yelled.

Often times, women came into the shop and created a diversion, upon which a second party would sneak around the store unnoticed and steal from under our noses.

Sure enough, when the woman fainted the child came in,

however, rather than scan the store shelves for pocket-worthy items, she ran toward the woman on the ground. The woman was convulsing and I was frantic.

Candy came down carrying a cup of tea, rushed toward the spectacle on the ground, and splashed the contents of her cup on the patron's face. The child nudged the woman's shoulders and begged her to open her eyes. Finally, the woman woke up, she was momentarily confused, but even in her agitated state she held tight to the child and looked into my eyes. "Pauli?" she asked.

I had never seen this woman before, and was baffled that she knew me.

"Yes, that's my name. Who are you?" We sat the woman up slowly making sure that she wasn't dizzy and faint. Candy went upstairs for a cold glass of water, not only was she pregnant but she was dehydrated. Her ankles were swollen and we had to take care of her and find out who she was.

"I knew it was you," she said. "He described you to a T, a gap between the front teeth, tattoo, and scar above your lip, that's how I knew."

"Who described me? Who told you about me?"

"Scotty."

Candy and I clutched the girl's arms and lifted her to our back room couch. We laid her down and propped her feet up and then she told us her story. She was searching for Scotty, who was looking for us. We were ecstatic to hear that he was alive and well and could even be in the city this moment.

"We have to find him, close the store; we will start looking right away." I started to pace, threatening to wear a hole in the floorboards, making everyone nervous.

"Darling, wait, she is in no position to be up and about just yet." I could read Candy's mind; she was afraid the woman would lose the child.

"You ladies stay here and rest. Candy, can you mind the store if the little one helps you?" We finally took notice of the young girl in tow and Mary explained that she was her shadow since she arrived in the city a week ago. She attached herself to Candy right away and became her helper for the day. But first she motioned toward the door where a small pup was wagging his tail and looking at them. Candy filled a bowl with water and put it outside the shop for the pup, tying her to the bench in the shade.

"Tell me everything Scotty said before he left. Where was he going to look for us?"

Mary said that Scotty was now nearly six feet tall, his hair was curly and black and he let it flow out behind his cap. He had filled out tremendously from all of his farm work and had broad shoulders. He was strong and competent. His plan was to search the Five Points, the brewery, and then the docks. He wanted to pick up work as well. He left Binghamton for numerous reasons, but didn't know his lover was pregnant. He was coming to New York to find us, but also to escape and find respite.

"Well," I cracked my knuckles deprecatingly, not happy with the situation in Binghamton that Mary described, but certain we could find a way through the nonsense. Scotty and Mary could live with us, we had a spare room we used for Candy's sewing, but it would be easy enough to clean out. I was already picturing a cradle and bed; the thought amused and delighted me. "I'd better be going then." I went to Mary and patted her arm, "I'll be back with your lad, have no worries about that. If Scotty is here, I will find him."

I hadn't been in the Five Points in years, preferring the fresher air in Manhattan to the polluted stench of the slums. I also feared running into anyone from the Roach Guards. I wouldn't be forgiven easily and wanted that part of my life to remain in the past.

I heard tell of a grand fire that destroyed half the shops several years ago, apparently the looting was out of control and shop keeps lost everything. Still, there were structures in place with signs depicting bakeries, grocery stores, clothing stores, and more.

I walked up and down Anthony Street before making my way to Cross, and then over to Orange Street. There was no sign of a man fitting Scotty's description. I hated to admit it but I was afraid that if a man came to New York for work and was unable to find it, he might be lured into the underworld of street fighting. Fighting was in Scotty's blood, I had put it there when I allowed him to train and get revenge on the gang that nearly took his life after they caught him spying for me. I encouraged him and watched him grow from a scrawny youth to a kid who was confident in the ring. There was decent money in the ring, especially for an unknown who would have a better split if he found the right promoter.

Fights always took place at dusk; they were even more prevalent now because of the increasing immigration problem. Men fresh off the boat jumped into the ring without hesitation in order to make quick money.

I asked around about the upcoming fights and heard tell of Vladimir the Victor, any man even willing to step in the ring with him was given a huge sum with no split. He earned it too, and most likely used it for medical bills if what the folks said was accurate. Vladimir was lethal, a hulk of a man with no empathy, he pummeled his opponents and had to be pulled off by three or four men before the man died.

I found the location of the fights and grabbed a beer from the tavern before heading to the arena. I would need a stout or two to loosen up and face the gruesome lifestyle once more.

A changing landscape of figures milled around the large arena that had three levels of decks. The top level had ladies entertaining men, as many as six per hour. Fight nights were very lucrative for the women. Bookies took bets, talked up one opponent over another and soon enough the first men appeared in the ring. It was a lightweight fight, the men were immigrants, speaking no English and looking weary before the bell even rang. The fighter in the red corner came out strong, he was scrappy and had his opponent against the ropes most of the round. In the second round, he knocked him out cold. The next fight started immediately, I watched both fights intently and was surprised that I had missed the sport. I asked around for Scotty, but no one knew him. I was determined to find him and slipped upstairs in case the ladies had heard of him. I paid a Jezebel for any information she had, and she whispered what she could do to me for just a few coins. "No thanks," I replied and noted her stunned reaction; surely she wasn't rejected often, for she was a beauty.

The bookies were busy, but I approached under the guise of placing a large bet on a fighter named Scotty.

"What's your wager, fella?" The bookie in the tan cap asked before spitting a wad of chew to his left.

"I'll wager my entire wallet on Scotty."

"Okay, then Scotty it is, he is in the ninth fight. He's got a tough match up, though, you sure you want to bet it all? Maybe you should spread it out."

"I'm sure." I said, handing the man all the money in my wallet.

Holy shit, Scotty, or at the very least, a fighter named Scotty was here somewhere. Fighters warmed up all over the arena, some doing it in front of the spectators to rile up their opponents, others in the quiet to calm their nerves. If I remembered correctly, Scotty liked quiet before his fights, so he could focus. I ducked into every corner, looking for anyplace that offered privacy, but had no luck. The eighth fight was ending and in just a few minutes, Scotty would be in the ring.

The applause settled down and the man in the blue corner wearing yellow knickers took center ring. Next, the man in red was called forward. Scotty was in the zone. He still looked like the kid I pulled off the streets ten years ago, but he'd lost his youth. Now he was a stone-faced man on a mission.

The bell signaling round one dinged. Scotty danced around the ring, assessing the skills of his opponent because he seemed to be far more experienced. Scotty was rusty but looked healthy and in shape. Hopefully, he still had the endurance he did when he was younger. The man in the knickers closed in on Scotty, nailing him with a series of body shots. Scotty gripped his gut and left his face open, he was punched in the jaw, spit went flying, but he stood strong. He came at his opponent and landed a long straight punch, followed by a few jabs. He always protected his kidneys, and after two minutes, the bell rang. I ran to his corner, "Clean and fast, Scotty. It's the only way to beat this guy."

"What the hell?" Scotty was breathing heavy and was shocked to see me.

"I'll explain later, now you have to get back in there and be quick about it, behind the ears alright? Knock him there and it'll mess with his equilibrium, then you'll have your chance on the body. You can do it." I massaged his shoulders and gave him a sip of water that he spit on the floor beside the ring before standing up and bouncing on the balls of his feet, renewed. The Gutter Boys in his corner stepped aside and let me coach him.

"Let's go, Scotty, you can do this," I cheered him on.

The man in yellow was named Roger, and he came out with more gusto as well, he was on Scotty before he could react. He pinned him against the ropes, but Scotty shimmied out from behind and hit him with a series of jabs and then an uppercut that forced Roger to stagger backwards. There was no time to think, Scotty just reacted, he followed up with a body shot, knocking Roger off balance. Roger stumbled to the outside of the ring, Scotty pinned him and pummeled him with jabs to the head, alternating with body shots. Roger couldn't protect his body because Scotty was too fast for him. When Roger put his gloves up to protect his head, Scotty would lead left and go right on his body, injuring his kidneys. It was a tough round for Roger. The bell rang and Scotty sat down in his corner, breathing heavily and bleeding profusely from the punch to the cheek in the first round. I taped it and gave him a sip of water. I encouraged him to keep at Roger's body, he was getting tired.

The third and fourth rounds were fairly even. Scotty gave as much as he got and both men were exhausted from the battle. Men in the arena were taking notice of Scotty and bets were placed rapidly. The crowd cheered him on and gave him energy to continue. He finished Roger in the next round, one strong right hook and the man went down for an eight count; in fact, he was still down when we took the winnings and left.

I put my arms tight around my son and then pulled back to have a good look at him. He was scraped up pretty badly, blood seeped out from his cheek, eyebrow, and mouth.

"Let's get you cleaned up, deal?"

"How did you find me?" Scotty mumbled through swollen lips, adrenaline pulsing through his veins dulling the pain.

"It's quite a story, first let me take care of you, then I'll tell you everything." We walked over to the doctor's station and waited for Scotty's turn. He had four stitches placed above his eyebrow; the gouge on his right cheek had congealed so stitches weren't necessary. I gave him ice for his lips and the doctor wrapped his ribs, even though they weren't broken, they were tender. The medical team applied ointment to his fists, which were cut open and bleeding at the knuckles. After he drank a few glasses of water, he started to look better.

Bookies were approaching us all at once. They asked Scotty if he'd be back and reminded him about Vladimir's offer of one hundred and fifty dollars just to get in the ring. There were numerous fights he could get if he wanted them. But now, the only thing he cared about was talking to me.

"I'm so proud of you, son. That was a great fight. You looked really good out there...have you been training?" It was as if no time had passed between us and we settled into a comfortable conversation right away.

"I'm not sure if you'd call it training, but yes, I have kept myself fit." Scotty didn't want to talk about himself, he had too many questions for me. "Is Candy here?" He scanned the crowd for her blond hair, but it was mostly just men on the bottom level watching the fights.

"No, she's at home waiting for you."

"How did you know I was here? I've been looking for you for months. Is my brother or sister there too?" Scotty looked so excited and I hated giving him the bad news. I shook my head and looked toward the ground, remembering how Candy's belly felt before the miscarriage. "We lost the baby, and there haven't been others. Boy, I have never been so happy in all my life, seeing you out there today, well, it was great."

We stood up and I directed Scott down Anthony Street toward home. He counted his winnings as we walked and I told him about the shop. Before his head cleared, he stopped dead in his tracks.

"Wait a minute, how did you know I was in New York? This doesn't make sense."

"It seems someone else was looking for you too, and that someone stumbled into my shop this morning, took one look at me, and fainted."

"What?" Scotty was confused.

"Mary. She recognized me from your description, she was dehydrated and a bit tired from all her walking in her condition."

"What condition? What the hell is she doing here?" Scotty breathed through his teeth. He was seething and I knew it was because he hated the thought of her alone in the city.

"Is she alone? Tell it to me straight, Pauli, what's going on?"

"Well, she is and she isn't alone, she has a shadow, a little girl around seven years old who has been with her for a week. That's about how long she had been here looking for you."

Scotty quickened his pace and was practically jogging he was so eager to see Mary. "She's been here that long alone, oh my God, how far uptown are you? I'm hailing a carriage."

Scotty looked around for a trolley or carriage, and sure enough, a trolley that was heading uptown stopped at the corner in front of us and we were able to catch it.

"You said something else; what is the condition she is in? Is she hurt, did someone hurt her?" My son had a far-away look in his eyes before he said, "I'll kill anyone who harms her."

"No, she isn't hurt. Candy is taking care of her now while she rests. I'll let her tell you the rest, relax, we'll be home in a few minutes." Home, the word stirred up images of chaos and boisterous little ones running around, even the word Grandpa suddenly etched itself in my mind.

"You look amused," Scotty said.

"I am. It's been quite a day."

CHAPTER 21

❧

SCOTTY: THE PROPOSAL

The Mr. and Mrs. Shoppe had a bright and airy feel. Pauli led me through the front door and I caught the eye of a little girl seated behind the counter at the register. Pauli nodded in her direction and asked her if everything was going okay. Then he held a curtain aside for me and led me through a narrow hallway and up a flight of stairs.

The space was colorful and cozy, but nothing warmed my heart as much the sight of Candy. She was in the den when we came in and hopped up immediately when she saw me.

"Scotty!" she whispered, cupping my face with her hands, "Look at you."

I picked her up and spun her around, she hadn't changed at all.

"Candy, it's so wonderful to see you. Where is Mary, is she okay? I have to see her right away, everything else can wait."

"She is resting comfortably, but I am sure you will be a welcome sight."

I opened the bedroom door and found Mary sleeping on her back, she looked more beautiful than ever. An avalanche of blankets was kicked to her feet. She had a protruding belly, could it be or were my eyes playing tricks on me? She must have felt my stare because she woke up with a start, speechless at the sight of me all beaten and bruised in front of her.

"Scotty!" she spoke my name and then the tears she'd been holding back spilled out.

I knelt at her bedside, kissing her, and placing my hand across her belly. She was a welcome sight to say the least, and she had the moxie to come here on her own.

"Is this what you came to tell me about then, Red?" I kept my hand on her belly, in awe that my baby was growing inside her.

"It is, are you mad?" she asked, peering directly into my eyes for an honest answer.

"The only thing I am mad about is that you came here alone, it's even more dangerous now than it was a decade ago. Am I mad about the baby? Never. I am delighted." I hugged her and crawled into bed with her, nervous and excited at the same time about becoming a father.

"Are you alright? Pauli said you fainted. Do you need anything? Water, food, anything at all?" I was rambling.

"I was dehydrated and tired, but not even that would keep me from trying to find you." The tears kept spilling from her eyes in torrents, she grasped at me fearful that I would disappear again.

"It's okay, I'm here now. We are going to be fine." I pulled out my winnings and showed her, and sure enough, the wad of money elicited a grin.

"It's Edna and Pap, I left them a note before I got on the train. I have no idea if they have disowned me or not. I am worried they will be disappointed in me and never want to see me again."

"God knows they'll hate me even more now. First things first, let me hug you a while, I have missed you."

Mary fussed over my stitches, traced the wounds on my cheek and knuckles, but all the caressing and hugging led to kissing and exploring. But before I put my hands on her woman parts, I wondered if it was safe for the baby.

"Perhaps this isn't the time?" I asked.

"I don't know if it's safe, but I will ask Candy. I have missed you too." We kissed and enjoyed being back in each other's embrace.

"Where did you learn to kiss like that, Mary?" I teased before pulling her to her feet and assessing her head to toe. "I just can't believe I am going to be a father!" We both laughed then and held hands as we went into the den to reunite with Pauli and Candy.

The sight in the den was bewitching. Candy had Sonya on her lap and was reading her a story. Pauli sat next to them smoking his pipe. This is what a family looked like.

"Congratulations, son." Pauli clapped me on the back and shook my hand. I noticed the tattoo beneath the rolls of his shirtsleeves but didn't comment on it because it was part of his past. I stared at the people in front of me and held tight to Mary's hand. Dropping to one knee, I proposed to her.

"Mary, I will love you forever, please marry me? Be my wife, Mary, please?" I looked into her eyes as I spoke, ruffling my hair with my knuckles, nerves getting the better of me.

"Yes, of course I will marry you! I love you too!" Mary stood there and hugged me and when she did I felt the baby pressing itself against my stomach.

"We would love it if you stayed here with us," Pauli said.

"Yes, we can clean out my sewing room and set you up comfortably in there, it would be so nice to have you." Candy clapped her hands together and stood to congratulate us.

"That's a rather generous offer, but first I need to speak to Edna and Pap about my news. I'm afraid I left rather suddenly." It was evident that Mary was worried sick about Edna, and her eyes pleaded with mine for understanding.

"Let's make sure that you're healthy first, and then we can travel to Binghamton together. Would that be easier for you?" Candy said, and her suggestion was most kind.

"You mean you would come with me? Golly, that is so generous, but I think I need to face my folks alone. Scotty, it would be nice if you came though."

"Of course, I'll be right by your side the whole time." There was a lot to consider, we had so much to plan and I had things to get in order. I felt suddenly overwhelmed.

The clock on the mantle said it was dinnertime, so we all sat together and ate. Candy made a roasted chicken, homemade butter rolls and potatoes. We even had brownies for dessert.

I watched Mary pick at her food and became nervous at the thought something was wrong. It didn't seem like she was eating enough and it wasn't just her ankles but her calves were swollen too. Later that evening, after Sonya had fallen asleep on the couch, I approached Candy and Pauli in the shop with my concerns.

"Candy, is she okay? She is hardly eating and is so swollen."

"Scotty, sit down. What she needs now is rest. She hasn't been to a doctor yet and I intend to see that she goes tomorrow. She is young and otherwise healthy so I am certain that she will be fine. Edema can be more of a nuisance than anything in pregnancy; she just needs to stay off her feet. We are all here to make sure she does that."

I felt a little better. "But why isn't she eating? Shouldn't she be eating for two now?"

"She is in her second trimester and her nausea is just now subsiding, things taste different during pregnancy, what she loved once she may hate now. Some pregnant women get by on milk and cookies alone, whatever she can stomach is fine for now. We just need to find what that is and make sure it's always available for her."

"Well, she liked your brownies," I said, and we laughed. "Can I ask you a more personal question, Candy?"

"You don't have to be embarrassed, Scotty, what is it?"

"Well, it's just that I don't want to hurt the baby if we... you know." I couldn't get the words out but Candy knew what I meant.

"Being intimate won't hurt the baby, and it might even be good for Mary. I will speak to her about it if you'd like."

"That's okay, I can talk to her. Thank you. It's just so good to be here with you, to have found you after all these years."

"Scotty, we've missed you so much, in fact we were just discussing you earlier today."

"I really don't know how I'll face Mary's folks, they hate me," I admitted.

"Who could ever hate you?" Candy stroked my hair and Pauli pulled up a chair to join our conversation.

"Pap for one, and possibly Edna too. For that matter, the whole town will hate me if they think I am responsible for harming the animals in my care. Pap says if I really love Mary that I should stay as far as possible from her. He says I need to let her go because I will never be able to provide for her the way she has become accustomed to living, and the way she deserves. On that note, he is right. She was raised in a home with handmade furniture and art and she is far more cultured and educated than I am. Did she tell you that she plans to be a teacher? How could she be happy living with me on a farm then? I just don't know what to do." I explained the situation with the Wright's Farm and told them about the money I needed for a down payment in order to make the purchase. Then I reiterated Pap's concerns.

"But she loves you, Scotty. She doesn't love a banker or lawyer, she loves you as much for your history together as for the man you are now. Money doesn't make a person happy, she would be miserable without you and now you have the baby to consider."

"I realize that, that's why I have to do something to make money and quickly. I can fight Vladimir. It pays just to get in the ring with him."

Pauli stood up and paced. "Absolutely not. I won't allow it. The man is a death sentence, just one punch could kill you, or leave you brain damaged and your child fatherless. That is out of the question."

On that note, Candy stood and said goodnight. She wanted to check on Sonya before getting to bed herself.

Pauli and I were alone. "There is another way," I said.

"What's that, Scotty?"

"I know the gold rush is mostly over, but there's a group of guys going to San Francisco this week to see if they can get lucky. I could take my winnings and buy gear and a passage out west. It may be my big break; I could become a rich man and never worry about being in anyone's debt. Pap would have nothing to say then, and everything would be easier for Mary as a result. If this works, she wouldn't feel so torn."

"Son, as you said, the rush is over. Yes, men are still heading west in hopes of finding new streams to pan but practically speaking, it's unreasonable."

"Maybe so, but I could get lucky. What else do I have to lose? If I leave now, before the baby is born, I can give myself half a year to make something of myself. I could be back in time to raise the baby and hopefully when I return it will be as a rich man. If not, I'll be no worse off than I am now."

"It's a stretch, but you don't know anything about gold mining. It's not like you just stick your hand in a river and pull up nuggets of gold. Nothing in life is that easy. And you have a lot to lose, Mary and your child for starters. Or your life, thousands of men have died trying to strike it rich out west."

"Like I said, a few fellas I met at the tavern are going, they are taking rolls to sleep on, a few pots and pans to cook with and use for sifting and the rest they plan to purchase along the way. It will be easier to travel light. They talked about saving their money for shovels, picks, axes, saws, ropes and possibly wheelbarrows, and knives to use on the job. A gun would come in handy, too. As a group we can pool our money for a cradle or sieve."

"Sounds like they know a little more than you do about it, but everyone is dropping everything and hoping for a quick fix, easy money, and that's just not how it works for most people. You know that."

"Maybe, just maybe, it's my turn for a little luck, especially with the baby coming."

"Are you going to talk to Mary about it? You already know what she is going to say."

"That's why I am not telling her, and neither are you. Not a word to Candy either. They'd tie me to a chair to make sure I stayed put."

"I wouldn't blame them either. I don't think it's the right thing to do, not now; Mary needs you. If you leave now it gives Pap more ammunition against you, can't you see that?"

"All I know is that he equates worthiness with money. He will never give me his blessing to marry his daughter as I am now. He will challenge me for the rest of my life and that's not fair to Mary."

"I suppose that's true, but what if you stay here in New York with us? You can raise your child here and be part of the family business. It does very well, we have a place to live and money left over for a few niceties every now and then."

"Pauli, while that's generous and I appreciate it, Mary and I talked about this and we want to raise our family in the country. She's grown to love it, and so have I."

"Sleep on it, alright? Don't do anything rash, give me a chance to think a little and see if I can't come up with a better solution." Pauli scratched his thinning hair and thought about my situation.

I hugged him and headed upstairs to my fiancé, who was positively glowing. She was waiting up for me. "What took you so long?" she asked. I crawled under the covers with her one last time before taking my leave and heading west. I would leave her a note explaining everything. I would beg her to forgive me for my sudden departure but prayed she understood it was for our future.

CHAPTER 22

※

GERT: POTIONS

The atmosphere in the house was strained. I knew Sarah was agitated because when she undressed my wounds to reapply the healing salve, her fingers were unsteady. Before she came in my room she spoke in hushed tones to Edna outside my doorway, attempting to soothe her sister's distress, this much I was able to ascertain. I worried their conversation had something to do with me; perhaps they had finally become tired of caring for me. I was becoming a burden because I had been here for weeks, I needed to get well and out from under foot. My mind was a hindrance; I was unable to cite any previous occupations or skills I had. It was almost like I was born again. I had no idea what I used to enjoy doing or how I spent my time. It was apparent I had little or no family, or I think they would have come to call by now, and claim me and return me to my proper home where they'd nurse me back to health. But that hadn't occurred and the ladies were tight lipped about my past and about my accident.

I studied my reflection in the looking glass the ladies lent me as if I were seeing myself for the first time. I noted my turned up nose and wide almond-shaped eyes. I had larger than average ear lobes with several holes for earrings. My chin was pointy but was offset by a matching set of dimples. I had all my teeth, albeit they were yellowing. Feature by feature I was not much to look at but all together, I would say I had an exotic look, which made me wonder about my heritage. The only thing with any familiarity was the brevity of my name, Gert. It was crisp like the first bite into a tart apple. I recognized "Gert" the same way an adult retrieves a memory from childhood, it is there, but clouded over and hard to reach. My past evaded me, and my future eluded me, it was a terrifying predicament. The tingling started in my toes and then rose up my shins, working its way to my torso, down my arms, causing a numbing sensation in my arms. My breathing became rapid as true fear took over my physical being. I wiped the sweat beads that formed on my forehead and tried to calm myself down. Panic was taking over and I felt the need to run, but didn't know where to go.

I need to gather my things and get out of this house. The women were generous and kind but I didn't belong here. They discussed bringing a special doctor from out of state to see me; they thought he could help me remember things through hypnotherapy. This scared me to death. I objected, exclaiming that I just needed more time.

I need to be up and around; surely then things will jog my memory. My wounds were nearly healed, only the tender area around my privates remained sore, but I had sat long enough on ice packs that the swelling was gone and the stitches removed. While I appreciated the discreet tender care, the women gave me I knew it was time to take matters in to my own hands now.

I had never seen the women rattled until today, and swore Edna had been crying before she entered my room to care for me. Her eyes were red rimmed and puffy, and she had a look of concern and utter sadness.

"Edna, are you okay?" I asked, my throat no longer sore.

"Darling, Gert, don't you worry about me, let's just get you better," she filled the basin with water and started my bath.

"But you look so sad, is it me?" I prayed I wasn't the culprit.

"Oh, heavens no." Edna put her hand across her ample chest before confiding in me.

"My daughter is in some trouble and has gone missing."

"I wish I could help you, Miss Edna, you have shown me so much kindness."

"Well, perhaps you will forgive me if I am not able to tend you in the next few days, I may need to do some traveling. I think my daughter has gone to New York City..." Edna began to cry, but wiped her nose with a hankie and continued, "she is pregnant and is searching for the baby's father."

"I see." Now this was a predicament, I thought Edna's daughter was close in age to me given the way she talked about her.

Edna told me about Mary and Scotty and confessed that she didn't understand why her husband was so against their love. She thought Scotty was a good boy; he just needed a little compassion given his situation.

"I completely understand, Edna. It's about time I get on my own two feet and start life anyway, I just don't know where to begin."

"Has Edmund been to see you yet?"

"No, Sarah suggested we wait a bit longer."

"Edmund is your very good friend. I know you don't remember anything, but maybe he'll be able to help. We have kept him away until you healed a bit more. He was one of the people who found you and it was quite distressing for him."

"Oh, I see. I should think I would like to meet this Edmund. Why yes, maybe he's just what I need to jog my memory."

"Very well then, after your rest today, we will dress you in something besides a shift and let him pay you a visit."

I was relieved to learn that I had a real friend. Thank God there was someone out there that knew me from before my accident. I simply couldn't fall asleep during my rest time because all I did was think about him. I tossed and turned until I couldn't take it anymore. I glanced at my wounds, the scarring had already begun and I wondered who could ever love me now?

A gentle knock came at my door several hours later. I was eager, and dressed in more than my undergarments so that I could finally receive a visitor. I wore a purple dress, with Spanish lace at the neckline and along the sleeves, the ladies said this color complimented my brown eyes.

"Come in," I bid Edmund to come in and prayed for a spark of recognition.

"Hello, Gert." Edmund took off his top hat and placed it on my bedside table before reaching out and taking my hands in a familiar manner. But he didn't look like anyone I had ever seen before. He was quite handsome, however, and looked to be my age.

"I am so sorry, Edmund, but I don't remember you." I desperately searched my mind for a flicker, but there was nothing.

"We were best friends, however, I don't blame you for forgetting me. I understand that the amnesia is meant to protect you; what you endured was pretty traumatic."

"I hadn't thought about it that way, but why would I want to forget my entire life? Can you help me put the pieces together? Can you tell me who I was, what I liked to do, even the little things would help, for instance, what was my favorite color?"

"I don't see how it would hurt; your favorite color was yellow, not a butter yellow, but a bright canary yellow. You had a beautiful straw bonnet with a yellow gingham ribbon on it; I think that was your favorite hat." I sat back and listened as this stranger described my life.

"Yellow, indeed. Please go on, tell me more. Did I have a favorite activity or any other friends that I can call on?" I felt starved for information.

"You volunteered at the church regularly and you adored reading. Why, you even read to me on occasion. Your favorite book was *Emma*. You look tired, maybe I should leave you for now. I can come back tomorrow. We have nothing but time, you must get well and soon you will feel strong enough to continue your volunteer work."

"Please don't go, Edmund. Stay here with me. I have so many unanswered questions and I am afraid they'll take over my mind and make it hard for me to concentrate. I am so overcome." I started to cry, but Edmund didn't startle, he just held me close to him and begged me to forgive him for telling me too much too soon.

"This is what my mother was afraid of, you've been through so much, Gert. No one wants to recount it for you."

He held me for a moment longer, then sat me in a chair and draped an afghan across my lap so that I could rest. I imagined my life as he described it but felt no connection to it.

"Visit me tomorrow?" I asked.

"Certainly, I will, until then," he kissed my hand and left me mesmerized.

The following day couldn't come soon enough. I was dressed and waiting for Edmund by mid-morning. Sarah bathed me and brushed my hair, parting it on the side and pulling it into a tight bun, loose tendrils curled at the sides. It looked rather nice, this hairstyle; I admired it and my new navy dress, both gave me confidence.

When Edmund came, I assaulted him with dozens of questions.

"One at a time!" he admonished, "I will do my best, but today, I wondered if you'd be up for some fresh air?"

"Oh, yes, indeed. That would be so welcome." My ribs were feeling much better now and my legs were at risk for developing bedsores, and needed the exercise. I bent to put on my shoes and winced from the pain I felt both in my ribcage and elsewhere.

Edmund could read the discomfort and bent down on his knees, gathering and placing my shoes on my feet.

Sarah lent me her yellow parasol and together we stepped out into the bright sun.

"You called me Eddie. It was your pet name for me I suppose," he said. I noticed he was a good head or more taller than I, his hair was thick and long, he was handsome and gentle.

"Did you like it?" I teased.

"I did, in fact. You and I walked along this pathway many times, we'd sit across from the pond and feed the ducks our left over cones."

"What flavor did I get?"

"Oh you never strayed too far from chocolate and jimmies."

We walked past the grocer's and the Ale House tavern, but nothing looked familiar to me. I caught a lot of people glancing my way but we ignored the stares and continued.

A black man stopped his sweeping at the grocery store and tipped his cap to me when we passed.

"Did I know him?"

"I don't recall, but you were kind to everyone in your path, so it was likely that you have exchanged pleasantries with him before."

"Hmm, nothing is familiar. It's so stressful."

"I can only imagine what you are going through. Here you are putting your trust and faith in me and yet you don't even remember me. That has to be hard." "It is hard, but your family has been nothing but kind to me, by taking me in and caring for me I trust them completely. Can you please tell me about my family now?"

"I really think that should wait. I don't want to set you back at all, remember, you were put through a traumatic experience."

"Did what happened to me also happen to them? Did I have siblings? Are they hurt, did they die?"

My questions came in waves, panic set in when I tried piecing together the puzzle of my life.

"You didn't have any siblings; it was actually just you and your mother. But that's all I will say for now. Please, can we just walk and enjoy the fresh air?"

I could tell I was getting on Edmund's nerves so I stopped asking questions. The sun was bright and I admired the window boxes full of bright flowers at each store in the village.

"Did I spend any time in these shops?" The stores held no memory and I promised to stop being such a pest, but I suddenly wondered about my personal style and taste in clothing and hair trends. I wondered if the shop owners would recall my purchases.

"I wouldn't know, you and I spent most of our time reading, walking, and helping those in need."

"That sounds sort of boring, doesn't it? Truly, is that all we did? What did we do for fun?"

"If you permit me to give you a kiss, your imagination might give you some ideas."

"Okay, then, kiss me."

Edmund leaned in to kiss me; his lips were slightly parted, and very soft. They searched mine for a flicker of remembrance. I kissed him back, recalling the motions. We leaned against a tree and continued to neck for a few minutes before he pulled away.

"Why did you stop? I was enjoying that," I said.

"I want to take things slow, Gert, trust me, please?"

"Kissing me was your idea." I said feeling giddy from the kiss.

"It was my idea, but it feels a little too good for me and I am afraid I won't be able to stop myself. I miss you so much," he confessed.

I grabbed Edmund's hand and we continued our stroll through town. Several passersby took notice of us and stopped to say hello. I may as well have been new to town, nothing and no one came back to me, which meant my amnesia was full blown. I was afraid I would never remember anything at all, but if that were the case and I were to live out my days here in Binghamton, it wouldn't be so bad. Edmund was devilishly handsome and kind; he showed that he cared for me and took pride in his appearance. I got the feeling he was well respected in town as well.

"Edmund, can we do some volunteering? Maybe if I jumped right back into my old routine I will remember something."

"Absolutely, I will call on the church and see what they need this week. Maybe we can stock the pantry shelves or put groceries together for families in need. I will look into it, but for now, let's get back home. I'm afraid you may need some rest after today's jaunt."

He was right, all the sights and sounds, not to mention the exercise, had me tuckered out. I ate dinner at Sarah's table, Edmund was to my right and Samuel was at the head of the table. The meal consisted of mashed potatoes, green beans, and roast beef with gravy. After dinner I perused Sarah's bookshelves and found a book with well-worn pages and went to bed for a nice long nap. I found it amazing that even with amnesia I still knew how to read.

That night I slept like a baby and woke refreshed and ready for a new day, a new beginning. Edmund came for me at ten o'clock in the morning and we went to the basement in our church that stored food for those in need. We lent a hand stocking shelves, and although everyone walked on eggshells around me, I knew it was because of my trauma and lack of memory so it wasn't unusual. Other volunteers asked about my health and I assured them that with Edmund's help I was feeling much better.

On our walk home Edmund asked me if I enjoyed myself today. The answer was yes, I did, being out and interacting with all sorts of people filled me with renewed joy.

"What else would you like to do?" he asked.

"Well, I have a crazy thought and I'm not sure where it comes from, but I have this desire to create potions."

"What in the world, like witch's potions?"

"No! I don't know if they're called potions, but I thoroughly enjoy the feel and smell of the lotions your mother and Edna have brought for me to use. I don't know why but I keep thinking about them. Does that sound ridiculous?"

"Not at all, but we could check the local stores and buy some if you prefer."

"No, I feel like I want to partake in the process of making them. Rose water for the bath, creams and lotions with varying scents, perhaps even night creams and lip balms."

"It sounds like you've been giving this some thought. Are you telling me when you smell roses that you can conjure a rose? Or when you think of an orange you can conjure both the smell and color? If so, that's progress!"

"I can! I have given this lots of thought, you're right. What else am I supposed to do while lying in bed staring at the butterfly shadow box?"

"Ha, so you like the butterflies then?"

"I do, I favor the bright blue moth, she is lovely, don't you agree?"

"Yes, she is magnificent. But let me see, sometime between staring at butterflies and getting well you came up with the grand notion that you should make products for women? How in the world did that occur to you?"

"Honestly, your mother has been so kind to me and she is the impetus for the idea. When she had to bathe me I was in so much pain, but the scented products she used distracted me from that state of fear; without them I would have fallen apart on more than one occasion."

"That makes perfect sense. Let's talk to Sarah when we get home and ask her if we can use the kitchen for some experiments."

"It sounds fun, maybe she'll even have some recipes we can start with."

"What's this 'we' stuff?" Edmund asked amused before leading me into the house.

"Sarah?" I called out to the woman of the house.

"Yes, Gert, is everyone alright?" She came bustling down the stairs and into the kitchen, her large frame taking up most of the doorway.

"It's just fine. It's just that I had an idea and I wondered if you would allow me to use your kitchen for some experimenting?"

"Of course, dinner isn't for several hours, go ahead."

Edmund and I had stopped at a florist shop on our walk home and I purchased a dozen red roses for my first experiment. I had a vague memory of doing this before, but pushed it aside for now, the more I tried to recall it the more upset I became. So instead I followed the florist's directions for making rose water. I plucked the petals from the stems and rinsed them thoroughly before layering them in Sarah's stockpot; next I covered them with distilled water and let them simmer. I stirred the pot so it didn't boil and watched until all the color disappeared from the petals. Oil skimmed the surface of my mixture and I turned the stove off, I strained my mix and squeezed the petals for any remaining oils and moisture. I let it settle for an hour and then dabbed the water on my hands, but the smell was too much like artichokes. I wondered out loud, "Huh, what did I do wrong?"

Sarah wandered into her kitchen to see how I was coming along and agreed that the water I created didn't smell like roses but had a musty vegetable scent instead. She suggested I try fresh roses and allowed me to pick a bunch from her garden out back. I scrubbed the pan and started the recipe all over again. This time the result was more promising, but still it wasn't quite perfect.

Before I knew it, Sarah needed her kitchen space to prepare dinner so I cleaned up my mess and thought about my approach. "Ha! I know," I exclaimed, "I have to pick the roses first thing in the morning before the dew has evaporated, that's when they are freshest." Everyone stared at me. "Wait, how did I know that?"

"Maybe you've made rose water before? With your mom, perhaps?" Sarah asked.

I searched my memory for images of a mother figure picking roses, but nothing came to mind.

"No matter, I'm sure it's what I need to do, is that okay with you, Sarah? May I pick a small bunch of roses tomorrow morning?"

"Of course, you don't have to ask, I have hundreds of roses out there with plenty to spare, help yourself."

"Thank you, Sarah," I ran to her and hugged her tight.

I started my recipe card index with:

Rose Water for Bathing
Rose petals plucked first thing in the morning
Removal of stems and leaves
Rinse free of dirt and bugs
Fill bottom of stockpot with petals two inches deep
Cover petals with distilled water
Simmer until petals are pale in color and a glossy oil
rises to the top
Strain and squeeze petals
Pour into glass jars

It was my first recipe! My mind raced and I got ahead of myself, I didn't have glass jars yet and needed them immediately.

"Edmund, after dinner will you walk with me into town? I need to go to the apothecary or florist and ask for glass bottles." Edmund and Sarah exchanged a quick smile, amused and encouraged by my sudden interest in working.

There was no end to what I could create. If I could create bath water then I could create facial toners and astringents by diluting the water or adding witch hazel. I could make rose petal soap and maybe even a lotion or cream. How did this idea come to me? What on earth would possess me to start a business?

Edmund and I found a dozen glass bottles at the apothecary's and he gave them to us free of charge. He only asked that I bring him a sample of my rose water for his wife. I did and she loved it! Sarah and Edna admired the subtlety of the scent as well and remarked how lovely it would be in a hand cream or as a perfume.

I spent the next several weeks experimenting and creating recipes in Sarah's kitchen. By the end of the month I had made rose water and rose milk for the bath, the two were differentiated by their textures. I made rose hand lotion and rose dust body powder. I also made a facial astringent that toned my facial skin making it feel and look smoother.

Rose Hand Lotion:
5 oz. rose water
3.5 oz. glycerin
1 droplet of red or yellow food coloring
Add drops of rose water gradually to glycerin
Mix color slowly
Whisk together until smooth
Bottle the solution and cap tightly

Rose Dust Powder:
4 fresh roses
1 cup cornstarch
3 tbsp. baking soda
3 dried roses
Layer petals and cornstarch in cardboard box, cover
loosely and leave for twenty-four hours
Sift petals and cornstarch and add baking soda
Grind dried rose petals and add to mixture
Blend with wooden spoon and pour powder into jar
For deeper scent add another batch of fresh roses

I experimented with rubbing alcohol and witch hazel to fine-tune a facial toner and found that one part alcohol or witch hazel to ten parts rose water worked the best. I now had a dining table full of concoctions and had received high praise from the ladies. I still had to concoct a recipe for lip balm and rouge, but if Sarah would allow it I would continue to experiment.

I always left her kitchen spotless and smelling fresh, I worked from early morning until mid-day before turning the kitchen back over to her. I had no idea how to sell my products but I knew that I loved making them.

Edna and Sarah got a kick out of it as well, suggesting I make chocolate soufflé hand cream or vanilla lip balm. We talked endlessly about the possible combinations and began to discuss recipes for healing balms as well. Eucalyptus for children with croup, or lavender tinctures for anyone who needed calming or help sleeping. "How about a peppermint cream for my hands?" Edna asked, she had arthritis and needed a product that was stimulating yet smooth enough that she could smear it across her knuckles.

Imagine my delight when customers came to Sarah's house and rang the bell to ask about the products I was making. They wanted to know if they could place orders or purchase them outright. The ladies and I sat together and poured over ideas for packaging as well as a name for the business. Edmund had been doodling for hours at the kitchen table, watching us make a fuss and giggle like kids ourselves. Before long he dropped a sketch in front of me and it read, *Heaven Scents by Gert*. His sketch had a scalloped edge, and the lettering was airy, which I liked.

"Heaven Scents! I love it, Edmund," I pulled him to me for a hug and the ladies watched our love bloom in front of their eyes.

CHAPTER 23

༄

EDMUND: SUSPECTS

"Sarah, she has so many products and everyone loves them!" I exclaimed. I admit I worried about her subconscious recalling the rose water, her favorite scent from her days as a prostitute. But so far I had done everything I could to convince her that she led a fairly normal and boring life with her mother.

"It's wonderful," Sarah agreed while she slathered her forearms with a new ginger-scented lotion that Gert made yesterday.

I had never seen this creative and fun-loving side of Gert. The doctors said she would keep her intelligence and personality, but she never had reason to be excited or creative until now. Before her trauma, Gert was rebellious and resolute. She was always thinking about survival, staying one step ahead of the game, money being her biggest cause of angst. I recalled how she would greet me in her room, smoking provocatively on her bed, sheets barely covering her naked skin, enticing me, daring me rather, to approach her. Gert never let anyone in, no one was allowed too close to her heart, building our friendship was a challenge because she was so closed. She lived to get through the day and not much more. She built a wall around herself; it was her greatest defense. The new Gert was adorable, charming, endearing, and engaging. She asked very few questions anymore, which made me think that she was finally settling into her life and accepting her fate. She felt secure among our family now and her passion gave her a reason to get up in the morning. Her energy was boundless and her idle chit-chat was amusing if not exhausting.

There had to be a way that we could get Gert's products to the public. She was feeling a tad underfoot and had admitted to me that she didn't want to wear out her welcome in my home.

I was on my way to meet the judge to discuss her case when I passed a vacant home with a storefront on the main street of town. It used to belong to the bakery but they moved when they outgrew the small space. I peered in the windows, and saw a refrigerated case, remembering that the store used it for pastries and cakes. The property had a large bay window, counter space, and a doorway to the back that housed a kitchen. I assumed the bedrooms were upstairs. The building couldn't have been more than five or six hundred square feet when all was said and done but I imagined Gert's sign above the doorway, *Heaven Scents by Gert*, and could envision her running a little shop here while living upstairs.

I would inquire about the rental price or purchase, but I had arrived at the judge's office and it was time to discuss more serious matters.

He brought me into his room, took my coat and immediately asked about Gert.

"She is doing very well, sir. She is keeping busy making bath products and women's lotions and makeup. Everyone loves them and it keeps her mind off what happened." I was happy to report good news to the judge and didn't have to lie to him, he was one of the few who knew her true story.

"Good, very good, I am glad to hear that. We still don't have any leads on the man who beat and raped her. It's mind boggling really, the sheriff would normally be all over this, but because the beating was on a wench, he appears to be letting it go."

"The perpetrator has to be someone who lives in town. He knew what she did and what her comings and goings were. I think he must have been watching her for a while before the attack."

"I agree. What do you say we go to the tavern and have some lunch?" I read between the lines and knew he was ready to take action on the matter.

The lunch crowd at the tavern was decent, the sheriff's deputy sat alone as usual. I never liked that man, he was unfriendly and there was something off about him. However, just because he rubbed me the wrong way didn't make him a suspect. Josiah sat eating a sandwich and drinking a beer, as did several shop owners. Mingled in were a few ladies having lunch with their book groups or volunteer organizations.

"I am going to go ask the ladies some questions. Why don't you talk to Josiah and the deputy?" the judge said.

I sat down next to Josiah, shook his hand, and told him we had no suspects. He shimmied a little closer to me and whispered in my ear. The deputy had blood on the hem of his pants, it was fresh, and droplets were forming on the floor as well. It was unusual indeed. I thanked Josiah for his keen observation and went to have a word with the strange man.

"Good day, sir. Any leads on Gert's case?" I removed my top hat and placed it on the table across from the deputy.

"No. We'll let you know when we find something out, boy. Don't you have school or someplace else you're supposed to be today?" he asked changing the conversation.

"No, sir, I finished my studies early today and am here having lunch with the judge. Please let us know if you hear anything. She is a friend of mine and I would like to see justice served."

"She was a friend of yours, huh? I find that funny." The deputy's body language changed and he suddenly sat very straight and became serious.

"Why so?"

"Being that she was a wench and all, I didn't think your uppity family would allow you to associate with someone so far below your station."

"She may have made some errors in judgment, but she was then and still is a good person." I wondered how he knew she was a prostitute; he wasn't on her client list.

"A good girl doesn't go around spreading her legs for the men of this town. That makes her a slut, nothing more. She is a sinner and deserved what she got."

I lay into the son of a bitch with a solid punch to his jaw. I grabbed his fine leather vest and pulled him to his feet, he was quicker and bigger, but I dodged his first punch; the second however, landed straight in my eye socket. It sent me stumbling backwards and I lost my balance. "No one deserves to be left dead, no one, you hear me?" I was screaming now and drew the attention from everyone in the tavern.

The judge hustled over and pulled me to a standing position but Josiah came out of nowhere and clocked the deputy, knocking him on his ass. Now everyone could see the blood on his pants, it left a pool on the ground and created a stir.

"I cut myself earlier today chopping wood, stop staring, Jesus Christ. You are all a bunch of no-good sinners in this town." He stood up and turned to face Josiah and said, "You, Nigger, are under arrest for assaulting an officer of the law."

"I don't think so, deputy, you assaulted this minor first. I do believe that's against the law." The judge was a quick thinker.

"Well, I guess we'll just have to call it even, then, but, black boy, if I catch you so much as looking at me again, I'll bring you in for questioning in Gert's case. Got it?" he threatened.

The deputy left the tavern and the ladies sat fanning themselves in disbelief. Jess, the tavern owner, brought me a slab of raw meat for my eye, which was already starting to swell.

"He did it, judge. I swear that man gives me the creeps. I just know it was him. I can't prove it but I feel it in my gut," my intuition was speaking loudly to me.

"You might be right, but we have to prove it. We can't just go around accusing people of rape, especially when that person is the law."

"But it makes perfect sense, that's probably why the sheriff isn't doing anything. His hands are tied because he knows it's one of his own, and that would make him look bad." Everything made sense now.

"Could be, let's chat with Jess and see if he knows anything about this deputy."

"Jess, do you have time for a drink with us?" I asked.

"Sure, let me fill a pitcher and I'll be right there."

"It was him, Jess, it was the deputy." I said, unable to hide my feelings.

"Now, Edmund, we can't be sure," the judge said being cautious.

"Well, it makes sense," Jess said, rubbing his hands on his temples. "He eats lunch and dinner here every day. He always sits in the same place, and I imagine he may have figured out what was going on. He never bothered anyone, but now that I think of it, well, never mind, I'm sure it's not related."

"Go on, Jess, anything could help," Josiah encouraged.

"Well, we always have to mop under his bench when he leaves."

"Why?" I asked confused.

"There is always blood on the floor. So I guess it's possible that he was whipping himself too."

I nearly leapt out of my seat. "He called her a sinner right? Do you think he could have been a customer?" I asked.

Jess tried to hide his embarrassment, but the flush in his cheeks gave him away.

"Jess, we were all her customers. It's okay." The judge said.

"Well, now that that is out in the open I could tell you who her regulars were. I mean, I did see them all come and go, and I can say for certain that the deputy wasn't on the list." Jess said with confidence.

We got some paper and a pencil and made a list.

CHAPTER 24

❧

MARY: STRIKING IT RICH

Dearest Mary,
I have gone west to mine for scraps of gold. Pap and Edna
won't ever welcome or approve of me until I am a man of
wealth. I have left you half of my winnings from the fight
so that you can start to prepare for the baby. I took the rest
with me and will buy my passage to San Francisco with it.
I will be home before the baby is born, hopefully a rich man
who is finally worthy of you and your family. I know you
love me as much as I love you, but I can feel your torment
regarding your folks. I am doing this for you, for us, and our
future. Be well.
Your loving fiancé,
Scotty

I held the crumpled note in my hands. I'd already read it a
dozen or more times. Sonya sensed my need for privacy and left
my room and closed the door behind her. How could he do this
to me again? How could he leave me alone, in the city no less?

I walked into the shop and handed the letter to Pauli and
Candy. Candy was shocked, but Pauli knew, guilt covered
his face.

"Did you know, Pauli?" I asked.

"I begged him not to go; he said that Pap told him in no uncertain terms that he could never make you happy unless he could provide for you as you have become accustomed. He was looking to fight Vladimir, but that would have killed him. Then he suggested the draft and told me that men were being paid now to sign up and fight for their country."

"Jesus Christ," I took the Lord's name in vain as I never had before.

"But then he heard a group of men talking about heading west. This was before you showed up, Mary. I guess they were willing to add him to their group. They left today."

"He doesn't know anything about mining, he could get hurt!"

"I know. I told him that too, but he felt he had nothing to lose, if he comes back without gold, he won't be any worse off."

"But what about me? What about the baby, doesn't he care about us?" I asked.

"He cares, Mary, that's why he left without telling you."

"He is just unbelievable," I said, and then threw a fit akin to a child before stomping out of the store.

Candy eyed Pauli and left the store as well. Only Sonya was left with him and she didn't understand what was happening.

I wandered around the city for an hour. I made my decision, I had to go home to Binghamton. It's where I belonged. I went back to the store, said my goodbyes to Pauli and Candy who were devastated to see me go. I grabbed Sonya's hand and told her we were leaving. I decided that she was in my life for a reason. I had come to love her in the short time we spent together, somehow she gave me strength and courage and I wanted to return the favor.

I would use the money that Scotty left for me to buy our train fare. Then I prayed the whole ride home that Edna was in a forgiving mood when she saw me.

Sonya sat beside me holding my hand, she had never been out of the city and didn't know what to expect. I suspected she was nervous. She was another orphan train rider now just like the rest of us. We did our best to communicate. I had started to teach her the English words for basic things and she was a quick learner. She did struggle with writing but it would come in time.

My belly was more obvious now and the note I left Edna was fresh in my memory; I walked in the front door of my home clutching Sonya for dear life. If no one else wanted me, at least I had her. No one was home. I dropped my bags and Sonya and I went to my room for a nice long nap. Hours later, my door creaked opened and Edna stood over me.

"You're back," Edna was a welcome sight.

"Yes, and I have brought a friend. Her name is Sonya." Sonya was awake and smiled at Edna.

"I see. Would you like something to eat, Sonya? Are you hungry?"

"We would like that, Edna," I rubbed my tummy so Sonya understood we were talking about food.

Edna prepared a chicken salad with small pieces of celery and red onion mixed with mustard and mayonnaise. She placed one scoop-full onto each lettuce leaf and set out three plates. A glass pitcher full of sweet sun tea was centered on the table and brownies were in the oven baking for dessert. I was able to eat all of my food and didn't feel even the slightest trace of nausea.

"How are you feeling, Mary?" Edna asked, referring to the baby.

"I feel much better now, thank you. Edna, please don't be mad at me! I couldn't bare it." My stomach was full after Edna's cooking but I didn't feel content and knew I wouldn't until I talked to her about the way I left things between us.

"I am just so happy you're home now where you belong. I suppose we better set up a room for your friend, Sonya. I assume she'll be staying here?"

Sonya had wandered from the table into the backyard and was picking the heads off the dandelions as we spoke.

"She was my shadow in New York, she never left my side once. I couldn't leave her there; it was pretty awful being back. Her English is coming along. We found out that she is German, her entire family died in front of her and I think she is still traumatized."

"Say no more. She is welcome, and seems to be adjusting."

"I found Scotty," I said, and then silence filled the air.

"And?" Edna paused, waiting for my reply.

"And we are engaged to be married. He went to California, however, to pan for gold. He is among a small group of men who left yesterday morning. They realize they missed the rush, but hope to find some scraps. He promised to be back for the baby." Saying this out loud and acknowledging my predicament made me cry.

"Should we talk about the baby then? Do you have any idea when you are due?" Edna asked.

"I haven't been to a doctor yet, but I think that I have less than five months to go. Pauli and Candy insisted I see someone while I was in the city, but I refused, I would only trust Doctor Robinson with my baby."

"Dr. Robinson will appreciate the compliment. A Christmas baby then, that will be nice," Edna was lost in thought, but then mentioned she'd have to get busy making booties and blankets.

"I hadn't thought of it, but yes, having a baby at Christmas time will be the only gift I need. Edna, Scotty left because Pap told him he wasn't worthy of me. He made him feel pretty low, saying he would never be able to provide for me. Does Pap really think I am that shallow?"

"Pap worries about you, he is concerned about you marrying someone without strong family ties, who may not be able to pay the bills and keep you comfortable." Edna wasn't being pretentious, just honest.

"He is the love of my life, Edna. Isn't that enough?"

"Ahh, young love, it's a beautiful thing. But love won't pay the bills or buy clothing for the baby. And you have dreams, Mary, you always wanted to be a teacher, now what?"

"The most important thing now is this baby and Sonya. I still plan to talk to Miss Kate and get her opinion, maybe I can graduate through a written exam before the baby's arrival. I am already ahead in my studies and feel confident I will pass."

The door flew open and a women carrying a basket full of glass bottles entered. "Pardon me, Edna; I didn't know you had company."

"Gert, this is Mary. Mary, this is our friend, Gert. She is staying with Edmund at the moment."

I felt a funny pang in my gut at the mention of Edmund's name. I had so much to explain to him and I owed him an apology.

"Goodness, I am so sorry for intruding; I just wanted to share my good news. I will come back," she turned to leave.

"Gert, stay, join us for tea," Edna invited her to sit for a while.

"It's so nice to meet you, Mary; Edmund and Sarah have told me so much about you," she sipped her tea and I noticed that she smelled lovely.

"Excuse me if this sounds strange, but you smell nice." It was hard not to notice the sweet smell of roses and I wondered if it she used a special soap when laundering her clothes.

"Thank you, here, have some rose milk for your bath," she rummaged through her basket and pulled out a pretty glass bottle. Then she gave me a second bottle that she said was a rose infused lotion. Now I could hardly wait for my bath. "I have been making these in Sarah's kitchen, and you'll never believe what Edmund's done for me!"

"What?" Edna and I asked in unison.

"He has secured a lease on a property in town, with help from his parents. Now I have a place to live and sell my products! Isn't that wonderful? Now I have my own kitchen for experiments and an actual storefront too. We are calling it, Heaven Scents." Gert was beautiful, but it was her energy and joy that was contagious.

"I can't wait to see it, Gert, let me know if there is anything I can do to help you get ready for your opening day." I would love to help and needed something to take my mind off Scotty.

"I am going to town now to take inventory of the space, would either of you care to join me?" she asked eagerly.

Edna jumped at the chance to go and offered to take Sonya with her so that I could have a quick rest. I agreed and promised to walk into town and see the property later.

I went upstairs and undressed for a bath. I added a quarter of the rose milk to the running water and dunked my big toe in to test the temperature. The water was seething hot and the fragrant aroma filled the room. I unpinned my hair and sunk into the tub. I laid my head back on the pillow I propped against the porcelain and relaxed. I didn't ordinarily care much for perfumes or scents, or even lotions, because they were too strong, but the pregnancy made my senses keener and this was luxurious. The bath felt nourishing and resplendent; normally I was in and out of the water quickly, but today I relished in the extravagance. I could feel the baby move, she rather enjoyed bath time. My body was filling out and changing daily, my breasts were full and heavy now, my middle was tightening and I had stretch marks already. I thought about baby names, and how I wanted to raise the child. What kind of parent would I be? Edna was an encouraging influence; she had the patience of a saint. She would spend countless hours with me while I sewed crooked stitches, or stumbled over words in poems that we were memorizing. Pap, on the other hand, was fairly stern. He was a stickler for manners and wanted everything to be perfectly organized and in its place. It took him years to accept me for who I am. He finally realized that while you can take the girl out of the city, you were less likely to take the city out of the girl. I grew up hungry, even on our farm we ate what we grew and if we had a bad crop, we risked starving. We always had eggs from the hens, but if it was a lean year we butchered our chickens and ate every last bit of them. Da would scramble to find odd jobs to earn enough money for sacks of oats, flour, and sugar, and if we were lucky there was coffee. Herbal teas were a high-ticket item and we reserved them for special occasions like Christmas. One year mama received a tin of herbal tea for the holidays and made it last the entire year. That was the Christmas that da made me a wooden top to spin, it was my only gift and I loved it. Pap didn't understand my need to clean my plate and ask for seconds or thirds, nor did he get why I would pick food from his plate or Edna's. Despite being well fed with Edna and Pap, I never felt full and grew up not knowing when my next meal would be. As a result, I hated waste and actually grew chunky as a young girl. Pap finally had enough and threatened me with a fork, I thought he was going to stab me for sure but withdrew my hand from his plate faster than he could propel the utensil into me. "No more," he said and I got the message. Pap also grew frustrated by my lack of interest in my appearance. I had given up on my untamed red curls, which frizzed whenever it was damp. I never wore a bonnet in town and while half the women gave me sideways glances, I didn't care. I preferred letting my hair flow freely, and not wasting precious time fussing over it. I wasn't sure why someone's looks mattered so much, my mama had always taught me that it was what was inside that truly mattered and defined a person. I preferred trousers to dresses and wore them around the house whenever I came home from school. I went against the grain of society with each layer that I unpeeled, starting with my dress, then corset, slip, and finally my undergarments. I was far more comfortable in Pap's old dress shirt and trousers. Pap rolled his eyes at me when he walked through the door and Edna told him to "leave her alone" but the way he shook his head at me said it all. I failed to please him. When I was younger, we would walk through town and I would hack up loogies just like the men. He admonished me something fierce, scolding me in front of the townsfolk for my awful manners. Why was it okay for the men to spit, or chew or smoke pipes, but not the women? When I was with Scotty I smoked his pipe and spit whenever I pleased. He accepted my unruly hair, the bridge of freckles across my nose with or without powder.

I didn't know if I would be a stickler for rules and organization, but I knew I didn't want this child to experience hunger. Mama used to brew nettle tea to curb our hunger and Mrs. Canter had her boys eat tissues on occasions when their bellies were growling. I would have to work; I would complete my studies and get my teaching degree one way or another so that I could be a good provider for my child. Our household would be atypical, most of the women in Binghamton who had children stayed home to raise them while the men went off to work after breakfast. They were greeted at the end of the day with steaming hot plates of food and the children were instructed to be seen but not heard. Our life would be far less traditional, my baby would be raised by Edna, Pap, Sarah, Edmund, and myself until Scotty came home; it would be a group effort.

The water was getting cold, so I stepped out of the tub and reached for a towel that no longer wrapped around my body. I was startled when someone knocked at the door. I knew

Edna and Sonya would be gone for hours and Pap was in town working. I scrambled to dry off and asked, "Who is it?"
"It's me, Scotty."

I dropped the towel, unlatched the door, not caring that I was fully exposed and dripping wet. I threw my arms around my fiance and welcomed him home.

"You're back!" I said, soaking him thoroughly, but neither of us cared. I grabbed him and pulled him into the bathroom with me, locking the door.

"I am, if you'll have me."

"Why did you leave? I was so worried and mad. I don't want this baby to grow up without a father."

"I know. I thought that going west and striking it rich would be the only way to earn Pap's approval, but then you know what? I was sitting at the train depot and thought, screw Pap, screw them all. This is my baby and I don't give a damn what anyone other than Mary thinks of me."

"So you never even got on the train?"

"No, I sold my fare and pots and pans and headed back to Pauli's but you had already left. I discussed the situation with them and we put our heads together. It didn't take long for us to come to an agreement and board the next train. I don't care what Pap thinks of me, but I do want to be able to take care of you."

Scotty looked me up and down, he put his hands on my growing belly and caressed my large breasts. "We will figure it out together. The only thing I need is you, all the rest I can live without," Mary said.

"You won't have to live without. I brought Candy and Pauli with me to look at the farm. If they like it, they said they would be willing to sell the shop in New York and help me purchase and work the place. Candy thinks she would like getting out of the city and they both want to be close to the baby. Pauli got a kick out of the idea of milking the cows and mucking the stalls. He said he was willing to put in the hard work. They think they can get over two thousand dollars for their store and all its merchandise. That would enable us to buy the farm outright and they would still have some extra money for traveling, which they want to do.

"Really? They would do that for you?" I was shocked.

"They would, they are the closest thing to a family I've got aside from you, that is. It was their idea actually."

"What are we standing around for? Let me get dressed and we'll go meet them!" I dried myself off and ran a brush through my hair.

Seeing Pauli and Candy was unsettling because they looked so out of place at the farm. But they said they wanted to give country living a try. Candy stood far away from the cattle, and pinched her nose because of the smell. She wasn't afraid of the horses and the little kittens that ran around made her laugh. She reached down to pick one up but it scurried away too fast. After seeing the farm, we took them on a quick tour through the village and then back to where I lived so they could meet Edna.

Edna was concerned that I hadn't shown up at Gert's storefront so she came home to check on me. When she came in she was surprised to see me with Scotty and his family, but she was polite as can be and shook hands with Pauli and Candy and immediately prepared tea and snacks to make them feel welcome.

Edna noticed the ring on my finger; it was a gift from Candy to Scotty, then to me.

"Edna, Scotty and I want to get married and run the Wright Farm."

"Is this really what your heart desires, Mary? You have worked so hard to be a teacher."

"I still can be. I can teach after the baby is born, I can tutor or find afternoon care for the baby."

Edna came around to the idea, but discussing my plans with Pap was another matter. I tried discussing the baby with him at dinner that evening, but he thought our approach was mutinous so he retreated to his office and hid behind a large stack of papers, pouring himself brandy after brandy. I gave him an hour to get used to the idea he was going to be a grandfather and then approached him carefully.

"Pap, can't you see that I'm different? Please just accept me for who I am. I love Scotty and I love this baby and I don't want to have to choose between you. You and Edna have given me everything I could have asked for and I am grateful. What I have learned is that I don't need stuff. What matters to me are the people in my life, especially the ones willing to stay by me when things get hard. Scotty has been there for me always, and Pauli and Candy have helped him. He and I, well, we're survivors. We're orphan train riders, we adapt."

"I just want you to be happy, that's all. I don't want you to struggle anymore. When you came to us you were so thin, we could count your ribs. Did you know that? It scared the bejesus out of us, what you went through as a child, I wouldn't wish that on anyone."

"Pap, I know, I remember. But look at me now. I am happy, truly happy, and I know what really matters in life. I have suffered from abuse and hunger. I have seen death and fighting. I lived in squalor, among filth and had few resources if any, yet here I am. I am here. I am not leaving. Pap, please accept me how I am. Accept Scotty too, please, for me. I can't lose any more people in my life." I began to sob. Pap pulled me into the wide berth of his arms, smoothing my hair and saying, "There, there, it'll be alright." I believed him.

We came to an agreement; he didn't want to lose me either and would do his best to get along with Scotty, although he was beyond angry for his lack of responsibility and putting me in this position. Plus, there was the question of the animal murders at the Wright Farm; no one had been arrested for that yet.

"Maybe everything happened for a reason, Pap. Or at least it's how I have to look at things. If my da didn't die, I wouldn't have made it to the city; if my mama didn't die, I wouldn't have gotten on a train and met you. Then you wouldn't have taken me in and you and Edna wouldn't be parents or soon to be grandparents."

He took out his handkerchief and dried his eyes. "Grandpa, that does sound rather nice."

We hugged once more and approached the crowd in the living room that now included Edmund, Sarah, Samuel, and Gert. We poured champagne and toasted to my pregnancy and engagement, then we congratulated Pauli for buying the farm. I had never been so happy in my life.

CHAPTER 25

꙳

GERT: HEAVEN SCENTS

Opening day for Heaven Scents was tomorrow! We were able to fit four small round tables into the store with plenty of room for customers to browse and move around. We covered the tables with bright white lace cloths to best showcase our merchandise. Each table held a display of soaps and lotions, creams, lip balms, dusting powders, and bath products. The ladies and I fussed with the packaging before settling on simple ribbons tied around the soaps that were placed inside a large glass canister with lid. The rose soaps had pink ribbons, the lavender soaps had purple, and orange ginger had orange and so on. My mind was racing; I continually thought of new products and recipes to experiment with daily and stayed up late at night fostering my culinary skills. I often created my best products from mistakes, as was the case with my orange ginger concoction. Similarly, the idea for soap for men came to me when I was using pine cones in an arrangement for the store window. I had a fleeting memory of a man smelling like clean air and pine and *voila*, the idea for men's pine soap was born. I woke in the middle of the night to jot my ideas down and then had trouble falling back to sleep. My adrenaline kept me moving throughout the day, as did the excitement coming from the ladies.

The shop sign that Edmund made was creative and fit perfectly above the doorframe. A sign with store hours was prepared and would be hung on the door itself beginning tomorrow morning. I borrowed money from Edmund to purchase a register and set it in the back of the store so I could check customers out and still see who was milling around. Edna and Sarah were more than willing to help with the register and so were Mary and Sonya. Sonya was impressing all of us with her ability to follow our conversations, so I knew she would be a good helper.

For the grand opening, we sent out handwritten invitations to every shop in town and we put them in every mailbox we could find. We prepared the food ahead of time and planned to make fresh coffee in the morning for our first customers.

I didn't expect to find a line of shoppers outside my door on opening day! It was overwhelming but not impossible for them to walk around the store in small groups, using the baskets we provided for their convenience. A rather elegant older woman wearing a hoop dress had difficulty traversing the aisles but otherwise everything went well. Ladies nibbled on fruit slices, cheese and crackers, as well as the raspberry tarts Edna made. Everyone who entered the store left with at least one or more items. One woman looked around pensively, then approached me with the idea of gift baskets. She wanted me to make up several baskets with a variety of products and she would pick them up later that day. I sent Sonya to the hardware store for larger baskets, she came back huffing and puffing, saying that everyone was talking about the shop. Gift baskets became a large part of my business, from then on I had several prepared and on display at all times. The first month flew by. If Edna didn't bring me dinner every night, I would forget to eat, I was so consumed. I was overjoyed, we all were. After I closed up shop in the evenings, I worked to restock my canisters with Sonya's help. She helped me mix and package new items. She knew precisely where each item was kept and was an excellent helper during business hours. Candy, our new friend in town, suggested that I keep a ledger for my sales, along with a list of materials needed for items that could be purchased in bulk to cut costs.

After a month or so of being open, Gentlemen started coming into the store. They often spent more money than their wives, who tried to whittle down my price or ask for discounts. They were matter of fact, and never haggled. One gentleman approached the counter when the store was otherwise empty and asked, "So, are you back in business then?" I deflected the question, rang him up and packaged his items, certain he had me confused with someone else. Another older man asked if I had any calling cards, and still more lurked around the store; they always made purchases but they acted like I should know them. I had a strange feeling they were after more than just soap.

It was four forty-five, almost closing time, so I started to dust the shelves and cap the samples so they didn't dry out. A man with a limp entered the store. A shiver ran up and down my spine and the hair on my arms rose. I desperately tried to work my way toward the front door, my only exit. I dusted and rearranged while I chatted with him as if everything were normal. "So how is business, Gert?" he asked, stepping closer to me and making me uncomfortable.

"Business is booming, as you can see. What can I get for you? Something for the Mrs. perhaps?"

"What I asked was, how is business?" He proceeded to pace the shop, he flipped my door sign over so it read "Closed" and asked me where the bed was.

I was confused. Why on earth would he dare to presume I would show him my private quarters?

"Sir, I am sorry, but I think you have me confused with someone else. I really need to close and get home, maybe you can come back another time."

He walked toward me and I noticed the trail of blood he left behind. Tiny droplets stained my floor and then I had a sudden flashback. He was the one; the man who hurt me, that man had blood dripping from his pants too, but why? I forced myself to remember but before I could he had me by the wrists and was pulling me through the kitchen and up the staircase to my room. He looked around anxiously, gripped both wrists and tied them together with his belt. He forced me into a chair in my bedroom and began undressing himself. I struggled to break my hands free and threatened to scream. He stuffed his handkerchief in my mouth and tried to rile himself with his hands, stroking his member up and down. I gagged on the handkerchief that tasted like sweat and stared at his scarred and disfigured body.

"You like it rough, don't you, sweetheart? I told you I'd be back. What's wrong? You didn't believe me?" He pushed me to the bed, lifted my skirts and began his assault. I remembered him on top of me, I remembered the pain and the sting of his belt's whip. He had no mercy when he attacked me before and probably wouldn't now either. He finished and got dressed, then he untied my wrists, and said he would be back to check on me from time to time to make sure my business stayed clean.

When he left, I filled the tub. I was recoiling from his stench and the filthy memories torturing my mind. There were so many men. I remembered taking money from them, inviting them to my room, even Edmund. My dearest Edmund, how could he? How could he look at me now and treat me with kindness? I was overcome with shame. I stripped and stared at my scarred body in the looking glass. I grabbed my kitchen knife and studied my wrists. I sat in the warm water and began cutting myself. I cut to feel pain and dull it all at the same time. My cuts dug deeper and the tub filled higher, turning pink from the blood. My breath was shallow and I flickered in and out of consciousness, suddenly I was desperate to leave a note for Edmund. I sloshed out of the water, grabbed paper from my nightstand and scribbled...I'm sorry...remembered...too much...crippled man...blood. Then I saw black.

CHAPTER 26

❧

EDMUND: TOO MUCH

I planned to tell Gert the wonderful news this morning before she opened the store. Mary had received her graduation papers and we were planning a surprise party in her honor. Her teacher agreed to a written exam and Mary not only passed but aced the test. Edna and Sarah were already working on the party menu, and they wanted Gert and me to address the invitations and find suitable entertainment.

It was a quarter to ten when I arrived to talk to Gert, but the store was locked up tight. Usually, she opened the windows and propped the door open by this time. I jiggled the door handle but it was locked. I went around back to peek in the windows and everything looked in order. I sat outside the store for half an hour and then panic set in. Call it a sixth sense. Never once had Gert failed to open her shop, and if she had to go somewhere she would have asked Candy to cover for her. Things were out of place. I jiggled the door handle once more, then ran to the hardware store and borrowed a screwdriver so I could break in. Once I got the door open I saw the blood, the pattern was unusual so I followed it in a circle and toward the back steps. Taking the stairs two at a time, I found Gert, lying in a pool of blood, dead.

I ran outside and waved down a boy who was walking past the shop. I told him to run for help immediately. I went back inside to Gert, held her in my lap, and cradled her back and forth. Why, God, why?

I saw the paper under her bed but someone else would have to retrieve it because I wasn't letting go of my beloved. Candy was the first to arrive. She checked Gert's pulse, stifled a sob, and got towels to sop up the blood.

"Your mother is on her way," she said, not knowing how to comfort me. She sat beside me, crying freely, neglecting the blood, lost in her own train of thought.

"Edmund?" Sarah's voice sounded frantic.

Candy went to the stairs and led her to the scene of the crime. It was a gruesome sight; not only was Gert dead, but I was covered in blood.

"Oh my God, are you okay? What happened?" Sarah ran to me, dropped to her knees and examined me to find the source of my bleeding.

Candy explained it wasn't my blood, she turned Gert's wrists over and Sarah could see that Gert took her own life, but why?

"She must have remembered, it was too much for her," I said, knowing the truth would eventually come out. Samuel and Pap came next, followed by Mary who heaved at the sight before her. Everyone tried to pull me from Gert but it was Mary who finally succeeded. Together we lay on Gert's bed, while the men took the body away and cleaned the mess. Mary rubbed my back and smoothed my hair as she used to do on the train. She told me that everything would be alright.

The women found the note and read it out loud so we could all hear. My suspicions were right, it had to be the deputy. He would pay, that was for sure.

CHAPTER 27

❦

MARY SAYING I DO

"Let's postpone the wedding." I had been thinking about this and now that we were all seated together for supper I shared my opinion on the matter. "It's just too soon after Gert's death, Edmund is in mourning and I don't feel right about a celebration right now." I placed my hands on my belly and thought about Edmund. His grief was palpable; he had lost weight and was gaunt. We were all surprised to hear the truth about Gert and her past digressions, but chose to remember her for the joy she brought to each of us in recent times. Edmund's connection to her remained a mystery but we all had our suspicions.

"Darling, I know, but the baby will be here soon and you want to be married before her arrival." Edna was convinced that I was carrying a girl.

"I agree with Edna, a little celebration is exactly what this family needs," Pap said.

"What if the judge marries us in a civil ceremony? Then we can have a reception later, after the baby is born?"

"I have dreamed about your wedding day," Edna said, "I can see Pap giving you away as you meet your groom at the altar. I have dreamed it so often I know the flowers in your bouquet," Edna sniffed.

"I have too, Edna, but I just feel that my celebration can wait. Edmund's feelings are far more important right now. He isn't the same; he has gotten so quiet, he doesn't visit me anymore, and he spends all his time alone. I am worried sick about him," I admitted.

"We are all worried, Mary," everyone at the table nodded in agreement.

The following morning I felt contractions, they were far too soon, and the doctor said it was premature labor. He was worried that I was stressed and that the baby could come early as a result. Now that I had graduated, that stress was gone, but Gert's death took its toll on all of us. I was put on bed rest for the duration of my pregnancy and it was agreed that the wedding ceremony would take place in my bedroom, with the judge presiding. The reception would take place after the holidays.

Edna insisted on flowers, and a new quilt for the bedroom. She fussed and cleaned profusely, laundering the curtains and fluffing the pillows as well as cleaning up all the dust bunnies that lurked in the corners and under my bed. The day of the wedding came and I was honored to wear Edna's ivory silk wedding gown, the lustrous fabric felt like a second skin. The gown's neckline and sleeves were embellished with saltwater pearl beads and tiny crystal beads. The bottom half of the dress didn't show so hemming it was not necessary. I allowed Edna the pleasure of styling my hair and she braided it around my head and gave me a halo made from baby's breath.

To my surprise, Scotty purchased his first suit, along with new rings for both of us. They were simple gold bands with our initials and the word "forever" engraved on the inside. I would wear Candy's ring as well and they fit beautifully together.

Before the judge performed the ceremony, we had a moment of silence for Gert, we prayed that she was at peace now and forever more. We didn't have any readings, and there was no music, just spoken promises and our family and Mr. and Mrs. Wright beside us as our witnesses. I was overjoyed when Edmund entered the room before we said our "I do's," he smiled at me and stood against my dresser wiping away his tears with a handkerchief I had embroidered for him with a navy blue "E".

He and I had spent the bulk of our lives together; he was my true family and came to be my side even though it was painful for him. The judge carried on with the service. "Do you, Mary, take Matthew Scotty Wright to be your lawful husband, in sickness and in health until death do you part?"

"I do," I said. I was propped up in bed, and stared straight into my lover's eyes. I held his hands and proudly took his last name as my own. He never knew his name so when Mr. Wright pulled him aside and suggested he take theirs, it was an honor.

"And do you, Matthew Scotty Wright, take Mary Pearsall to be your lawful wife in sickness and in health, until death do you part?"

"I do." We placed our rings on each other's fingers.

"Then you may kiss your bride." Scotty leaned in and kissed me with every ounce of his soul; my family clapped and cheered us on.

Everyone hugged and wished us well. Even the baby kicked during all the commotion.

The day's business, however, was not complete. We had the judge write up official adoption papers for Sonya and while we were all together, he performed a simple adoption ceremony. Sonya was now under our care and was part of our growing family.

When we cuddled in bed that night, we thanked God in our prayers for bringing us together under the stoop in the Five Points so long ago. We made sweet love for the first time as husband and wife and kissed goodnight.

Life went on peacefully. We were married now with one child to look after already and another soon to be here. I stayed at Edna's until the baby's arrival because it was easier for her to care for me in her home while I was on bed rest. Sonya never left my side unless it was to help Edna in the kitchen where she was becoming quite the baker, or to help Candy, who was now running Heaven Scents. The name of the store was not lost on any of us. I was anxious to get settled into the farmhouse and put my own touches on it, but happy to have Edna's care for now.

The men worked tirelessly on the farm, increasing the head of cattle significantly and raising a third barn for them before their purchase. We had over one hundred acres, which was more than enough land for the cattle to roam and grow fat for slaughter. Every night, Scotty saddled his favorite horse and rode him through the fields, down the trails, and back across the streams to check the property and exercise the animal. Pauli was nervous around the large animals but Candy was fearless and took to Savannah, our newest mare, riding every morning before going to work in town.

Bart was arrested for the brutal beating of Gert and the murder of the animals, although he denied that. He was sentenced to death by hanging.

The judge asked Edmund to clerk for him, and he did for a short time. They had developed a nice relationship; the judge was a mentor for him and encouraged him to go to law school. But Edmund remained depressed after Gert's death and confided in me that being in Binghamton was too hard for him and he was no longer interested in obtaining his degree as a lawyer. He intended to leave as soon as the baby was born.

He wanted to head west, not to pan for gold, but to sell merchandise to those who still did and who chose California as their permanent home. He had devised a well thought out plan; he would purchase Levis jeans, pots and pans, cradles and sieves, along with bedrolls, tents, and food in bulk. He would set up shop in San Francisco and sell his product for double his cost. He would send word to Pauli, who had connections in the business, when he needed more supplies and by then he hoped to have a permanent address where the merchandise could be sent. I didn't want to see him go; it would break my heart because it would be the first time we were truly apart. I worried about his lungs and his well-being, but I knew he couldn't stay. He had loved Gert, and wherever he went, her image haunted him.

The day after Thanksgiving, I had a great deal of indigestion followed by labor pains that were hard and fast. The women called the midwife, who came at once. After an internal exam, she said I was dilated five centimeters. The men paced and waited anxiously in the parlor for news. I cried in pain and was covered in a slick layer of sweat; when the time came to push, Edna held my hand and I did as instructed by the midwife. Our daughter fought her way into the world on November twenty-eighth. Her birth was easy and I was grateful that Edna, Candy, and Sarah were by my side.

My daughter's tiny face was precious. She had a full head of black hair, like her father. I placed her to my breast and she latched on perfectly.

"What should we name her?" Scotty asked, overwhelmed and looking at me for an answer. "How about Tabitha?" he wondered out loud.

"No, I think it's time," I cleared my throat and wiped my eyes, "it's time for forgetting Tabitha." I hadn't been called by my birth name in nearly ten years; it held a special, yet painful place, in my heart. It always brought my parents to mind, as well as our farm in Westchester, my animals, and all the people I loved in the city, even the Canters called me

Tabitha. It's who I was, Tabitha Colleen Salt, and yet I was Mary Pearsall Wright, too.

"I was thinking of something different." I gazed at my newborn, into the depths of her heart and soul and wanted only one thing.

"Well, then, out with it!" Scotty waited, but his patience was dwindling.

"I was thinking of Lilith Gertrude. We can call her Lilly, which means new beginning." My daughter had a bright future in front of her, while I was sure it wouldn't be without strife, it would be full of love from doting parents and grandparents, aunts and uncles, and of course her big sister, Sonya.

EPILOGUE

MARY

Symbolic of my journey is the locket that I wear everyday around my neck, close to my heart. The treasures within engender the joys and sorrows traversed in my seventy years. I fondle the grooves thoughtfully honoring the memory of the woman who gave me life, my mama. I kiss the piece of jewelry and allow the evening's gentle breeze to caress my skin while I rock on the porch with my great-grandson. The air has a cool, dewy quality signaling a storm.

"Time to get the laundry off the line, Lilly," I called into the kitchen, careful not to wake the baby.

At forty-nine, Lilly basked in the glow of all her triumphs. She was a local schoolteacher, a wife, a mother, and now a grandmother. She sat at the well-worn kitchen table grading papers just as I once had. She put down her marking tool and grabbed the sturdy basket I wove forty years ago for such a purpose, hustling outside to undo the clothespins and bring the laundry in before the storm.

In Lilly, I fostered a love of reading, as a child she absorbed books like I did. She joined the literary society and even authored a series of short stories. When I left my position as head teacher of the elementary school, Lilly filled my shoes. She also took over my work at the library, which was one of the first to circulate books in our city. Lilly met a wonderful man whose daughter she taught over the years. When he became a widow, they fell in love. We embraced our first granddaughter and welcomed the baby they had together the next year. Baby Beatrice was a joy for us all. Motherhood suited Lilly; she was not easily flustered, took things in stride, and laughed loudly and often. I couldn't have asked for more.

Sonya was the first woman in our family to graduate from college. She attended the esteemed University of Binghamton and graduated with honors, her degree was in linguistics. Not only was she fluent in English and German, but Spanish, Italian, French, and Chinese. She was in high demand for her ability to communicate with people from other countries. Everyone from government officials to merchants hired her to decipher contracts and look over shipments, or help write letters to enhance business relationships. Her husband is a highly regarded college professor, a lovely man by the name of Frank who adoringly calls me mom. They gave us our first grandson, Lenny, who today teaches at the university just like his father did. Imagine her fate if she had not become my shadow all those years ago...

Scotty and I never had more children. Not for a lack of trying. Oh, we had fun in the trying, but God didn't see fit I suppose, we were busy loving the two girls we had and taking care of other business.

Candy closed her shop when she was fifty-five years young, and she and Pauli took their savings and set out to travel the world. They sent us postcards from all their stops along the way, so we always knew where they were. The details are unclear, but sometime while visiting Paris, they both fell ill and passed away. Thankfully, we have their bones in our backyard, close to us, where they belong.

Edna died in her late seventies; it was a peaceful passing. Pap woke up one morning and found her still, hands by her side. She lived a blessed life and told me many times, "Mary, you are the most splendid thing!" I remember her voice and her kindness always. Each year on my birthday, she gave a special thanks to my birth parents for bringing me to her, keeping their memory alive in my heart. I was grateful that Edna loved me as if I were her own child, regardless of my past.

Pap died two years later, he had chest tightness and difficulty breathing but shrugged it off as a bad case of indigestion. It was a heart attack and he was admitted to the hospital. He died in a hospital bed, with his family all around him.

Sarah and Samuel passed on shortly after Edna and Pap. Sarah from a ravaging cancer and Samuel from heartache. It was a difficult time for everyone because we all knew how much Sarah was suffering.

Edmund left the day after Lilly was born and never came back our way again. Over the years, he sent gifts to the girls for Christmas and birthdays, but otherwise his correspondence was sparse. We encouraged him to come back home when Sarah was sick, but he was unable to for reasons only I could understand.

I still think of Eddie as one of my life's greatest blessings. If I didn't have him to look after on our train ride west I would have become an indentured worker; no doubt I would have lead a very difficult existence. Eddie nuzzled his way into my heart where he remains. I identify with him, though few others do, orphan train riders have coping mechanisms few understand. He survived by escaping pain; everyone he ever loved has been taken from him for one reason or another. Even me, for I married Scotty. Eddie's proposal made me realize that he always thought of me as his future wife, not his cousin. His parents abandoned him, Gert came in and out of his life, and in one of his few letters that was addressed only to me, he professed that he loved me still and couldn't stand to live so close while I was married to another man. I still worry about him and pray that I will see him again one day, but as time presses forward, the likelihood of that wanes.

Next to raising my girls, and now caring for my great grandbaby, teaching was my greatest joy. How wondrous that a girl from the slums could earn a teaching certificate. I owe it all to Edna and Pap for taking me in when they did.

Scotty remains my one true love, my soul mate if you will. We are among the lucky few who find this in their lifetime. We were destined to meet under our stoop and forge a friendship that would last as long as it has. He is my dearest confidant, most trusted companion, and he never fails to make me laugh. We don't have much in the way of material goods, but we have each other and the farm, and for us, this is all that matters. Our children understand that we view things differently from the townsfolk, we aren't better or worse, just different. We prioritize family above all else, and have a fierce loyalty to one another. Our resilience and love was embedded in our early years and is the reason we survived.

My husband is out on his old gal, Sugar, roaming our property checking the fences as he does each night regardless of the weather. His arthritis has flared up again making it difficult to hold tight to the reins, but Sugar is reliable and steady of foot. The dewy evenings are his favorite for riding and he says it keeps him young. He still flexes his muscles for me and calls me "Red" when we're alone.

We sold the cattle and pigs years back, but kept a few horses for the children, who love to ride like their father. Our days working the farm are over, now it's ours simply to enjoy.

Scotty taught me many things, beginning with the definition of family, which in our case was not tied by blood but rather kinship and respect. He made me realize the importance of a work ethic, that no matter how large or small the job, you do it well and consequently will be given the respect you deserve. Scotty didn't believe in short cuts. He showed me how to put faith and trust in another human being even after so much loss and devastation early in our lives. He taught me to love unconditionally and enjoy life. Most important, he taught me that while it's okay to look back, it's divine to let go, look forward, and breathe in the life around me. That's just what I do.

ABOUT THE AUTHOR

Author's photo by Marnie Carter

Julie Dewey is a novelist residing in central New York with her family. Julie selects book topics that are little known nuggets of U.S. history and sheds light on them so that the reader not only gets an intriguing storyline but learns a little something too.

Julie's daughter is a Nashville crooner and her son is a student. Her husband's blue eyes had her at hello and her motto is, "Life is too short to be Little!"

Her works include *Forgetting Tabitha*, *The Back Buliding*, *One Thousand Porches*, *The Other Side of the Fence*, and *Cat (the Livin' Large Series)*.

To follow Julie, visit www.juliedewey.com and sign up to get regular updates and reading guides.

BOOK GROUP QUESTIONS

❧

1. The orphan train riders in this book are each flawed in some way. Do you attribute this to their lot in life, or do you think it is innate? Discuss the flaws as they pertain to each character.

2. The author paints an image of time and place, richly detailed with descriptions that evoke emotion; which portions of the book are the most vivid to you and your experience when reading about the orphans' journeys?

3. How was New York City's treatment of the indigent different in the 1800s than it is today? Do you agree that the orphan train movement established by Reverend Brace was the impetus for our modern foster care system?

4. What surprised you the most about Tabitha and her journey?

5. Tabitha had many men in her life, her father, Scotty, Edmund and Pap, what do they all have in common?

6. Love and loss are themes throughout Forgetting Tabitha, not just between individuals but families. Discuss how this affected and was significant for each character as portrayed in the story.

7. Was Mary every truly able to forget Tabitha and would you want her to?

8. The author reveals that hundreds of thousands of orphans were sent on trains west. Were you aware of this time in our history?

CPSIA information can be obtained
at www.ICGtesting.com
Printed in the USA
FFOW04n0912210616
25183FF